South
OF
Reason

CINDY EPPES

WASHINGTON SQUARE PRESS

New York   London   Toronto   Sydney   Singapore

WSP

A Washington Square Press Publication
1230 Avenue of the Americas, New York, NY 10020

ISBN: 0-7434-3973-2

First Washington Square Press trade paperback printing February 2003

WASHINGTON SQUARE PRESS and colophon are
registered trademarks of Simon & Schuster, Inc.

For information regarding special discounts for bulk purchases, please contact
Simon & Schuster Special Sales at 1-800-456-6798 or business@simonand-
schuster.com

Printed in the U.S.A.

ACCLAIM FOR CINDY EPPES AND *SOUTH OF REASON:*

"Kayla Sanders' family has moved 'south of reason,' which is bad news for Kayla but good news for readers. . . . A charming, funny book."
— Debra Spark, author of *Coconuts for the Saint*

"*South of Reason* maps out not only the specific flora and fauna of South Texas, but also all the zones and regions of the human heart. Cindy Eppes explores the fault lines that pull a family apart and the bonds of love and memory that keep them whole. This is a warm and lovely book."
— David Haynes, author of *Somebody Else's Mama* and *All American Dream Dolls*

"Eppes writes about the emotional intricacies of family with a rare generosity and deceptively light touch. *South of Reason* introduces Eppes as an extraordinary storyteller, fluent in the uncertain gestures of love."
— *The Seattle Scanner*

"Intriguing and beautifully written. . . . An amazing adventure."
— *Booklist*

"A likable and earnest debut. . . . This is a fine portrait of adolescent confusion and small-town anxiety, narrated with a fine, light touch."
— *Kirkus Reviews*

"What starts out as a simple coming-of-age tale soon grows into a complex tug-of-war. Told by first-time author Eppes with an evocative sense of place, Kayla's story forms a novel as poetic as it is piercing."
— *People*

For Mack McClaren, Mack Mandell,
and, most of all, Mac Eppes

Acknowledgments

To the following people and to others I fear I've left out, I am very grateful:

For wisdom, encouragement, and timely humor, Richard Russo, Kevin McIlvoy, CJ Hribal, Debra Spark, Peter Turchi, Ellen Bryant Voight, Suzanne Segal, Susan Kelly, Eva McCollaum, Paul Michel, Judy French, Kathryn Schwille, Marjorie Hudson, and the faculty and students of the Warren Wilson College MFA Program.

For rare friendship and lengthy conversation, Donna M. Gershten.

For seeing something in these pages and working so hard to ensure their success, Sandra Dijkstra.

For her sustained enthusiasm for this novel, for her loving and tireless work on its behalf, for making the editing process both constructive AND enjoyable, Rosemary Ahern.

For a thousand acts of friendship during the writing of this book, Karen and Jack Albright, David L. Lott, Beverly and

John Awalt, Collin Evans, Martin Buchanan, Becky Corder, Mary Cryer Awalt, Doris Smith, Diana Kimble, Jim and Suzette Freeman, Fletcher Gruthoff, Matt and Miranda Eppes, Leslee and Charles Knight, Eddie and Roxie Logan, LaTreece Mandell, Clifton Brown, Clarke Knowles, and the many Merins, young and old.

And finally, for driving her child to the public library, day after day, summer after summer, Joy Ray Logan Brown.

Jealous heart oh jealous heart, stop beating.
Can't you see the damage you have done?

—JOHNNY RODRIGUEZ

1

Charles Dale Perry's mother was known for washing her hands. The summer that Charles Dale came to live with my family, she was up to at least forty times a day. If she forgot and took the mail out of the box before the sun had time to bake off the postman's germs, or if she had to give Charles Dale's little brother an enema, the count could go as high as fifty.

When my mother told me that Charles Dale was coming to stay with us and that his mother was going to North Austin to a psychiatric hospital, I cried like a kid Charles Dale's little brother's age. It wasn't that I didn't want him to live with us—he was my second best friend—it was that his mother was my *best* friend.

Lou Jean Perry was the only person I ever knew who could scare both my mother and my grandmother. Neither of them was afraid of Jesus, and only one of them was afraid of God, but both were afraid of Lou Jean. My grandmother was afraid of her because of the effect Lou Jean had on my mother. My mother was afraid of the black hair that hung over Lou Jean's shoulder and straight down the center of her cleavage, a braid as thick as a woman's arm, and of the black pencil, soft as a Crayola left on a hot sidewalk, that Lou Jean used to color the pale white skin around her blue eyes.

When Lou Jean left that day, sitting with her right shoulder blade against the passenger door of her mother's white Cadillac, everyone on the street noticed just one thing. She didn't wave to Charles Dale or David, who stood with me on our lawn. My mother stood behind the three of us, her arms spread out to catch me on my right shoulder, Charles Dale on his left. With David in between us, where he could feel it too, she sent waves of motherly concern down her hands, out her fingertips, and into our August-brown bodies. The neighbors watched and thought how lucky Charles Dale and David were to have my mother step in. My mother watched and thought how lucky she was to have Lou Jean drive off. My father stayed at work.

Just as the Cadillac got to the end of our block, before it pulled on to Fifth, Lou Jean turned in her seat and leaned through the window, her hair crow's-wing shiny under the noon sun. And still she did not look at us.

Instead, she tilted her head back further and further, lifting her chin until her eyes were locked on the tallest point of her house, where the second story was capped by a tiny bell tower. She stared at a point high up on the hot stucco, and seeing where her eyes went, Charles Dale, David, and I turned to stare at the exact same spot. While the neighbors poked each other to make sure nobody missed this, her last broad daylight act of craziness, and my mother tried to decide what we were staring at and if she should herd us on into the house, we looked at the spot and then back at Lou Jean, making sure we knew exactly where she was looking. When we could no longer see the car or hear its motor, my mother took David by the hand and led us inside, away from the twelve-o'clock glare of neighbors' eyes. I tried to glance at the spot one more time as we started to the door, but I couldn't see around my mother's body.

"My mom said you can come over if you want" was the first thing Charles Dale Perry ever said to me. I was sitting on the curb the day we moved in, hoping kids would come out of one of the houses. In the three and a half hours we had lived there, I had seen none. He spoke from directly behind me, and I had to turn all the way around to look up at his face. The late afternoon sun was so strong behind his head that I couldn't see what he looked like, but I was so ready for company that it didn't matter. I said, "Okay," got up, and followed him into the house next door to ours.

The Perrys had lived in that big Spanish house since before the boys were born. "Old money," said my dad. "And crazy as peach orchard boars, every one of them," said my grandmother. My mom said nothing.

The house had been bought for Lou Jean and her husband by her parents just before Charles Dale was born. When I followed Charles Dale through that door for the first time, Lou Jean's husband had been dead a year and a month, the first and only person in Rosalita to be killed in Vietnam.

Lou Jean was in the kitchen, a huge room covered in

Mexican tiles and hand-painted wooden cabinets. The floors were spotless gleaming saltillo. The counters and walls were cobalt blue with small touches of terra-cotta and forest green. The cabinets were painted with jungle birds, toucans and macaws and parrots, with tiny hummingbirds feeding at the knobs. Even the ceiling was painted, in swirls of icy blues and greens. It was like walking into a magic cave with a stream flowing through it, where birds and animals come to get out of the heat. I wanted to lie down on that tile floor and turn my face side to side, press each cheek against the shine until I soaked up all the cool.

Lou Jean turned from the carrot she was grating and saw me staring at the floor. "Hi, Kayla," she said, surprising me by knowing my name, and then added, as if she could read my mind, "I just mopped it. It's clean." Thinking she meant it was all right for me to lie down, I did, stretching out on my stomach and extending my arms so my elbows and palms could feel the cool too.

Charles Dale laughed, a snort really. His voice was shocked. "She's lying down on our floor." It dawned on me then that his mother must not have meant for me to lie down on her tiles; she was just saying that they were clean. Now I was stretched flat on the kitchen floor of a house I'd never been in, in front of the first kid I'd met, whose name I didn't even know, though for some reason, his mother knew mine.

I pushed myself to my knees as quickly as I could, wanting to be up and out of there before I did anything else stupid, but just as suddenly, Lou Jean was at my side, her hand on my shoulder. "Charles Dale Perry. What do you think you're laughing at? This is what tile floors are for. This is how they do it in Mexico. Down in *old* Mexico, I mean. Away from the border." She lifted her braid from where it hung between her breasts, threw it out and around her right shoulder to her back, and got down on the floor in the same position I had been.

I looked at Charles Dale to make sure they weren't playing some kind of joke on me, but he was staring at his mother, as surprised as I was. Slowly, I got down on the floor beside her, moving over from the last place I'd lain, to make sure the tiles were as cold as possible. I turned my face on its left side and out of the corner of my right eye, I could see Charles Dale staring at us, a grin on his face. His smile was familiar, like someone I knew, and I decided he wasn't really mean, just not sure how you were supposed to act when people lay down on your kitchen floor.

"Y'all are crazy." He shook his head and sighed as he climbed down beside us, slowly, shyly, although by now I could tell he was dying to try it too. Pressing against the floor, his face was dark, tanned, almost the color of the saltillo. His hair was the same color as mine, the kind of hair that bordered between brown and blond, depending on the time of year. His eyes were also brown, with golden flecks, as if the sun had claimed them too.

We lay there until our undersides were cold as grass snakes, grinning at each other and occasionally changing the position of a foot or arm to let another part get cool. Finally, Lou Jean got up, stretched her arms back over her head until they touched the floor, a perfect backbend in the middle of a kitchen, then rose up and went to the sink. She washed her hands and said over her shoulder, "If you two will go drag

David out from in front of that television and wash his hands and yours, and wash them *good*, now, I'll make you raisin-and-carrot salad with baby marshmallows in it."

I believe it's possible there is no such thing as crazy. Or maybe that there are degrees of craziness, some worse than others. And I also believe that what some people think is crazy is not really crazy at all. To me, that June afternoon, when temperatures were already in the hundreds, it seemed like the most sane thing in the world to keep a kitchen floor clean enough to lie down and cool off on.

I was thirteen that summer, and had begun to claim and proclaim all the ways I was different from my mother. I was especially interested in things that she, with her increasingly poor taste, might find abhorrent. Lying down on a kitchen floor certainly was one of those things.

When we had washed up, the three of us stood in the light of the kitchen window and watched Lou Jean finish the salad. I was enchanted. In my house, a salad was iceberg lettuce and cherry tomatoes, or maybe, if we had company, canned pears with Miracle Whip and grated cheese on top.

At home, marshmallows were only found floating on hot chocolate, after dinner. *After* you had eaten your iceberg lettuce salad. And now, as Lou Jean's smooth pale hand, clean as a Bible, reached into the bag and came back out, I felt as if it were telling me a secret. "Listen closely," it said. "Most people wouldn't tell you this, may not even know it themselves, but marshmallows *can* be salad. Watch this." The hand opened above the bowl, marshmallows fell down like pearls, and I stood speechless, entranced. Until the spell was shattered by my mother's voice, calling me home.

I crossed their yard and ours, hands wrapped tight around Lou Jean's gift, a turquoise Tupperware bowl of salad, so focused that I did not notice my grandmother's Buick parked out front until I heard her voice in the kitchen. She grabbed me before I was all the way in the door. Her arms around me, she buried my face in her stomach and kissed the top of my head, then stood back and looked down at me seriously. My grandmother was a large woman. Tall and sturdy, she reminded me of a water tower, her white fluffy hair sitting like a cloud around its dome.

"Do you know how glad I am that you're going to be living back here? Do you know how much fun we're going to have? You've got to spend the night with me on Fridays when football starts and ride shotgun to the games. We've got to help those Panthers win. Will you do that for me and those poor old Panthers?"

I nodded yes to every question. "And, Gran," I shot out before she could go on, "I already met some people. A woman. And a boy. Two boys, one's my age. And the lady's gorgeous. She can do backbends. Maybe they can go with us to the games."

She looked at my mother over my head, then back down at me. "Well, that figures—that you'd not even be here one whole day before you found a friend. And you're going to make lots more, do you know that?"

"I know, but these people are right next door. I never had a friend that lived next door before. She made *this*." I turned toward my mother, who had just lifted a blue enamel turkey roaster out of a cardboard box.

"What is that?" She looked at my grandmother before she looked at me.

"Carrot-and-raisin salad." I didn't tell her it had marshmallows in it. "Now you don't have to cook."

For a moment, it was quiet, then my grandmother, behind me, said, "Well, isn't that nice."

"Just lovely," said my mother, shoving the empty cardboard box across the kitchen floor with her foot and pulling a full one toward her.

Something about the speed of the boxes wasn't right. "What's the matter? Do you have a headache?" I asked.

"Not yet." She ripped apart the folded flaps of a box, then slammed both hands down into its newspaper-wrapped contents. I glanced at the side of the box to make sure it wasn't marked BUTCHER KNIVES. She looked at the bowl in my hands and shook her head, as if I held something dangerous. "Put that in the refrigerator and go start unpacking your stuffed animals. Dad's gone to get hamburgers."

"Okay," I said, "but I'm having it for supper *with* my hamburger."

Mother stood with a cheese grater and a colander in her hand. She gave me a long look before she spoke. "By all means, Kayla, you can have it for supper with your hamburger."

"What's wrong with you?" I asked. Silently, she put her hands on her hips, and looked at me with her eyebrows raised to their full I'm-waiting-for-you-to-remember-I'm-the-boss position.

As I passed through the swinging door into the dining room, I heard Gran say, "What do you think you're doing?"

I stopped on the other side of the dining-room table as I heard another box slide across the floor and, above it, my mother's voice: "What does it look like I'm doing?"

"Being mean to your daughter, it looks like to me. What are you mad at her for?"

The sound of the boxes stopped. "I'm not mad at her."

"It sounds to me as if you are. It sounds like you're mad because she met your next-door neighbors and liked them, although why they're your next-door neighbors, I still don't understand."

"Leave me alone, Mother," I heard as the noise of flying boxes started up again. "I haven't been back a whole day yet, and already you start in."

My grandmother's voice was louder now, "Sarah Jo, listen to me. Stop kicking those damn things, and listen to me." Her voice grew calmer and slower then, as the noise from the boxes stopped. "I don't know what you've done. I don't know why you've moved *here*. In this house, of all places. Why have you done this?"

"How many times do I have to tell you? Because we liked this house best, of all the ones we looked at."

"Who the hell is *we*? You can't mean Kayla, because she hadn't even seen it when you bought it. And I know good and well Phil wouldn't choose to live here. He just did it to pacify you."

"Are you sure, Mother?" my mother's voice interrupted. "Are you sure and certain that Phil didn't want to live here, that it wasn't exactly what he wanted?"

For a long time they were quiet. Then Gran spoke again. "I meant what I said about Kayla. You can't expect her to take sides. You can't get mad at her for liking the neighbors *you* chose." Then very slowly, she said, "You can't expect her to hate somebody just because you do. It isn't right."

The kitchen was quiet then, with no sound coming from my mother or the boxes, and my grandmother continued, "Let her be a child. And you be a grown-up."

When Mother didn't respond, Gran asked, "Honey, why did you do it?"

The boxes started flying again, and over the noise, almost shouting, came my mother's voice. "I'm not telling you *again*. Because we liked the *house*."

Hearing the jingle of Gran's key ring, I ran for my bedroom, and just as I cleared the door, I heard her as she left the kitchen. "Sarah Jo, you are my daughter and I love you more than life itself, but I swear to God you would worry the balls off a brass monkey."

2

Unlike my mother and grandmother, my father did not enjoy confrontation. He avoided arguments the way that I, until the year before, had avoided baths, an activity I'd considered boring, a complete waste of time. Behind a locked bathroom door, I would take off my clothes while the tub filled, then sit naked on the floor, swishing my hand in the water, carefully wetting the soap, the wash rag, the bath mat, and finally pulling the plug and donning pajamas to the sound of clean water being sucked down the drain. I consistently went to much more effort than the actual bath would have required.

In the same way, my dad would do whatever it took to avoid a confrontation: ignore his wife's snappish "What took you so long?" as he carried a Dairy Queen bag into a hot and chaotic kitchen. Dive to catch a Tupperware bowl that skidded off the table as she slammed it there. Avoid asking, "Where did this come from?" as the lid was ripped from it, though he must have wondered. Decline a serving of carrot-and-raisin salad, though he had to want it—who wouldn't? Carry his dinner out to a hot front porch, unfold lawn chairs for himself and his daughter, and eat while sweat dropped onto the paper plate in his lap. I turned my own plate so that the carrot-and-raisin-salad faced outward, safe from my own sweating face.

I had stopped avoiding baths in seventh grade, on the day that I heard James Chestnutt whisper in the lunch room line, "Kayla Sanders has a *huge* mole on her neck," and reached up to find a clot of mud left there by a game of touch football played two days earlier and miraculously undiscovered by my mother. My normal response would have been to wash my neck that night, checking myself a little closer in the bathroom mirror, if I hadn't also heard how Mike Spivey answered James. "I don't care. I still like her."

Mike Spivey had blue eyes and, unlike the other boys in my class, muscles. Girls at school buzzed around him. His Valentine sack overflowed, not just with cards but with candy. King-size Butterfingers, boxes of Whitman's Sampler. And he was always polite. He thanked every girl brave enough to sign her Valentine, her Whitman's box. But it was *I* who received the only box of candy that *he* gave that year, a Pangburn's heart wrapped in red cellophane. And when he bought a see-through ice blue ruler exactly like my own, so that we were the only two people in the room with matching rulers, he suffered the teasing of James Chestnutt with good humor and what seemed like pride. By *that* time, I was bathing con-scientiously and daily.

"How's the salad?" Dad asked. His forehead was smeared with dirt. His jeans were dusty gray from kneeling to hook up the washer and dryer. His head leaned back against the lawn chair, his eyes closed. He didn't seem at all interested in the house next door. He just seemed tired.

"It's good. Why was it such a big deal to Mom?"

He opened his eyes. "Why is anything?" he asked, but it didn't sound like a question. His hands now worked his empty paper plate, torturing and twisting it, then straightening it out to fold into a wrinkled misshapen airplane.

"Why did we move here?"

"What do you mean?" He concentrated on a wing that refused to stay folded, the paper made too soft by a grease stain. "You know why we moved here. Because I got a good job. Because it's where we want you to grow up."

"No," I said, loud enough that he looked up at me. "Why did we move *here*?" I pointed through the porch boards to the earth underneath. Dad's hands jerked away from each other, and with a solid pop, the plate split in two. He stood and walked to the door. "Because your mother wanted this house," he said so loudly that I thought he meant to go inside and confront Mother about her bad mood. Instead, he spun toward the steps. Mike Spivey had been enough to make me change my mind about baths, but it seemed that nothing could make Dad change his mind about arguing with Mother. As he passed my chair, he wadded the ruined paper into a ball and launched it through the air. It arced perfectly, landing on my plate with his words: "And your mother *always* gets what she wants."

The next morning I woke to a house full of nothing but me, eight unpacked boxes, and a hundred others still full. On the kitchen table was a note under a box of cereal: "Dad's at work. I decided to get my hair done. Will bring you a surprise. Love, Mom." The idea that my mother would go off and leave a house full of unpacked boxes, just to get her hair done, was odd enough, but when I found unwashed breakfast dishes in the kitchen sink, I was shocked enough to wash them, along with my own. I had just finished putting them away and was thinking about going over to visit Lou Jean and her boys when I heard Mother drive up. She called as she came in the front door, "Kayla, come see what I brought you."

I walked into the living room and saw someone I did not know.

My own mother, as she was fond of telling me, believed in natural beauty. She had a coloring she was proud to call peaches and cream, and a body that looked fine without girdles or Cross Your Heart bras, devices she claimed were meant only to be provocative. She believed that makeup was unsuitable and unnecessary, except for lipstick, pale pink or coral. She did not wear eye makeup, simply using an eyelash curler. She said that mascara was worn only by tramps or people practicing to be. Her blond hair, which would not come straight no matter how long she left it rolled on orange juice cans, was always worn halfway between her ears and her shoulders, a length she said was ladylike. Any shorter and it might have seemed too mod. Any longer and it might have seemed flirtatious. She rolled it under, so that it framed the six-millimeter pearl earrings my father had given her for Christmas. She had asked specifically for six millimeter because any smaller and they might have seemed cheap. Any larger and they might have seemed gaudy.

The woman who now stood in front of me was not gaudy or cheap, but neither was she the mother I recognized. She wore a dress that *my* mother would have considered inappropriate, if not disgraceful—a sun dress, pale blue gingham checks. The bodice was tight, fitted to the waist. The skirt was full and stopped above her knees, something none of her dresses ever did. Most surprising were the spaghetti straps, made of the same gingham and tied in bows, leaving her entire neck and both shoulders out in the open for the whole world to see.

Her hair was up, pulled toward the crown of her head as far as its ladylike length would carry it, then left to curl its way wherever it wanted to go. Above each ear and along the back of her neck, more curls were loose.

And she wore makeup. Her eyelids were shaded with the palest green shadow, and her brows, normally as blond as her hair, had been filled in with a darker pencil. Her cheeks were pink and her lips were a frosted shade that she'd never worn before. Her eyelashes were coated in mascara.

"Come sit beside me and open your present," she said.

I sat down on the sofa, pushing back against the arm at one end, and stared at the naked neck and shoulders, the clumped spiky lashes.

"Oh, quit looking at me like that," she said, reading my mind, "new town, new look. Besides, the mascara's water base. And brown, not black."

She handed me a white box with gold lettering. TEENS AND QUEENS, LADIES' APPAREL. I opened it, separated the pink tissue paper inside, and found a blue gingham sundress, identical to hers, except smaller.

"Won't it be fun?" she said. "Mother and daughter." As if she hadn't really wanted an answer to her question, she got up and headed for the kitchen, humming under her breath. "Well," she called, "these boxes aren't unpacking themselves. Go try your dress on, then come show me."

I walked across the lawn, thinking that until now, I had known my mother. Put in a room with a hundred other kids, asked to select my own from a hundred hooded mothers, I'd have had no problem recognizing mine. She'd be the one dressed like a grandmother rather than a mother. The one wearing a sensible heel rather than a sling-back pump. The one whose legs were crossed at the ankles, gloved hands resting discreetly on her lap. And the one most intolerant of the whole affair, ready to have it done so she could go back to more important duties. Cranky, determined, used to getting her way, and responsible. Mother was always the same. As if she were a competitor in some life-long contest for Most Responsible, she went about her days dressed the same, acting the same.

And she and I were very different. I had discovered that difference at the age of six. Preparing for my entry into first grade, Mother and I had strolled the school supply aisle at the local Ben Franklin. We gathered pencils and lined tablets and scissors and glue, with no dissension regarding choice. But halfway down the aisle, our agreement ended, when I spied a bright red lunch box, adorned with the smiling visage of Hopalong Cassidy. In each hand he held a Colt Peacemaker, barrels pointed responsibly toward the sky. I clutched it tight in my arms, certain that at any moment some kid would run through the door and grab it. Without question, it was the best lunch box ever, and I was just lucky to have claimed it before someone else did. Running down the aisle to where Mother had stopped, I held it up to her. "This one," but she couldn't take it, because her hands were occupied by an alternate. A pink one, portraying a grand painted staircase down which charged Cinderella, her face a picture of moronic distress, forgotten glass slipper somewhere behind her.

I marched determinedly past Mother and set my treasure on the counter, knowing that she wouldn't call me back. Causing a scene in public was the last thing she'd do. Instead, she simply carried her own choice to the counter and paid for two. On the first day of school, I took Hopalong Cassidy, but the next day found my lunch packed in Cinderella. It was a battle that lasted all year, and I remember that she won as often as I did. She wasn't mean, my mother. She didn't want me to be unhappy. She simply had responsibilities. And one of them was making sure that her daughter carried a lunch box made for girls.

That she now had abandoned responsibility by leaving dirty dishes in the sink and had gone to purchase a new dress and *makeup* was out of character and was odd. That she stood in hose and heels, organizing a hot kitchen, wearing her newest dress, was absurd. That she insisted that I wear *my* newest dress to go out and play was pure science fiction.

I had mentioned, cautiously, after last night, that I might go over and see what Charles Dale and David were doing. I did not mention Lou Jean. Mother agreed that it sounded like a good idea, and why didn't I wear my new dress and she'd put my hair up like hers before I left. Having little desire to go next door dressed for a tea party, but having even less desire to make her mad enough to make me stay home, I didn't argue. But I did wonder.

I knocked on Lou Jean's back door and heard her yell, "In here." The kitchen was empty, but on the far wall was a door I'd not noticed before. Made of rough gray weathered cedar, its hinges were heavy black iron. Painted just above the handle, so that it looked like it would light on your hand as you opened the door, was a dragonfly, blue, green, and purple.

From behind the door, I heard clanking noises, the ring of glass against glass, and I called again, "Lou Jean?"

"Come on in, love." I opened the door. When my eyes adjusted to the darkness, I saw that she was not there. The wall ahead of me contained another door, just like the one I'd come in. The walls to either side of me held shelves lined with pre-served food, mason jars full of potatoes, green beans, pinto beans, corn, and what looked like a hundred jars of tomatoes and tomato sauce.

"Did you do all this?" I asked as I made my way across the dark floor.

From behind the door she laughed. "Yes. I did. And there'll be more to do before long. Do you want to help?"

I opened the door and stepped over its threshold. On the floor rested a large aluminum tray. Bending over it was Lou Jean, and as she stood, she changed colors. Her head and arms, which had been green as she bent over the box, became blue, then turned to purple, to pink, and finally red, as she stood up straight and smiled at me.

I gazed down at myself and saw that I was colored the same way. When I looked back up, past Lou Jean, I saw the source of all that color was a great rainbow of light, as large as a stained glass church window. Looking closer, I realized that it truly was a window, a great picture window across which Lou Jean had hung narrow glass shelves. On the shelves, like giant sapphires, rubies, and emeralds lined up side to side, no space in between, were rows of tiny jars, all the same size, filled with something as clear and bright as jewels. The shelves were just tall enough so that a row of jars could slip in between, and there were no gaps, so that each color seemed to flow into the next.

The result was solid bands of colored light, bottom to top. On the bottom two shelves were green jars; the next two, blue;

the next two, purple; the next two, pink; and the top two, red.
"What do you think?" asked Lou Jean, taking a final pink jar
from the tray and putting it in its place.

"What is it?" I moved my arms up and down at my sides,
straight out like a scarecrow, watching my hands as they
changed through all the colors, like a revolving Christmas tree
light.

"Jelly. I just put up the last of the plum." Her hand turned
green as she plucked a jar and handed it to me. "Mint," she
said. "With jalapeño." I took the jar, and her hand moved up
to the next rows and turned blue. "Mustang grape." She
handed me a blue jar. "Blackberry." Her hand, now purple,
offered me a matching jar, then, before my eyes, turned pink.
"This is the plum," she said, as I rearranged all the jars in my
hands to take it. "And, finally, strawberry." She took down a
red jar, the brightest of all, and her red hand looked just as
bright, translucent, as if I could see through it too.

I carefully balanced the last jar among the rest. "Red's my
favorite color," I told her.

"Mine too. And I'm thirsty. Do you want a Big Red?"

"Sure." I nodded toward the load in my hands. "What do
you want me to do with these?"

"Whatever you want to do with them, they're yours. We'll
put them in a bag before you go home."

While I loaded my treasure into a paper sack, Lou Jean
washed her hands and poured the sodas over ice. "The boys
went to see their grandmother," she said, as we both sat down,
"so I'm glad you came to visit." She leaned her elbows forward
on the smooth dark wood of the kitchen table and, resting her
chin in her hands, looked at me as if I might say something

important. As if anything I might say was exactly what she wanted to hear. Her eyes were a blue I hadn't seen in a person's face before, a shade I'd only seen in movies. They were the color of water in nighttime swimming pools, reflected out and up onto people wearing cocktail dresses and white dinner jackets, drinking pink champagne and dry martinis, and waiting for someone to have too much to drink, to get angry, or simply to become bored with all that perfection, those gleaming silver trays, chignons with not one hair out of place, shrubbery clipped to look like jungle animals—and to push somebody else in, so the party could really get started.

"So. Tell me about Kayla."

"What do you mean?" I'd never been asked that question.

"What do you like? Who *are* you?"

I was stumped, so I started out safely, politely, I thought. I looked at the bag at my feet. "I like jelly."

Lou Jean laughed. "*Everybody* likes jelly. What do you *really* like that's just you and nobody else?"

I thought about it. "I like secrets. Not like things somebody tells you about somebody else, but real secrets. Ancient things. Things other people don't know." I thought some more. "And mysteries."

"Ooh," she said, "good stuff. I knew you were smart."

She picked up her glass, just off the top of the table, and rolled it between her palms so that the frostiness came away and it was clear again. "I think you're right. The best secrets are the ones you learn on your own. Or the ones somebody special teaches you. Someone either much older or much younger." She cocked her head back and stared up at the swirled ceiling, as if trying to remember something. "I don't think I've ever learned anything worth knowing, or really important, from anyone my own age."

Before I could ask what she meant, she said, "Ever have your fortune told?"

I shook my head.

"Never?" I shook it again.

"Well. We'll have to fix that."

"You can do that?" I asked, and held out my palm for her to look at.

She took it in her two hands, looked down at it, then folded it back into itself, kissed my closed fingers, and set them down on the table. "Not like that. Another way."

She stood and carried her glass to the sink. "I'll show you some day when we have lots of time."

"How did you know my name?" I asked quickly. I knew I should go home soon.

"Because I knew your mom and dad, growing up."

"Very well?" I asked, twisting in my chair to face her.

"Pretty darn well." She cocked her head to one side and staring at a point above us, where two walls joined and touched the ceiling. If she had left her head straight up and down or if she had looked at me and not into that corner, I might have asked her more. Instead, I stood, hoisted my jelly sack, and thanked her.

"You come back whenever you want, Kayla Marie Sanders." She looked straight at me as if I were important to her, every bit as precious as the jeweled rainbow in her pantry. "I promise," she continued, "there'll never be a day when you're not welcome in this house."

☙❧

Regarding Mother's change in appearance and attitude, my father seemed as confused as I was. By the time he got home that day, she had finished unpacking, last night's bad mood apparently thrown out with the empty boxes. We still wore our new dresses, though Mother had stepped out of her heels and into a pair of pink satin mules.

Dad found us in the dining room, where, my mother had just proclaimed, we would be having dinner from now on. New town, new look, new dinner routine. I was setting the table, and Mother was arranging roses she'd cut from the bushes out front, still humming the same tune she had hummed all day, something I didn't recognize.

Dad hadn't quite cleared the door when he saw us. He looked at Mother first, then at me, a shorter, breastless, unsmiling replica, then back to her.

"What do you think?" asked Mother. "Don't your girls look lovely?"

"Um . . . yeah." Face blank, Dad stood at the door with both hands holding onto the frame, leaning just his head and shoulders into the room as if testing the atmosphere before fully entering. "Yeah," he said again, his face still void.

Before we'd moved from Cameron, my mother had been president of the First Baptist Church Ladies' Prayer Circle, even though she was the youngest woman in the group. She was elected, the preacher's wife had told me one Sunday, for her stalwart belief in the importance of feminine virtue, something, the lady said, that most young women seemed to have forgotten. My dad said she was elected because she was the thinnest and the only one in the group who could get by without wearing makeup, something the circle considered the product of the devil.

A 1960s apple, designed to tempt not only the woman who wore it but also any man who stood before her.

Now, little more than twenty-four hours since we'd left Cameron, my mother stood in front of her perplexed husband and child, nude from the collarbones up, her hair sprayed and teased, her face covered in makeup that had become more garish in the afternoon's heat. Her cheeks blazed. Her mascara-smeared eyes looked wild, and I wondered what the Cameron First Baptist Church ladies would think if they could see her. Their former poster child had clearly been dipping in the devil's paint box.

My father must have been thinking these same kinds of thoughts, wondering what on earth had caused this change, and, like I was, worrying what he was supposed to say about it. As my mother gave him her shimmery new smile, reminding him that she expected more than two measly "yeahs," Dad looked like someone the teacher had just called on. Someone who hadn't read the assignment and didn't even have his book open to the right chapter.

"Ya'll look . . ." His eyes went to me, then to my mother, then back to me, as he fished for the right word and tried to think of the safest place to focus his attention when he said it. "You look . . ." He steadied his eyes on me then and smiled hopefully, like he thought I could tell him what to say. When I didn't, he simply reiterated, ". . . Yeah," and smiled really hard, as if *yeah* could mean something grand if the smile was big enough.

Then he pushed himself out of the doorway and headed toward the kitchen and outside. "If supper's not ready yet, I think I'll go put the sprinklers on. Backyard looks a little dry."

You big chicken, I thought, as the screen door slammed.

Everyone liked my dad. He was the guy who, at get-togethers and picnics, was surrounded by kids. People trusted him, grown-ups and children. If someone got a splinter, Dad was the one to extract it. If someone scraped a knee, Dad was the one to apply the Merthiolate. When a tooth needed pulling, parents drove their kids to our house, because Dad was the only grown-up the kids would allow to touch it. And around campfires, *his* ghost stories were the scariest, but the little kids, terrified by the story *he* was telling, still chose to sit in his lap, the safest place, while he told the story.

He had a sense of confidence that extended to others, whether he was pulling a tooth for one of my friends or fixing a flat tire for one of Mother's friends. He always knew *exactly* what to do. Except when it came to Mother's moods.

All through dinner, tuna in cream of mushroom soup on puff pastry, a dish you'd eat in a dining room, I suppose, Mother smiled. When he caught her looking at him, Dad smiled back. The rest of the time, he looked at his plate, or at me, as if he still thought I might clue him in.

When we were done, we all went out on the front porch, leaving the dishes to soak. Mother and I still wore our matching outfits, and she hummed that same song. Again, Dad chose a chair facing the street. Mother's eyes were the ones that glanced repeatedly toward the house next door.

The lightning bugs were out, and as I went back in the house for a jar, I heard my mother say, "You know what we should do tonight? We should play old records. I unpacked them today and set up the stereo."

My father answered, "Yeah," and I wondered if he'd forgotten every other word he knew.

Mother was breaking off the spent heads of rose blooms when I got back to the porch. Little David, home from his grandmother's, had come up and was talking to my parents. David looked nothing like his older brother. His hair was black and straight, cut long so that his bangs stopped just short of his eyes. His body was stocky, arms and legs thick and muscular, bare feet wide and brown, now solidly planted on our sidewalk. When he saw me, he opened his tiny mouth and, in a voice too deep for a five-year-old, asked the first intelligent question of the day: "Why are you and your mother dressed alike?"

I looked at Mother. Dad, clearly wondering the same thing and glad someone else had asked it, looked at her too. She just kept snapping off those rose heads, throwing them down on the ground, humming that stupid song.

I shrugged at David, and he seemed satisfied with the only answer I could give him, though his eyes kept returning to my busy mother.

Later, after I was in bed, Dad stopped by my room to see the lightning bugs. On my dresser in their mayonnaise jar, they reflected against the mirror and back out into my room, across the jeweled jelly jars that sat around them. As Dad started from the room, we heard the sound of the record player from down the hall, the same song my mother had hummed all day.

A man began to sing. "Some enchanted evening . . . you may see a stranger. . . . You may see a stranger . . ."

"No joke," said Dad.

❧ 3 ❧

One of the first things I learned about Charles Dale was that he did not believe in killing anything. Cockroaches, yellow jackets, spiders, even coral snakes and copperheads—all were safe with him. He claimed they wouldn't harm you if you didn't harm them. He told me this on the third day I lived in Rosalita, while the two of us sat on the ground under a giant mulberry tree that grew in my backyard. We were watching a tiny hole in the bare ground between us. It was after eight o'clock at night, but the sun seemed caught on the wires of the chain-link fence that ran along the alley, making the shade of the mulberry tree the only comfortable place in the yard.

In the three days I'd lived there, Charles Dale had gone to what I thought were great efforts to make me feel at home. We had spent the whole afternoon in his room, him showing me photo after photo of kids in our grade at school. "So you'll recognize people on the first day," he'd said. "So you won't be lost. And even if you *feel* lost, you won't be, really, because I'll be there." He didn't look like his mother, but they had strong similarities. Like her, he was kind and very certain about some things.

Like the fact that whatever was in the dirt hole we watched would soon emerge, so that he could show me just how safe the thing was, something I wasn't yet sure about. "When it comes out, I'll show you." Charles Dale's eyes never left the smooth dirt between us. His gaze was serious and focused, and he didn't seem to notice the dirt sticking to the sweat of his crossed legs. I lifted my own, circling my knees with one hand while I brushed away dirt with the other. "Be still," Charles Dale said in a low voice, "here he comes." Out of the hole protruded two black antennas. More than an inch of them came out of the hole before a black head followed. The body behind the head was spotted orange and black, like some garish Halloween creature. Fully out of its lair, the insect measured almost two inches, antenna to rump. It made a slow circle around its home, its bent black legs leaving minuscule imprinted dots in the sand, then lifted orange wings away from its body and took loud buzzing flight straight at my face. I fell backward as the thing looped over my head and back toward its lair. "It won't hurt you," said Charles Dale as it landed and stayed on the ground, walking around and around its home. "It's a cowkiller." So calm were his words, he might have said, "a mother sheep." Noticing the dirt I plowed as I pushed myself away, he said again, "It won't hurt you."

"You mean it just kills cows and not humans?" The cowkiller continued to walk around and around, packing the runway for a quicker liftoff, I was certain.

"It doesn't kill anything. Except other insects." For proof, he laid his index finger on the ground and didn't even flinch as the thing lifted its front legs onto his skin and climbed over. It then walked directly to its hole and entered head first. The last thing I saw was its black stinger. I watched with apprehension, hoping the creature was in for the night, thinking Charles Dale was watching too, until he said, "Your mother sure dresses up a lot."

Mother stood beside our house, holding a water hose over a rosebush. The sun had finally freed itself from the fence, and the light around her was dim. She wore heels, little slingback sandals in a shade of raspberry that matched her dress. An A-line princess style that, like the gingham sundress, stopped just above her knees, and also like the sundress, was something she'd never have worn in Cameron. With her free hand she smoothed her dress, disciplined hairs that had sprung loose from her upsweep, wiped what must have been a splatter from the toe of one sandal. Even in the dusk, I could see the swing of her neck away from the plants she watered and toward the house next door. She had suggested to Gran that Dad was the one who wanted to live next door to Lou Jean, but it was *her* good shoes being splattered because she'd suddenly developed a fondness for gardening wearing her finest, and because she couldn't keep her eyes on what she was doing. With running water and ruminative stares, she might have been willing Lou Jean to come out and see her dressed up.

Charles Dale eyed her as if she were some sort of insect he'd not seen before, as if making mental note of every characteristic so he could go back to his room and look her up in one of his field guides. She moved to the end of the flower bed nearest us, and I lowered my voice. "Did your mother say anything about us moving here?"

His response was slow, as he studied Mother. "No. But your grandmother did."

"My grandmother? You know my grandmother?"

"Of course." He looked at me as if I'd asked a very dumb question. "She practically lives at my house."

"My grandmother lives at *your* house?" Mother's head whipped around and she stared out into the darkness around us. "Kayla? Are you still outside?"

Her voice was bright and cheerful, a raspberry trill that matched her outfit. Which might mean she had heard only our voices and not what we'd said. When I didn't answer, she moved away from us again, along the length of the house. Charles Dale lowered his voice so that I barely heard it. "She doesn't live with us. She just comes over. She's my mom's best friend."

Mother moved into the glow of our dining-room window, so that we saw her clearly as she bent to the faucet on the side of the house. The handle squeaked as she twisted it, and as if in accompaniment, her neck turned one last time. When no one came out, she dropped the dead hose, stepped from the light, and walked out of our view. We heard the cap-gun cracks of her heels across the front porch, the *whap* of the screen door behind her.

"What do you mean?" I asked Charles Dale. "How could my Gran be your mother's best friend?"

The first time my mother saw Charles Dale was later that week when he came over to form a band. I played ukulele, he played guitar, and we were pretty sure we'd make a great duo. For two days before he came, I worked to learn a new song. The song I knew all the words to and could play best was "The Eve of Destruction," but I couldn't play that for Charles Dale. I was afraid the "bodies floatin'" part would remind him of his father.

That afternoon, I sat in the living room with Mother and practiced "In the Misty Moonlight." It was happier, and the man who sang it was a famous golfer. My mother sat on the sofa looking at the high school yearbooks she'd found in the unpacking. Between refrains, I asked, "What was it like growing up here?"

Mother laughed. "Well, I don't have any place to compare it to, since I never lived anywhere else until after I married, but it was fun. A lot of rodeos. A lot of team roping. Every January, the whole high school went to the San Antonio Stock Show on school buses."

"Does it ever get cold here?"

She nodded emphatically. "Yep. But don't try to guess when. On Thanksgiving you might wear shorts. On Christmas you might wear a heavy coat and earmuffs." She shrugged. "Or it could be the opposite, depending on the year." She turned a few more pages. "Look at this," she said. In a photo that took up half a page, she sat with two other girls on the wings of a crop-dusting plane. "You know that a lot of vegetables are grown here?" she asked. "Cabbage and onions and carrots?" She gave me a sideways grin. "Well," she drawled, "if we wanted to be *really* bad, we stole a cabbage from a field."

I made a face. Who would want to steal a cabbage?

She laughed. "We weren't all that bad, really," she said. "The field belonged to the father of the girls who were with me."

"They stole their own father's cabbage?" Again, she nodded. "Did you take it home and cook it?" I asked, wondering how a teenager explains coming home with a cabbage.

"No. We always gave it to Beto's wife. Beto worked for my

friends' father. He brought home all the cabbage he wanted. But his wife thought it was funny that we'd swiped it. She'd fry it with onion and peppers and tomatoes. She said our stolen cabbage always tasted better than what Beto brought home."

"Did you ever steal a watermelon or a cantaloupe?" I could see myself stealing something that tasted good, that didn't stink when you cooked it. I lay my ukulele in my lap and strummed it like a steel guitar, hoping she'd talk about something more fun than stealing cabbage, something I myself could look forward to doing someday. When she didn't answer, I looked up. She had stopped turning the pages and was staring at one certain picture, and her smile had disappeared.

Just then, Charles Dale knocked on the door. I went to help him in with his guitar and Mother, solemn-faced, followed me.

"Hello, Charles Dale Perry," she said, and then righteously humiliated me by staring at his face and saying, "You look just like your father." I was horrified that she would bring up his dead father, but Charles Dale, instead of being upset, seemed proud. "Thanks. Most people say I look like my mother."

"Do they?" Mother's voice was pensive. "Well, I guess I'll go make you two some Kool-Aid."

Mother had left the open yearbook on the coffee table. While Charles Dale tuned his guitar, I looked at the face-up picture. Two high school boys clowned for the camera, acting as if they were throwing their schoolbooks into a garbage can. I recognized my own dad but had to read the names under the picture before I realized the other one was Charles Dale's dad. I closed the book and put it back in the credenza.

Charles Dale played his song first, "Ferry 'Cross the

Mersey," a song I loved and knew every single word to, because the week it made number one, I was home in bed with the measles. About halfway through the second verse though, just after "People they rush everywhere," a sound came up from outside. A howling. Like something very sad or in pain.

"Is that a dog?" I asked.

"Just ignore him," said Charles Dale. He glanced back over his shoulder and shook his head, but kept playing. The howling continued, but I couldn't see any dog.

The moment Charles Dale finished, the howling stopped. I started my song, but I wasn't three words into it when the howling started again. Charles Dale went to the open window and stood with his back to it as if to block out the sound, motioning for me to keep singing. The noise only grew louder, coming through the window on both sides of his body, and when I got to "I know I'll be happy anyplace anywhere I don't care," the howling turned into crying. Human crying. As I tossed my ukulele on the sofa and ran out the front door, the crying changed to laughter.

Behind a lavender althea bush stood a kid with a face that was gray, the color of cigarette ashes, the color of someone who lives under rocks. Framing the gray were long narrow ears, as red as raw hot dogs. He was wearing, in the middle of the week, navy blue Sunday school pants with a skinny black belt that missed two or three loops.

Charles Dale came up behind me. "Go home, Thad. You're not invited."

"Who wants to be?" he asked, and his breath was stinky from three feet away. "You two sound like a couple of dogs hung up together. Everybody on the street's closing their windows."

He walked up and stuck his ratty, smelly face in mine, then looked at Charles Dale. "Well," he said. "My old lady may just be right this time." He walked around and around us, his arms folded across his chest, one hand propped under his chin, like a scientist on television.

A look passed between Charles Dale and me, and in it was concurrence. Neither of us wanted to give him the satisfaction of asking what his mother was right about. "Come on, Kayla," Charles Dale said, and started for the house.

I turned to follow, then realized I had not said a word since I'd met this creep. Needing to show some guts and my loyalty to Charles Dale, I said over my shoulder, "Try to keep your putrid breath on your side of the street. You might kill my mother's roses, and besides, I want to live."

I was impressed by my own wit, and Charles Dale must have been too. As we climbed the porch steps, he said, "Good one," even as the creep called to us, "See you later, Bobbseys."

"What's that supposed to mean?" I wondered.

"Who knows? He's a weirdo."

Thad Howard's mother was the high school librarian. His father, who was supposed to be an expert on the Civil War, did nothing but stay home and eat. Lou Jean's opinion was that Thad couldn't help being obnoxious. She said his mother spent so much time gossiping that she'd notice Thad only if he ran off with a pregnant nun and his father would notice him only if he climbed between two slices of bread.

Lou Jean was always saying stuff like that. You couldn't call it gossip because it was true. And she never stopped talking when we came in the room. She didn't believe in words that were okay for grown-ups but not for kids. She said the same words to both, a practice that seemed remarkably sane to me.

She told us that life was a gift from God and if you didn't enjoy it because you were afraid of what people might think, it was like slapping God in the face and saying, "Here. I don't want your stupid old gift." She also said there was no proof God was a man. He might be a woman, and in case He was, she was covering all bases. In the backyard, in front of a blooming pink bougainvillea, sat a concrete Jesus. In the front yard she kept a Goddess statue, terra-cotta, the color of real skin, and naked. My grandmother said she didn't understand why Lou Jean couldn't put Jesus out front and give the bitch the backyard. When a group of high school boys couldn't resist and painted a black triangle between her goddess's legs, Lou Jean still didn't take her in or even try to scrub off the paint.

When Charles Dale left that day, I got out the annual, looked at that picture again, and decided all that mascara must have affected Mother's eyesight. Charles Dale didn't look anything like his father, whose hair was much lighter and whose eyes, even in the black-and-white photo, seemed a pale shade of blue. When my mother walked in, I told her so. She came over to where I sat, looked across my shoulder at the annual in my lap, a funny smile on her face, and said, "Oh, really? I think they look a lot alike."

"Look at his hair," I started, "his eyes—"

"All little boys want to look like their fathers," she interrupted, "just like all little girls want to look like their mothers. Isn't that right?" Her voice was very quiet, the strange smile still on her lips.

I kept quiet. I wanted to look like Lou Jean. Lou Jean's body was like the green rolling hills we'd left in Cameron, with rounds and hollows. Covered in the Mexican peasant blouses she wore, the hand-embroidered flowers, her body looked like springtime earth. But where Lou Jean's body had hills and valleys, Mother's had icy cliffs and crags. The edges of her body were sharp, like the rock walls of a garrison. Impossible to climb. The very piece you clung to could chip away and send you plunging.

I think this is one of the reasons that people didn't joke with my mother. At barbecues in Cameron, when we'd get together with other families, the men would all cut up with their own wives and each other's, tease them about their cooking, a new hairstyle, or what "honey-do" jobs they had lined up for the next day. But no one ever teased my mother. One of my dad's friends, who liked to joke even more than the rest of them, and who also drank more beer, had started calling my mother The Citadel, although not to her face.

Perhaps she was trying to soften the edges with the new clothes and makeup, to file off some of the rocky points. But if so, it wasn't working. The new look only made her seem more remote, as if the fortress that was her body now wore camouflage as well.

I started for the door, carrying the annual with me. "Kayla," she called, before I could get away. "Why don't you invite Charles Dale over for supper? Daddy hasn't met him yet."

This sounded like fun. "David too?" I asked.

"I don't think so. Just Charles Dale will be fine."

She turned and looked not at me but at the annual. Then, she came across the room, took the book from my hands, and walked away with it. She sat down in the chair closest to the window, opened the cover, and began reading what people had written, where they signed their names. She seemed to travel across a distance greater than the mere width of a living room. And when she began thumbing through the pages, finding again the picture she'd stared at earlier, she moved even farther away. It was as if she, the yearbook, her weird smile, and the chair she sat in were enclosed and separate from the rest of the room. From me. From the mockingbird song coming in the window. From the sound of the washing machine changing to the spin cycle. Not as if they were on another planet, but as if they *were* another planet. One incapable of supporting any other life.

4

She was humming again, draping the bougainvillea vines between the roses so that they trailed down the sides of the vase. She had made me cut the flowers, and my fingers were sore from the thorns. It was beginning to seem as if she and not I was the one having company. "There," she said, standing back to admire her artistry. She'd taken the same pains with her makeup and her hair, and she wore another new outfit, red pedal pushers with a blue-and-white-striped sailor top. "Why don't you go change?" she asked, turning to look down at my cutoffs and T-shirt, clean ones I had *just* changed into, my normal summer supper clothes.

"Just go," she said, pointing toward my room. As I dug through my dresser, looking for something normal enough not to embarrass me but dressy enough to please my mother, I heard Dad come in. I pulled out a pair of culottes and a striped top. The culottes were old, but the top looked a little like the one Mother was wearing, a fact that might save me from having to change a third time.

"Kayla's having company for dinner," my mother was saying when I came into the room.

"Oh, no," said Dad, grinning, jumping back onto one leg, then forward onto the other, faking punches as usual. "Who is it? Let me guess . . ." He danced around me, as if I were punching back. "Sonny Liston? Cassius Clay?"

I turned with him as he danced.

"Raise your arms. Where's your guard?" He grabbed my arms and brought them up to the proper position, then continued, "Floyd Patterson?"

"Charles Dale Perry," called my mother, from where she washed lettuce at the sink.

My father stopped his dance and dropped his guard, and I moved in and let him have one. "Where's your guard?" His hands came down and rested on my head, his fingers spread over my ears, and he stood very still, looking at my mother.

Then he spoke. "Sarah Jo, I don't think so tonight. I'm really tired."

I tilted my head back and looked up at him. In my whole life, I had never heard my father say he was too tired to meet one of my friends. I had heard him say he was too tired to have the preacher, who made him nervous, over for supper. I had heard him say he was too tired to drive some of the prayer circle members, who *really* made him nervous, to Houston to hear Billy Graham.

Mother was looking at Dad with that same strange look she'd given me earlier. "He's just a little boy, Phil. And he's lost his father."

Dad *did* look tired, I thought. In fact, he looked ill. "Charles Dale can come another night," I said. "Or maybe he and I could just have a picnic in the backyard."

"Nonsense." Mother's voice was unusually smooth in the

face of argument. She looked at us and gestured with the veg-
etable knife. "He's already been invited. What would Lou Jean
think?" Then she turned back to her tomatoes. "Go sit down,
Phil. Have a beer."

Before Dad could move, someone knocked on the back door.

"Kayla, that must be your company," said Mother, her face
alight. She looked like someone had just handed her a tiny box
with a jewelry-store label on it. Dad really looked as if he felt
bad, but she didn't seem to notice. His hands on my head had
tightened. "Kayla . . ." Mother said again.

I ducked out of Dad's grip and answered the door. Charles
Dale handed me a jar of bread-and-butter pickles. "My mom
sent these." He wore a pair of madras shorts and a pale blue
T-shirt that made his tanned arms even darker, the blond
streaks in his hair even lighter.

As Charles Dale came toward him, Dad seemed to retreat
without leaving. As if he took up less space where he stood. I'd
always thought of my father as a big man. In fact, he was well
over six feet tall. But now, as he stood before us, gazing first at
Charles Dale, then at me, then again at Charles Dale, he
seemed small, young, and terrified. Like a barn kitten trans-
fixed by the first human it sees, in the split second before it
turns and scrambles behind the hay bales.

If Charles Dale, at that moment, had looked at my father,
he would surely have thought Dad didn't want him in our
house. And I was beginning to wonder if I really wanted him
there myself. My mother looked like she had a fever, and my
father looked like he had the flu. I was confused and grouchy
from all the work I'd had to do getting ready, no longer in the
mood for company. Nothing seemed right.

Mother put her hands on Charles Dale's shoulders, then, and staring down at his face, said, "We are so glad you could come," her words as slow and pronounced as if he were royalty. As if she were the mayor, welcoming the governor. Then she turned him around to face my father. "Phil," she said, "this is Kayla's very special friend. Charles Dale Perry."

My dad's smile was small, tight, and the hand that reached to shake Charles Dale's seemed stiff and fearful, afraid to extend itself. It reminded me of my own hand once, at the Houston zoo, when the zookeeper had demonstrated how to pet a boa constrictor. I had wanted to stroke it, but my hand shook when I reached out, my arm frozen at the elbow, not fully extended, so I could pull it back if I had to.

Charles Dale didn't seem to notice anything. He grinned, the grin that took up his whole face, and said to Dad, "Your picture is on our wall."

The smile left my mother's face.

"It's in our hall."

Mother looked at Dad, who seemed unable to do anything but stare at Charles Dale.

"It's you and my dad. And you're wearing football uniforms."

Mother smiled again. "Well, isn't that nice?" she breathed, her hands patting Charles Dale's shoulders. "Charles Dale," she said, leaning around him to look into his face again, "why don't you go with Phil into the living room and get acquainted, and Kayla and I will finish getting supper on the table?" Dad didn't move. "Phil?" she prodded.

"We'll help. Won't we, Charles Dale?" Dad opened a drawer and pulled out his barbecue apron. He unfolded it and,

with his right hand, slipped the apron over Charles Dale's
neck. With his left hand, he reached around my head, drawing
me closer and tousling my hair like he'd done a million times
before. Except it didn't feel the same. As his right hand slid
down Charles Dale's face, settling the apron loop at the base of
his neck, Dad's left hand suddenly stopped against the back of
my head, tightening around my ponytail, circling it and holding on, the same way my free hand had circled and clung to his
fingers the day my other hand petted the boa.

At dinner, we sat like quarter-hour marks on a clock face.
Mother flirted and told lies. She told Charles Dale that he'd
have to come camping with us when the weather turned cooler,
even though she hated camping, griped from the moment we
got there till the moment we left. She also promised to get Dad
to make his famous venison chili during deer season, even
though she hated venison, didn't even want it in the house. If
he killed a deer, Dad knew to have it processed before he ever
brought it home—and not to even ask to cook it inside.

Each time she got up from the table to get something, she
made a point of walking behind my father's chair. She'd brush
her hand across the top of his head, lay the backs of her bent
fingers against his cheek. Once she even stopped and rubbed
his shoulders. "Your neck is so tight, sweetheart. Did you have
a rough day?"

He didn't answer, but a chatty Charles Dale did. "You
ought to put some peppermint oil on it. That's what my mom
uses." He asked for more mashed potatoes and, as I passed him
the bowl, said, "I have a tent. Well, really, it belongs to David
and me. It was our dad's. Where do you go?"

My mother sat back down and, beaming, passed him the meat platter. "I don't know, but you'd better have some more chicken to go with those potatoes." She turned to Dad. "Phil, where should we go?"

My father looked all the way down the table to me. The smile kept slipping off his face. "I don't know. Someplace close. Kayla, where do you want to go?"

I shrugged. "I don't know." I didn't. And I wanted them to just shut up and eat, so that I could watch Charles Dale. There was something about him that I hadn't noticed until tonight, something that seemed familiar, as I'd noticed before, but that now seemed misplaced, as if he wore clothes I was used to see-ing on someone else.

He dropped one of his shoulders, tilted his head, and with his eyes rolled up toward his brow, as if perusing his brain, said, "Well, let's see. We could go to Garner State Park. It's not too far away. And there's ConCan. It's about the same distance. Or we could just go to the county park outside of town. There are campsites there." He stabbed two more slices of red tomato, raked them onto his plate, and turned to my dad. "Do you like to fish better in a lake or the river?" he asked.

This time, Dad held on to his smile, a wide one that relaxed as it spread and that didn't stop until it reached his ears, the way his smiles normally did. He dropped one shoulder, tilted his head, looked up toward his brow, and said, "Well, let's see. I like a lake for largemouth. Big old black bass. But most of the time, the river's better for catfish."

Now I watched Charles Dale's grin spread. "Can we set out trotlines when we go? I've got lots of line, and some old plastic jugs we can use for floats."

Dad's face grew very still, and his eyes shone as he listened to Charles Dale rattle on. Then he shook his head, as if clearing some clouded thought, and joined in the conversation. I put down my fork and simply followed their movements. Like partners on a well-practiced relay team, they passed a single grin back and forth. Smoothly, naturally, the transfer itself invisible. Just as easily, they handed off the dropped shoulder and raised eyes, while they mulled all the things they'd need for the trip. As it dawned on me that disgusting Thad Howard might have a reason, besides insanity, for the things he'd said that afternoon, my throat tightened past the point of swallowing chicken, and I coughed a little, trying to loosen it.

Mother turned to me, and the smile she'd lavished on the fishermen fell away when she saw my plate. "You'd better get started, young lady. You haven't touched a thing except pickles."

The night breeze came warm onto the porch, bringing smells of huisache and honeysuckle across our faces. "You and Charles Dale go outside and play," Mother had said after dinner. "Dad will help me with the dishes." I stood on the top step and stared at Charles Dale, now searching for ways that he *wasn't* like my dad. A dropped shoulder and raised eyes could be coincidence. And a lot of people had wide smiles.

"Want to catch lightning bugs?" he asked.

"Nah." Standing on the lawn below me, he looked very small and very young, though he was only three months younger than I was. His ears were flatter than Dad's, and his hair was lighter, if only a little. It was dark out, and I was glad, because I didn't want him to see my face, the way I could feel it closing off against him, the way it sometimes set itself against my mother.

Charles Dale pointed to the far end of the street then, where it dead-ended into a vacant lot, a pool of light there from a street lamp. "I know where there's a momma skunk that brings her babies out to eat June bugs every night. If we're really quiet, we can hear them crunch."

"I don't think so. I'm kind of tired."

"Okay." He looked at me sympathetically, probably thinking skunks made me nervous, as tall trees made him. The night before, we had climbed the mulberry tree in my backyard. I had gone all the way to the top, where the branches were so thin that they curved under my weight, but Charles Dale had become nervous, wanting me to come down. When I'd encouraged him to follow me, he'd declined. "Naw," he'd said. "I'm kind of tired."

The top step of our front porch suddenly felt no more solid than the thinnest branches of a mulberry tree. I sat down quickly and looked at the lower step between my knees.

"Are you okay?"

I nodded. A clanking in the street drew our attention. Thad Howard, his rusty bicycle creaking like a corpse, rode by, staring at us silently. He circled once in front of my house, then pedaled off toward his own. "Numbnuts," said Charles Dale.

I leaned my elbows on the porch, still looking past him. The moon had risen above the house across the street, turning things ghostly. The white petunias my mother had planted around the roses, the white caladiums under the shade trees, my father's white Chevy pickup, all of them looked eerie in the moonlight, drained of color and yet glowing, as if they had no life except what the moon gave them or were only bits of moon dropped in the yard. Through our porch slats I saw Lou Jean on her own porch. She wore something long, a robe maybe, and it was white also. She stood there with her hands and arms turned out, as if to catch the light, and her face very pale, no different from the robe, really. Her loose hair drifted in the breeze, but was so dark, so nearly invisible in the night, that it gave the impression that her body was swaying, moving at the discretion of the wind. With no more volition, no more strength, than the caladiums.

When I got back to the dining room, my father stood with his back pinned against the far wall, his eyes closed, both arms outstretched, one hand trying to balance the gravy boat, the other, the cut-glass bowl holding Lou Jean's pickles. Pressed tight against him, her back to me, was my mother, her hands on either side of my father's head, flat against the wall her body pushed him into.

She kissed him, not on the cheek as she usually did, but on the lips and for a long time, while he held the dishes out and away from the two of them. Finally, she pulled away, and my father's head dropped back against the wall, his eyes still closed. "Sarah Jo . . ." he said, as if he wanted to complain about something but couldn't quite, his voice hoarse, like something was wrong with his chest.

The dishes he held were no longer upright. The pickle juice slid further up the side of the cut-glass bowl as it tilted, as my mother's head tilted too and moved down, her mouth to my father's neck. Her head turned and her teeth raked his skin, as he said again, "God, Sarah Jo," and then, so hoarse I could barely understand him, "What brought this on?"

The pickle juice inched slowly, thick as syrup, to the top of

the bowl and hung heavy between the sharp points of the ruffled edge, then flowed over the side and clung. Bringing her
mouth back up to his, my mother kicked off her sandals and
stepped, barefooted, onto the tops of my father's boots. The
pickle juice, clear and bright as tears, ran down the outside of
the bowl and dropped, a shiny steady stream, to the carpet.

5

I awoke before daylight the next morning, with a raw throat and a head that throbbed. My parents weren't awake yet. It was the coolest time of day, and I shivered a little on my way to the bathroom for aspirin. I climbed back in bed and reached for the light blanket that covered my sheet, my arms turning to goose pimples as I settled down under the covers and tried to go back to sleep.

The cool air made me think of Cameron, all the way across Texas, almost in Louisiana, about as far from Rosalita as you could get and still be in the same state. Cameron summers were hot and humid, but the winters were cold. Cold enough for fireplaces and heavy sweaters. Sometimes it even snowed. In my mind, I could see a Cameron snow, heavy on a Saturday morning, the first week in January, and I mentally walked out of our old house, which sat at the edge of a piney woods, and gathered a handful of that clean perfect snow, opened my mouth, and stuffed it in, packed its frozen calm against the back of my throat, the pain melting and trickling away as the snow did.

My parents had seemed happier in Cameron, or at least more like the people I knew. My mother had always been moody and set on getting her way, as Dad had said, but at least predictable. I always knew what to expect. Here, she was either moping, staring at the photo faces of people she hadn't seen in fourteen years, or frantic, donning first one new outfit and then another, her hands nervously roaming her body, searching out imperfections. One minute, she was angry, yelling at my grandmother or my father. The next minute, she was out the door, smiling like the largest problem in her life was keeping aphids off her rose buds. In two months, I would begin my last year in junior high. And not once had she mentioned shopping for school clothes.

For the first time since I'd walked into Lou Jean's magic kitchen, I really missed Cameron, the place, and not just Cameron, the home of Mike Spivey. I missed the people my parents had been, and I missed the person *I* had been. Someone who thought mysteries were fun and romantic. And, at this moment, with my throat burning and my head aching, I especially missed the protective isolation of the woods behind our house. The trees that grew there were tall and thick, red oak, loblolly pine, chinquapin, hickory. In the spring, white dogwood and purple redbud had decorated the hideouts I made. In the fall, leaves of all colors covered the ground and I had to walk slowly, cautiously, to keep from frightening squirrels that worked and played all around me. Now, lying in bed, I could see the entrance to those woods on the backs of my eyelids, the place where the light stopped and the darkness started, the narrow trail that I kept worn down. In my mind, I stepped onto the trail and moved off through the trees, weaving around them, walking under familiar branches that measured my growth as I measured theirs, year after year, traveling the quarter mile or so to the one tree I wanted. I sat down on the cool damp earth, leaned back against an oak older than both my parents put together, and fell asleep.

I awoke later, hearing my mother come out of their room and go to the kitchen to make coffee. I did not call out to her or say I was sick. Above the bubble of the percolator, I heard her low voice to my father and his to her, as he followed soon after, their voices whispering. In our house in Cameron, I remembered them whispering only twice, both times when my mother had miscarried babies, when they were trying to decide how much to tell me. The second time it happened, Dad and I whispered too, after Mother came home from the hospital quiet and sad, when the sound of our normal voices seemed too loud to be in the same house with her.

My grandmother had whispered also, coming across Texas to cook for my dad and me, to sit by my mother's bed and try to get her to eat more than dry toast and fruit juice. It had taken several weeks for my mother to seem herself again. Then, one afternoon, she simply climbed out of bed, washed her hair, put on a dress, and announced that she felt well enough to make Wednesday-night prayer meeting. On her way out the door, she looked at me and said, "I guess you'd better not count on ever having a brother or sister."

After that, my mother began to talk about moving back to south Texas. A few months later, Dad was offered a job as branch manager for the agricultural lending company he worked for, and the particular branch was in Rosalita. Mother was ecstatic, but at first Dad was hesitant. Finally, though, she'd won him over, and then they had both shown nothing but excitement as they discussed his taking the job, our moving to the town where they'd grown up. There had been no hesitation, no sense of apprehension, so that now I wondered if it was different here from what they'd expected. If there was something in Rosalita that they hadn't anticipated. Or if we had actually moved to the wrong place, somewhere they hadn't intended to go at all.

It was as if my parents and I, leading the van carrying our belongings, had moved farther than just across the state. Had traveled longer than the distance it took to go from pine trees to prickly pear. As if somewhere between Cameron and here, we had crossed some ghost line and now lived south of reason. I wondered if they were becoming the people they'd been growing up, or if moving to the town of their childhood was making them children again. I seemed to be the only one in the house getting any older.

Later, I heard my mother and grandmother's voices, low but clear, coming from the living room. "She's a kid," I heard my mother say. "Kids are so wrapped up in their own world, they don't pay any attention."

"She won't have to pay attention once school starts. Somebody will be glad to pay attention for her. You think kids talk any less than adults?"

"Well, Phil can tell her. Except he won't. You should have seen him last night. He was scared to death. You'd have thought I'd invited Castro to dinner."

"Can you blame him?"

Mother's voice was edgy. "You'd better believe I can."

"It has to be hard for him, Sarah Jo. And who knows how it's going to affect those children. You're asking for trouble."

"How am I asking for trouble? All I'm doing is including Kayla's friend in some of our activities, making him welcome, giving him the chance to be around a man his father's age. Some people would say it's the Christian thing to do."

"Yes," said Gran, "and some people would say if you're such a big Christian, you should have listened to Christ thirteen years ago."

"That is mean." Mother was almost yelling.

"Well, it's true. In my experience, when people say they're doing something simply because it's the Christian thing to do, they're lying to somebody, most probably themselves."

"She started it. Not three hours after we moved in here."

"Started what?"

"What she always starts. What she's so good at."

Gran's voice was angry now. "Sarah Jo, this isn't Cameron. This is Rosalita. And people know you. *And* they know Lou Jean. *And* they know Phil. You can't expect Kayla not to find out. Especially with you living next door, of all places. You should all be thinking about what you can do to make life easier on these two kids."

"I have been thinking about that, Mother. I've decided we're going to join the church next Sunday. I'm going to transfer our membership from Cameron. And I'm going to ask Charles Dale to come with us. His mother evidently doesn't have him in any kind of Sunday school program. Kayla is used to having a church home. I think it would be good for him to have the same thing."

"You're going to walk into the church with Phil and Kayla and Charles Dale like one big happy family?" asked my grandmother. "What makes you think Lou Jean will stand for that?"

"Because Charles Dale will want it," said my mother. "She might not like it, but she'll let him go. She'll just have to wash her hands a few more times."

"Now who's being mean?"

Mother's voice softened. "Don't look at me like that. Please. It wouldn't hurt you to come with us."

For the second time in two weeks, I listened to my grandmother stomp out of our house. "I'd rather crochet barbed wire."

~ 6 ~

My grandmother, like a lot of older women in town, had a river camp. The camps were built back in the '30s, when materials were cheap and labor was even cheaper. Stucco cabins, painted in cool colors, mint and peach, sat behind deep green lawns thick as mattresses, along the banks of the Nueces, where the river pooled and pouted under ancient oaks and pecans. The water was blue-green during times when there was rain, muddy brown when there wasn't. In the summer, the river barely moved, dragging its feet all the way to Lake Mathis, and below that, to Corpus Christi and the Gulf of Mexico.

When the camps were built, they had been welcome retreats, a cooler place for families to spend weekends and holidays. Back then, the camps were open as much as they were closed, used by everybody in the family. The men had cookouts to celebrate opening day of deer season, fish fries during the rest of the year. The women held bridge club and study club luncheons, folding the legs out on card tables and setting them in the shade of the giant trees. The children had birthday parties there, swinging wooden bats at piñatas, jumping into the river from rope swings, cooking hot dogs over campfires.

The first day I felt better, my grandmother showed up at nine in the morning, wanting me to come to the camp with her, to air it out and dust. I couldn't help noticing that just like me, Gran wore a pair of denim overalls, cropped off and dangling uneven fringe at the knee, over an old T-shirt. "Bring your bathing suit," she said, putting a hand on either side of my face, cupping my jaws and turning my eyes up to hers as if she had something important to tell me. "I would bring mine, but it's got a hole in the knee."

My mother, who stood behind the screen door watching Gran and me on the porch, held the door open as I rushed in for my suit. "Wait," she said. "Why don't you ask Charles Dale to go with you?"

I turned and looked through the screen at my grandmother, who was shaking her head. "I just saw him with his mother and David. In the car. Headed toward town."

As I ran on into my room, pulling open a drawer and digging for my swimsuit, I heard Gran again, "Give it up, Sarah Jo." By the time I made it back to the porch, she was already in her car, the engine running and the windows up. I ran down the steps, jumping the last two.

"Aren't you going to kiss me good-bye?" called Mother. I turned and walked back up the steps to where she sat in the glider. She cocked her cheek toward me so that I could kiss it. I turned and ran down the steps, opened the car door, and slid into the air conditioning, Mother's scowl skewering the windshield.

The drive to the river went through Mexican town, tiny houses with perfect yards. Most of them didn't have grass. Instead, the entire yards were taken up with flowers, roses, daylilies, zinnias, and rosemary plants as big as trees. Just past a yard that was especially pretty, where two orioles drank from a concrete birdbath and a statue of the Virgin of Guadalupe took shelter in the shade of a weeping willow, my grandmother surprised me by hitting the brakes. She stared at my face as if trying to decide something. Then she threw the car into reverse, backed up in front of the pretty yard, and stopped.

"Can you keep a secret? From your mother, I mean?" When I nodded, she shoved the gearshift up into park and killed the engine. We got out, opened a chain-link gate topped by a metal pheasant, and went up the brick sidewalk. The orioles flew up into a chinaberry tree. The front door was open, and through the screen, itself decorated with an aluminum heron, I could smell something wonderful. Gran knocked on the door frame and yelled, "Carmen? You've got company."

The woman who opened the door was as tiny and delicate as my grandmother was tall and big boned. She wiped her hands on a green gingham apron, pushing the screen out for us. *"Ay, que chula,"* she said immediately, grabbing me and pulling me against her as if she'd known me all my life. She was so small that her head pressed against my chest as she hugged me. Her voice, though, rang as if out of a megaphone. She pushed me away from her, holding onto my shoulders, and looked up into my face, then dropped her head back even farther to look up at Gran. "Rose. How did *you* get such a pretty granddaughter?"

"Because I deserved her, that's how. There's not much use in having an ugly one. What do I smell?" She strode off. Carmen and I followed through a living room where every possible surface was covered with crocheted doilies, not just white ones, but pink and green ones that looked like the roses in the yard, and pale yellow ones with fat purple clusters of grapes. Atop the television, on a ruffled doily that dipped and flowed like ribbon candy, sat framed photographs, all of the same person, as a boy, a teenager, a man.

Carmen saw me looking at them.

"Joe Vincent Ayala," she said. *"Mi hijo."* I noticed that the pictures were only of him, no wife or children, though he looked old enough to have a family of his own.

In the kitchen, Carmen pushed us into red vinyl chairs that matched the red linoleum on the floor and the red Formica on the countertops, then she turned immediately to the stove, flipping a tortilla that was browning in a cast iron skillet. "You're just in time, Rosie, like always."

"We were kind of hoping that." Gran winked at me. From under a damp cup towel, Carmen took a ball of dough. In about three swipes of the rolling pin, she shaped the dough perfectly round and flat, flipped the finished tortilla out of the skillet and onto a pile staying warm under a different cup towel, then tossed the raw one into the hot skillet. Her tiny hands never stopped. While the tortilla cooked, she walked to the refrigerator, took out a pitcher of lemonade and an ice tray, and before it was time to flip the tortilla, there were full glasses in front of Gran and me. The whole time she worked, Carmen kept up a conversation with my grandmother, their voices jumping back and forth across each other, one word on top of the next, like baby frogs on a sidewalk after a rain. Newly hatched and out to explore, going in all directions. There was a closeness about their words, a playfulness, that was different from the way grown-ups usually talked.

"You get your peaches up yet?" Gran leaned out of her

chair and looked through the kitchen screen to a large tree in the backyard. "There's still peaches on that tree, woman. I thought you were canning last week."

"I did, Rose, I did, but this year I got too *many* peaches." Carmen was back at the stove, flipping tortillas. "You see those boxes? You see all those boxes?" She looked at me to make sure I was paying attention, then pointed with the egg turner to a stack of Ball Jar boxes almost as tall as the refrigerator. "That's all peaches. Canned peaches, peach preserves, pickled peaches. I got peaches for the whole neighborhood." She slammed the rolling pin down on another round of dough, flattened it, and tossed it into the skillet. "You like peaches, Kaylita?"

I nodded, looking out the door at peaches as big as grapefruit. "Yes, ma'am."

"*Ay, que chula,*" Carmen said again, dropping the egg turner and coming back toward me. This time she cupped my cheeks almost exactly as my grandmother did. "She's so polite," she said to Gran.

"Yeah, a natural wonder, isn't it?" Gran swigged her lemonade, then set the glass down hard, like a saloon drinker on *Bonanza*.

"Rosie, you be nice." Carmen rolled her eyes, then peered over her shoulder at her tortillas.

"What do you mean, a natural wonder?" I asked Gran.

"Just that some kids aren't so polite," said Carmen quickly, patting my shoulder with one hand. "There's a little girl lives down my street that is rude all the time. To her mama. To her sisters. To everybody. Not like you, sweetiepie." She patted the top of my head, then turned totally around, her back to us, and pounded another tortilla.

Gran grinned at her back, never having answered my question, then looked at me. "Never mind," she said. "Don't listen to old women."

"That's right," said Carmen, still not looking at us. "Just two old *viejitas*, two old women. With no old men to remind us we don't make good sense." She repeated the tortilla steps, then turned back to me. "You want to do me a favor?" I nodded. Putting one tiny hand between my shoulder blades, she pressed me up and out of my chair. With the egg turner, she pointed out the back door. "You go out there and get that basket, that big one by the dog house, and you pick every one of those darn peaches, every one, *bueno*? And you take them home with you because I am *through* with peaches for this year. *¿Me entiendes?*"

Thinking I understood that last part, I finished my lemonade and went out the back door. Carmen shouted to me, "Don't be afraid of that dog. He's old, like me and your grandma."

"Hell, at least *we* get out of our damned beds in the morning," called Gran.

As I went to get the basket, the dog so far up in his house that I couldn't even see him, Carmen said, "Rosie, you need to quit saying bad words in front of your little granddaughter."

"Me? You're the one that just lied to her. Little girl down the street, my hind foot."

"Yes, and that's your fault, Miss Big Mouth. Now I got to go to confession for telling whoppers."

"Hell, you tell whoppers every time you go. You're too old for confession. You worry yourself sick around here every Friday, trying to think of something to confess. Usually, you end up having to make up something. Which makes you worry about whether you ought to confess that you lied about whatever it is you're confessing because you really didn't do it, because you're too old to do anything worth confessing. So Saturday morning comes, and you drive off to the church with your face all in a frown, worrying what to lie about, and whether to lie or tell the truth about the fact that you're lying in the first place. This week, I just saved you all that worry. You ought to butter me one of those tortillas out of gratitude."

"Only somebody who was never in her whole life a Catholic could spout a bunch of mess like that. There's the butter. Get your own."

They might have been kids, I thought as I picked peaches, except most kids couldn't talk to each other the way they did without one of them getting mad. They were like the best kind of kids. Crazy enough to have fun, but wise enough to not get mad at each other. Young enough to act goofy, but old enough to not hurt each other's feelings.

"When's Joe Junior coming home again?" Gran asked.

"Labor Day," said Carmen. "How many peaches you got so far?" she called.

"I looked in the basket. "A lot. You sure you don't want to keep some?"

"None!" Then her voice lowered. "I saw Guess Who yesterday. In front of the dress shop. I said hello, but you know, she seemed in a really big hurry. I guess she just didn't hear me."

My grandmother snorted.

"Who?" I called. There was silence, and then they burst into laughter again. Without answering me, they moved on to the year when they had ended up with no peaches. A rattlesnake had crawled into Carmen's backyard, and while Gran had gone out to her car to get a pistol to shoot it, Carmen had tried to keep it from getting away till she got back. Afraid to get too near it, she kept grabbing green peaches, still hard, off her tree, pelting the snake every time it headed for the fence. But Gran had forgotten that she'd taken her pistol out of the car, and by the time she remembered and came back carrying a garden hoe, Carmen had pulled every single peach.

"Like it made a big rat's ass. You still had enough canned peaches from the year before to last till the next summer."

How long had they been friends? I wondered. Maybe they had grown up together, raised children together, been widowed together. They lived on opposite sides of town, one in a huge house, one in a tiny one, yet seemed to have so much in common. My mother and Lou Jean had grown up together, had children the same age, and now lived next door to each other, yet they seemed as different as Gran and Carmen seemed alike. I couldn't imagine them sharing anything.

"Is Carmen your best friend?" I asked Gran. Charles Dale had said that Lou Jean was Gran's best friend.

Her answer was nonchalant. "Next to you." She dropped her arms over the side of her webbed plastic lounge chair, stretching her feet and legs out toward the river. We had left Carmen on her front porch, laughing and flapping her apron as if we were errant chickens. We had cleaned the river camp, and I had eaten four peaches, then jumped into the river to wash off the stickiness. Taking a deep breath, I turned bottom up and kicked my way down into the green that grew cloudier and darker as I went. Little white flecks and pieces of something, vegetation, algae maybe, moved away from me as I dove, my hands and arms pushing them to the side. I wondered if the flecks were dangerous, dirty, the very things that caused ear infections, and I imagined that my hands were a shield, clearing and cleaning the water I swept through. I pushed off the bottom with one hand, then turned toward the surface, looking up to the light. Feet against the floor of the river, I shoved off, and mud exploded on every side of me. The water around and between my legs clouded and cooled, as if I had kicked up buried ice cubes. In the current I created, something rough brushed my calf. Against my skin, it felt like something backward, like stroking a cat's fur the wrong way or running a hand up a bream's scales. It caught and clung to my leg, then was gone, and I sped for the surface.

Gran leaned forward in her lounge chair, her chin resting on fists, elbows lodged against spread knees. She gazed over the top of my head to the far side of the river and didn't seem to notice my hasty arrival. Then, she spoke. "So. How do you feel about your new house? Is it all right so far?"

I scanned the water around me, without mentioning what had happened below. I wasn't sure if I was scared enough to get out. "It's okay. It'd be better if we had a peach tree."

She laughed. "Well, maybe we'll plant you one." The water was clearer on top, and I saw no movement beneath the surface. Gran's laugh died away. "Do you have a good time playing with Charles Dale?"

"Yeah." I turned in the water so that I too faced the opposite bank. "He's nice," I said, hardly breathing. "But how come my mom doesn't like his mom?"

Gran's long sigh sounded as if I wouldn't get an answer, and

I turned back toward her and moved nearer the bank. Her own eyes shifted downward, as if periscoping the water around me.

"Don't get too close to that old log. It's a perfect place for a cottonmouth nest." I quickly treaded back out into the river, to a patch of sunlight that fell between the tree branches, but Gran's eyes never left the surface of the water. When I was almost ready to repeat my question, she spoke. "It's complicated, love. I'm not even sure if I understand it."

"What do you mean?" Still treading, I closed my eyes, so that it felt like my body was in two different worlds, the top of it in bright sunlight, warmth that flooded my face and steamed my hair; the lower part of it, my feet and legs, in a cold dark place. Icy streams threaded between my toes as I made small, cautious kicks.

"I mean that it goes back so far, it's hard to remember." I leaned my head back onto the water and floated. The river moved so slowly that I barely had to fan my hands to stay in one place. "The first time your mother met Lou Jean, they were three years old. I took her to Lou Jean's birthday party."

Water flowed in and out of my ears, and Gran's voice sounded as if it came through a tunnel. The sun made me heavy. "And what happened?"

"Your mother took one look at a little aluminum dinette set Lou Jean had gotten for her birthday and decided she had to have it. She picked up one of the chairs and started for the door with it. I had to spank her to make her put it down. Each time I got it away from her, she'd go right back to it. Pick it up and head for the car." She spoke slowly, thoughtfully, as if, thirty years later, she was still confused by her daughter's actions. "She was so damned determined."

"Couldn't you have just bought her a set?"

"I did. For Christmas, we bought her one just like it. But it didn't matter. She didn't want the one we got her. She wanted Lou Jean's. And after that, it was always something. Never the item, not the dinette itself, or the bicycle, or the exact prom dress. It was whatever Lou Jean had, whatever she seemed to care the most about. *That* was what your mother had to have."

I stretched out on to my back again, thinking about this. The sun came through my closed eyelids so that red lights danced against them. Gran kept talking, as if mulling it all over. "And of course I couldn't get her what Lou Jean had; I could only get her one *like* it."

"Did Lou Jean ever take anything of Mother's?"

"No," said Gran. She was so emphatic that I opened my eyes and looked at her. She had resumed staring at the opposite bank, and her voice dwindled, as if she were backing away. "She did try, once or twice, to reclaim what was hers in the first place."

Ground doves drank from a sidewalk puddle left by the sprinkler, and the mockingbird sang from his usual place on the telephone pole. The whole neighborhood seemed so peaceful that Gran's "Oh, brother" startled me. She wheeled into the drive and jammed the gearshift into park. The car rocked forward and back before it stopped. Across a gap in the ceniza hedge dividing our lawns, Lou Jean and Mother faced each other.

Lou Jean waved to us, and the gold hoops in her ears danced from side to side. She wore a pair of cutoffs and a white gauze painter's smock. The long shirred sleeves billowed like summer curtains. Mother wore the blue sundress.

Reaching for the door handle, Gran said, "Stay behind me in case there's stray fire." We carried the basket, heavy with fruit, across the lawn. The wire handles dug into my palms, and I set my end down hard enough for some of the peaches to roll out.

As I bent to gather them, Mother told Gran, "Lou Jean goes with her mother every Sunday to Uvalde, to see her uncle in the nursing home, so I've suggested that she let Charles Dale come to church with us. Don't you think that sounds like a good idea?" The quickness of her voice, its edge, made me think that Lou Jean had already said no.

Gran grinned at Lou Jean, as if she hadn't heard Mother's question. "Lou Jean, how in the world are you?" You'd have thought she hadn't seen Lou Jean in months.

"I'm fine, Rose." She wore a matching grin. She lifted the thick braid off her neck and coiled it around and around on the back of her head, twisting the tip end of it back into itself to form a knot that somehow held. She nodded at the basket of peaches. "You two must be doing all right."

Mother, who had been glaring at Gran, and then at Lou Jean, as if it made her angry to see hair long enough to tie in a knot, as if Lou Jean tied it just to vex her, finally noticed the basket. "What in heaven's name is that?"

"Peaches," I said, just as Gran said, "What does it look like?"

"We can't possibly eat all those peaches. Where'd you get them anyway?"

I stuttered.

Gran saved me. "A friend gave them to us. She had more than she knew what to do with."

"Well, they're certainly more than *I* know what to do with. You'd better find somebody to give them to, Mother, before they ruin."

"I'm going to put them up. To can them, I mean," I said.

Mother put her hands on her hips, her body facing Lou Jean but her scowl aimed at me, as if I'd brought home a basket filled not with peaches but with puppies. "Kayla Marie, that's a lot of work, and you have no idea what you're doing." Lou Jean smirked at Mother's turned head. I couldn't tell them that I knew how to put up the peaches, that Carmen had given me a recipe for jelly.

"Can't *you* help her with them, Sarah Jo?" Gran asked Mother.

"No, I can't," she fumed. "I have enough on my plate already." Her voice rose and fell, plodding up and down the hills of all the things she had to do. "We're joining the church this Sunday, Mother, in case you've forgotten, and I do not have time to be fooling with peaches."

Lou Jean's expression was different now, her smirk turned hard, as if she no longer enjoyed what she saw, or as if she were seeing something that she'd seen before and never had liked. Then her gaze shifted to me. "I have time."

I looked at Mother as quickly as Gran did, both of us expecting explosion. Instead, she looked at Lou Jean for only a moment, then dropped her hands from her hips and lifted one to rest on my head. "Well, isn't that nice, sweetheart?" Her voice changed as fast as her face did. "Would it be okay with you if Lou Jean helped you with the peaches?"

I nodded, speechless, thrilled at the prospect but dumbfounded by Mother's behavior. Gran stared at Mother, as confused as I was. The look on Lou Jean's face, though, was as strange as Mother's behavior. Her head tilted down, chin tucked, her eyes raised all the way to her thick dark brows, she smiled at Mother, a smile that involved only her lips, just a tiny careful lifting. An expectant knowing smile, like a mother watching her two-year-old try to decide whether to again fling his food bowl off the high-chair tray. The smile of someone who knows the person she watches even better than the person knows herself—and enjoys watching her struggle.

When Lou Jean looked at me again, her face was back to normal, her smile merely cheerful, and she said, "We can do them now if you'd like, Kayla. The boys have gone to my mom's for the night."

"Okay." I grabbed one wire handle. Lou Jean walked directly in front of Mother and lifted the side of the basket that Gran had held. Mother radiated a smile gracious and generous and smug, like the winner of a race gives the person who came in right on her heels.

As we started to Lou Jean's door, the peaches swinging between us, Mother called, "Lou Jean, I really appreciate this. And it's settled." Her voice rivaled the mockingbird in cheer. "We'll take Charles Dale with us on Sunday. Turnabout."

As Lou Jean opened the screen door, leaned back against it, and waited for me to go in, her hair came unknotted and tumbled, a black velvet rope, down her shoulder. She leaned against the house, and across the bounty of her braid, gave Mother a very flat look. As if she saw nothing there.

As I scooted in the door, I looked too. And I saw Mother's smile turn liquid and drain down her neck and onto our grass, then pool itself and reemerge on my grandmother's face, as Lou Jean finally answered. "Oh, I almost forgot. This is the one Sunday out of the month when we have a church service at the nursing home. And Charles Dale lights the candles. Maybe some other time."

7

Twelve jars sat on the kitchen table. Eight of them held preserves. Four held pie filling. Mother, not awake yet, still hadn't seen them. It embarrassed me that she had tried to con Lou Jean, but it didn't surprise me that she'd used the church to do it. Almost everything she did involved the church, though her labors seemed more about spectacle than service, as if she had deemed herself Most Faithful and had to work diligently to retain her title.

In Mother I saw none of the quiet joy I had seen in people who felt their religion, in some of the older ladies in Cameron, and also in Carmen, in the way she talked about going to Mass, as if she couldn't wait to get there, each and every week. As if she gained something that informed not only her days but her life, the woman she *was*. She tolerated my grandmother's teasing about confession with the patience of someone who owns something she doesn't expect anyone else to understand and who values it so much that all the ridicule in the world could cause no doubt. In Mother, I never saw this joy. She responded to Gran's ribbing by enumerating accomplishments and duties rather than by professing or defending her faith. There was this fierce energy in Mother's relationship with the church, hurried and fraught with all the things that would go wrong if she weren't there to take care of them. Gladness of heart, the joy of doing, the radiance on Carmen's rouged face when she climbed into her Sunday-clean car, gloves and mantilla tucked into the side pocket of her handbag, these things I never saw in Mother.

In Cameron, Dad had been a big part of Mother's church plans. The fact that his enthusiasm never matched hers, that he'd have been content showing up on the occasional Easter Sunday, Mother took as proof that he *needed* the chores she assigned him. The construction of manger props, the painting of rectory walls, the flipping of pancakes at church suppers, the travel to nearby towns to help the "less fortunate." Mother used religion as a wifely whip, flogging my indentured father into doing the things she thought he should do. As if, left to his own choices, he would surely squander his free time.

Most of the time, he simply went along with her plans. Dad's basic personality was so cheerful that he could find something to enjoy in almost any activity. It was also his natural inclination to make the best of the situation. But a few times he had balked. Once, after several weekends devoted to a spring cleanup campaign, he had refused to start the truck to drive to the church to plant azaleas until Mother promised him he could skip church the following morning for a fishing trip. Another time, when she'd agreed we'd leave a Saturday-night church social early enough for Dad to watch a boxing match and then had reneged on her promise, he had arranged with one of the church ladies to bring Mother home. At ten minutes to eight, he announced that he and I were leaving and that anyone wanting to see the Frazier fight was welcome to follow us to our house.

He had been alone when I, carrying a large cardboard box, had returned from Lou Jean's the night before. I was triumphant, proud but a little nervous about Mom's mood after her loss to Lou Jean. Dad sat in his recliner in front of the television. On a tray beside his chair was a foil-wrapped TV dinner, its unopened surface still smooth. Around it, carefully positioned at the four corners, sat four beer bottles. Uncapped and empty. Someone, Dad, I guess, had taken rubber bands, the large loose ones that came on the Sunday papers, and had looped them over the beer bottles, so that the whole thing looked like a boxing ring, complete with ropes. With one finger, he plunked the rubber bands, as if sending a fleeing boxer back into the ring.

When I'd set my box down gently on his outstretched legs, he'd put an arm around me and said, "Whatcha got, Sunshine?" I'd opened the box and shown him my jars.

"Where's Mom?"

"Had a headache." He'd lifted each jar out carefully, naming each one, as if each was different, each significant: "Preserves. Pie filling."

"Is she mad at me?"

"Why would she be mad at you?"

"Because I went to Lou Jean's, because I brought the peaches home." I didn't say, *Because she didn't get her way about Charles Dale going to church with us. Because she didn't get something of Lou Jean's.*

"Why would that make her mad?" I knew he knew. I knew

she'd been mad when she went to bed. I also knew that he didn't want to talk about it with me, or didn't think he should, so I'd carried the peaches to the kitchen and had gone to bed myself. As I went down the hall, the *ping* of the "ropes" started again.

And now, I still wanted someone to admire my jars, to be with me when I uncapped the first one. I hadn't seen Charles Dale since the night he'd come to supper, and I wasn't sure how I felt about seeing him. If he *was* my half brother, if *that* was the reason for Dad's worry about meeting him, if Charles Dale *himself* was the secret Gran and Mother kept talking about, it certainly wasn't his fault. As half brothers go, I could have worse, Thad Howard being the first to come to mind. I just wasn't sure how I should feel. The idea of suddenly having a brother was too ridiculous, like something that happened on a television show my mother wouldn't allow me to watch.

I wondered how Lou Jean felt about Charles Dale's meeting my mom and dad, about us living next door. About his coming to supper, and about my mother wanting him to spend so much time at our house. And I wondered about my mother's motives. You couldn't just pick up a thirteen-year-old boy and walk out the door with him, like you could a child's aluminum dining chair, even if he halfway belonged to your husband. The whole mess was confused and murky and, next to the clean smooth jars on the table, seemed dirty. I took a fresh tea towel from a drawer and polished each jar again, then left them and went to dress, passing my parents' room on tiptoe.

When I knocked next door, no one answered. The front door was closed, and the air conditioner ran full-tilt. I headed toward the backyard, keeping close to the house to avoid the itchy leaves of a fig tree. Across the lawn was Lou Jean. She sat on the ground, her back against the trunk of an oak, and she wore cutoffs and a striped halter top. With her bare feet dug into the grass, her knees drawn up to her chest, she looked no older than I, but just as I started forward, she dropped her head onto her knees, her shoulders shaking.

8

The itching was like something alive. As soon as I scratched one place, the itch jumped to another, up and down my legs and arms, on my face, even against the back of my neck. From her place on the edge of the tub, Mother stuck her hand under the tap. "That's cool, but I'm going to get another tray of ice cubes." She grabbed my arm, then dropped it and headed for the kitchen. "Stop scratching. You've already got it bleeding." I kicked off the rest of my clothes and stepped into the tub, then climbed right back out.

"It's freezing," I yelled. "It doesn't need any ice cubes."

I bent over and raked long comforting scratches all the way up the outside of my legs as I stood. I had just stooped to repeat the process when Mother came back in the door, swatting at me with the ice tray before pulling its lever. The cubes made thunking splashes as they hit the water.

"Quit that *now.*" She turned off the faucet and reached to help me into the tub. "If they get infected, they'll make scars. Do you want scars up and down your legs?"

My right foot entered, my left reluctantly joined it, and I stood ankle deep in misery.

"You have to sit down."

"I can't," I screamed. With one hand, I scratched my legs. With the other I clawed the red welts that crisscrossed my neck and chest.

"You look like you've been flayed with a whip. I could just throttle your grandmother. Her and her damn peaches. Are you going to sit down or do you want me to get a glass and pour this water over you?" Without waiting for me to choose, she chunked the ice tray on the floor, grabbed both my arms and pulled me down into the water, so cold I lost my breath. An ice cube poked a frozen dent in my flesh, and I grabbed it and threw it against the pink tiled wall, screaming as loud as I could. Mother covered her ears.

When she brought her hands down, she planted fists on her skinny pointed hipbones, and I knew I was going to catch it but didn't even care. Seeing Lou Jean crying in her backyard was too much. I hadn't known what to do, whether to go to her or let her be alone, so I had moved into the fig tree and watched until I was sure she was okay. Then I had gone back into my house tired of mysteries, for the first time in my life. I was tired of Mother's moods, I was tired of trying to figure out how all this had happened, and after only sixty seconds, was more than tired of sitting in a freezing tub of water trying to get rid of a miserable rash that I couldn't even reveal how I'd gotten. I launched another ice cube, and above its explosion, heard laughter.

Mother backed herself onto the closed toilet. Knees together, ankles apart, she leaned forward, her face in one hand, the other propping its elbow. "What's so funny?" I demanded. She pointed at me with one hand, pushing her index finger against the air between us. The other hand covered her mouth, as if trying to contain the cackles. I didn't seem to be in trouble, but I wasn't sure I wanted to be this funny.

Finally, she dried her eyes, smearing brown mascara on the powder blue toilet paper she peeled off the roll. "Oh, God," she said, standing up to look in the bathroom mirror.

"You said *God*," I said accusingly. Her eyes met mine in the mirror, and she struggled to keep from starting all over again. Finally, I did what I knew she wouldn't find so amusing. "What is so *damn* funny?"

She whirled, the laugh gone, her eyes startled. She stiffened and glared at me. For a second. Then she leaned against the sink, bracing herself as the laughter took her again. "Oh, God," she said one more time, weakly now, almost wheezing.

"It's you," she managed between gasps. "You are so much like my mother that it isn't even funny."

"You act like it's funny. You act as if it's hilarious. And anyway, I'd rather be like her than like you."

Her back to me, she took a washcloth down from the cabinet, held it under the tap, and began removing her ruined makeup. The laughter died away, flowing down the sink with the mascara and blush, and the room grew very quiet. I wondered if Lou Jean was washing her face right now, or if she was still outside, by herself and under the tree. There was a slap as the wrung-out face cloth met the towel rack.

"It's so funny," said Mother, "because it's just what I deserve. I got what was coming to me." Her voice was sad, and she looked about to cry. First Lou Jean, now her, and me with not a clue why or about what to do. I scoured the water for one more ice cube to hurl and came up empty-handed. All the damn things had melted.

By the time I got out of the tub, my itch gone, my bad mood intact, Gran had come in the front door and was arguing with Mother. "If she's allergic to peaches, she'd have broken out yesterday."

Mother was making coffee, and Gran sat at the table. I walked to the counter and opened the bread box. "Anybody else want toast?"

"I'd love some," said Gran.

"Not me," said Mother. "And don't think you're going to eat any of those preserves. You'll not touch another peach until that rash is gone."

"That's not fair," I said, turning to Gran for support.

"Sarah Jo, you take the cake."

Mother took the bread from my hands. The sadness had left her voice. It held only its usual bossiness, edged with the mild anger that accompanied Gran's visits. "Go get the brush and a rubber band. I'll do something with your hair." I stormed out of the kitchen, thinking that I never *walked* anymore. I either stomped or tiptoed.

By the time I came back, the toast was in the toaster, the coffee was perking, Gran was glaring at Mother, and Mother was pretending she didn't see her. She smiled when I came in the room, as if glad for a reason to ignore Gran's hostile face. "Sit here, honey," she said, pulling out a chair from the table, angling it so that my body was between hers and Gran's.

Combing my hair, she noticed my overalls. "Overalls again, Kayla? You look like the little matchbox girl."

"Match*stick* girl," said Gran, reaching for a jar of preserves.

"Whatever, Mother. *You* could set a better example. I never know what you're going to show up wearing. Someday I'll get a call from the sheriff's office: 'Come pick up your mother. We found her wandering down Main Street nude.' "

Gran ignored the slur. She picked up one of the jars. "These sure turned out pretty. But then, Lou Jean's always do. Canning is something not many young women bother to learn anymore."

Mother's grip tightened, and the brush raked my ear.

"Ow," I yelled, grabbing my ears, covering them both.

"Damn, Sarah Jo, you don't have to take the hide off. I promise not to wander naked if you'll just leave her ears intact. Hell, I'll go check myself into the nursing home right now if you'll let her eat these preserves." The brush strokes grew more vigorous, my eyebrows moving up and down with the tug. A loud pop announced the opening of the first jar of preserves.

"She's not eating those," Mother warned in a singsong voice. She dropped the brush over my head and into my lap.

"Yes, she is." Gran's lilt mimicked Mother's.

"No, she isn't," said Mother, and this time her voice was hard, all melody gone out of it. She began braiding my hair. "Make yourself useful," she said to Gran, "and answer that phone if it rings. I'm expecting Brother Rhodes to call."

"What does that old windbag want?"

Mother ignored the insult. "He's calling to discuss our joining the church on Sunday. And he needs someone to head up a new committee."

"What kind of committee?" Gran set the open jar on the

table. The smell made my mouth water. She rolled her eyes and poured coffee.

"One to organize fellowships for Friday nights in the fall. Something to get the high school kids off the streets. So they won't be in parked cars somewhere. Or out at La Campestre, dancing."

Gran laughed out loud. "What are you going to have them do? Make jewelry out of dry macaroni? Serve them Kool-Aid and graham crackers?"

"Very funny."

Gran set a cup on the table, close by Mother. "I seem to remember somebody who did quite a bit of dancing in high school. And quite a bit of sitting in parked cars."

Before Mother could answer, the phone rang. Gran picked it up, and Mother's fingers moved faster. She was almost done when Gran greeted the caller, her voice soft and angelic, "Naked Acres, Nudist Nursing Home . . ." I jerked and my braid flew out of Mother's fingers, unraveling before it hit my back. Gran glanced heavenward as if for divine inspiration. Then she smiled angelically at the phone and continued, ". . . where you can go out the same way you came in."

9

I sat on the living-room floor, yearbooks in my lap and on the carpet around me. The idea of Mother dancing and sitting in parked cars had cured my aversion to mysteries. Almost immediately, I found a snapshot of her. Grouped with a number of photos, an uncaptioned collage of people in the high school halls, she leaned against a locker. A guy with his back to the camera, his eyes and hair dark and vaguely familiar, stood with her. Across his shoulder, Mother's face concentrated on his. If she knew the camera was there, she didn't show it. With a ponytail and a smile, she was very pretty. She looked nothing like the woman who had spent the last three hours clomping around in a pair of pink mules.

I turned the pages, hoping to find more pictures, some knowledge of who he was, wondering why she had ended up with my dad instead of this guy. Before she'd left for her meeting, she had marched over and over to the window facing Lou Jean's, ankles flexing back and forth, satin slapping heels with each step. Each time, she'd summoned a glare strong enough to bore wood and stucco. Then she'd whirled around, the floor squeaking like a dying rabbit beneath her shoes, and flapped back to the kitchen. She'd sat at the table, drinking another pot of coffee and declaring in a prim and accent-free voice, not her own voice but the superior voice of an English teacher or news commentator, how difficult it was to deal with an unstable mother. What a trial it was to suddenly find yourself more mature than your parent. I sympathized with her on this one. I had better sense, however, than to think swapping stories would be in any way pleasant for either of us.

Halfway through the annual, I found another collage, this one containing scenes from her junior prom, and in one of the photos, the same familiar guy. Eyes closed, he danced with a girl. His hand rested on her back, his head leaned against hers, oblivious to any camera. The girl's face was turned away from the camera, but her back and shoulders, I recognized.

How had she gotten from there to here? From someone who wore a strapless gown and buried her face in a guy's shoulder to someone who believed dancing was evil and who *lived* for the preacher's call? She had salvaged the morning's situation by grabbing the hook on the wall phone, slamming it down, and holding it there so that the Reverend Rhodes would think he had reached a wrong number, some kids at home unsupervised. He had called back almost immediately, and Mother had been on top of the phone, having snatched it away from Gran. One hand held down the hook, the other cradled the receiver against her chest, like a mother who'd just snatched her baby from a kidnapper, until the phone rang again.

She had been so rattled that she said nothing about the preserves I ate. If the shining concoction I'd spread on my toast had been made from the family goldfish rather than peaches, she wouldn't have noticed. The lower half of her face carried on a cheery but responsible conversation with the preacher. The upper half carried on a conversation with Gran, and there was nothing cheery about it. As soon as she finished her breakfast, while Mother was still on the phone, Gran had left, but only after joyfully and loudly pronouncing the peach preserves the best she'd ever eaten. As she went out the door, she'd mouthed at Mother, "You really ought to try some, Sarah Jo. They are delicious. Take the preacher a jar."

I flipped to the Junior Class Pictures section, still looking for the gorgeous familiar boy who danced with my mother. It didn't take long. On the first page, in the A's, he smiled as if the whole world belonged to him. Just as he did from atop Carmen's television.

❧ 10 ❧

In my room were two lists: all the ways that Charles Dale was like my dad, and all the ways he wasn't. The list marked SIM-ILARITIES was longer, and the first item on it was the need for peace, an almost desperate desire to avoid conflict, no matter what. Charles Dale gave in to David's demands the way my father caved in to Mother's. In the short time we had lived in Rosalita, I had twice seen Charles Dale hand over his half-finished snack, once a frozen Milky Way, once a Coke float. David had gobbled his own like some barnyard animal, then started at his older brother's with fake tears in his eyes. The look on Charles Dale's face when he handed over his food was the same look on my father's each time he changed the televi-sion channel from his fishing show to Lawrence Welk. A look of apprehension, as if hoping that the usual wasn't about to take place yet again, followed by a look not of resentment but of resignation. As if there *were* no other way.

Mother, of course, had not let up on Charles Dale's spend-ing more time with us. She might have conceded the first round, the round of the church service, to Lou Jean, but she had already begun planning strategy for the next. When she returned from the preacher's office, late enough that my father was already home, she held big greasy bags of chopped barbecue sandwiches and French fries, Dad's favorite.

"Sorry I'm late." She handed the bags to Dad. "I got caught up talking to Brother Rhodes. That poor man has more good ideas and absolutely no one to help him with them."

Dad opened one of the sacks, grabbed three fries and stuffed them into his mouth. "But now *you're* here, right?" he said to Mother, winking at me. Her busyness, her projects, those that didn't involve *him*, he always found comforting.

"Well, I don't mind telling you, he is glad for the help." She took the bags out of Dad's arms, carrying them with a handful of paper plates and napkins to the kitchen table.

"What? We're slumming? No more dining-room elegance?" Dad grinned over the milk carton he handed me.

"Give it a rest, Phil. I have too much to do tonight to worry about dishes."

As we sat down at the table and he reclaimed the bags, dumping their contents and passing plates around, Dad said, "Just don't sign me up for anything. I have plenty of new things at work to worry about. You and the preacher will have to battle sin and corruption on your own."

Mother said nothing. She kept her eyes on her paper plate, carefully pouring catsup into one of its divisions.

Dad's voice was apprehensive. "Sarah Jo?" He stopped stuffing potatoes into his mouth. He gripped his sandwich gingerly.

"I didn't really commit you to anything." Mother lifted the top of her sandwich and removed the onion, putting it on Dad's plate.

"Keep your bribe. I'm not doing it, whatever it is."

Mother cut her sandwich in half, gently pressing the bun along either side of the knife. Dad had eaten half his sandwich and she'd yet to take the first bite of hers. He dropped what was left onto his plate, and said, "Okay. What is it?"

Mother looked up, her face tentative. "It's baseball. Church league."

Dad lifted his sandwich again. "All I have to do is play?" he asked. "Not coach?" Mother shook her head reassuringly. "And not be in charge of getting umpires or raising uniform money or any other damn thing?" She shook her head again and handed him the other half of her sandwich.

He took it and bit into it, looking young enough for Little League himself, making me laugh by lifting what was left of his own sandwich, taking a bite of one and then the other, rolling his eyes in clowning relief. "Okay. I can do that. Be good to get some exercise. So, is it all old guys or will there be anybody young enough to get around the bases?"

"Oh, there'll be young guys and older guys. But really none much older than you." She put her sandwich back on her plate and began cutting it up with a knife and fork. Then she stopped, dropped her implements onto the table and, looking straight at Dad, said, "It's a father-and-son league."

Dad, his hands now free, laid his fingertips onto his paper plate, pressing them down so that they left reddish stains. "But," he said, looking carefully at me and then fully at Mother, "I don't have a son."

"I know that." She looked at me too, then quickly back to him. "And Charles Dale doesn't have a father. So why can't the two of you play together? Brother Rhodes thought it was a good idea."

"Well, I don't." Dad got up from the table, went out the back door, and surprised me by letting it slam. Mother immediately rose and left too, the bedroom door slamming behind her. I stared at their abandoned plates and wondered why Mother hadn't married Joe.

An hour later, I sat on the porch steps and leaned against the banister. The front yard held the peace I'd sought the night before. The mockingbird was again on the telephone pole, and the doves drank from a puddle. Charles Dale and David played on the sidewalk in front of their house, David wearing skates over his red tennis shoes, holding his brother's hands as Charles Dale walked backward and pulled him along. Muffling their voices, the water sprinkler droned the sound of early evening, a pretwilight hum that preluded the coming chorus of cricket and frog.

Inside the house, Mother moved about, her steps loud and determined. I heard her go into the bathroom and close the door, then come back out. She was like the sprinkler head, never still. Twisting one direction then another, spraying orders, commands, complaints, and cons. The odd thing, though, was that in the photos I'd found that afternoon, the ones with Joe, she *was* still. The camera, each time, had caught her at peace. There was a calm to her, a relaxed concentration, a focus on *him*, as if *he* were the only important thing. Seeming happy, as if simply being with him was enough, hers was a face I scarcely recognized. It wore none of the familiar agitation, the set readiness that Dad and I took as warning, recognized as advance notice of her latest plan.

The boys' voices climbed over the sprinkler noise as they

moved down the sidewalk toward our house. As they drew parallel with our lawn, our screen door flew open, and Mother
sailed by me, down the steps, and out toward the street. The
breeze she created was frenetic but intent. She might have
been some crusading warrior, too obsessed with her assigned
quest to notice the doves she scattered, the water spray she
stormed through. "Charles Dale," she called. "Do you like
baseball?"

"Sure." He didn't even look up, carefully pulling David
across a grassy crack in the sidewalk. Mules planted on the concrete, Mother stood very close to the boys.

"Well, I have a problem," she said. "Or really Phil does."
She shuffled along, keeping pace with the slow progress of the
skating lesson. "Our church has a baseball league. For men and
their sons. But Phil . . ." She paused.

Though he held onto David's hands, Charles Dale stopped
tugging, looked seriously at my mother, and said, "Doesn't
have a son. Just like I don't have a father."

I held my breath and waited to see what Mother would say,
if she would care enough to be embarrassed. Maybe she did,
because her voice grew soft and her hands, mounted on her
hips, dropped to her sides. Or maybe this display of empathy
was only part of the new *her*, like the makeup and the clothes.
"Yeah, I guess so," she said.

A look passed over Charles Dale's face, and I thought that
he, like my father, might finally be angry, and my mother
thought so too. She stepped back from him, fully onto the wet
grass, at the same time reaching out to touch his shoulder. "It's
okay. If you don't want to, I understand."

When he got down on one knee in front of David, though,

without seeming to hear my mother's comment, the look on his face held no anger. "David, can we do this later?" he asked in a very soft voice, almost a prayer. "I'll help you twice as long, if it's okay. If we can do it after a while. Instead of now, I mean."

"No," said David, pulling up on his brother's hands. His voice was not pleading and held no prayer. It was matter-of-fact, without question. As if Charles Dale had no choice in the matter and was an idiot for thinking he might.

Charles Dale stood again, his shoulders hunched, his face the face of my father forfeiting yet another fishing show. The doves had just settled again when I stood and walked down the steps. Though I stepped onto the grass, trying not to disturb them, they flew anyway, down the street to another yard. "David," I said, as I came to the sidewalk, "how about if I help you?"

As Charles Dale streaked home for his glove, Mother said, "That was really sweet of you, Kayla." She moved toward me, stroking my cheek with the back of one finger. Pointedly, I turned David and moved away from her hand. Toward Lou Jean's house.

On our knees in the soft gray garden, we gathered the last of the snap beans. David, worn out from skating, was inside, asleep. Dad and Charles Dale weren't home yet.

Somewhere in the alley, a bobwhite called. The doves, finally settled, drank from a stone bowl at the feet of the concrete Jesus. "You know doves mate for life, don't you?" Lou Jean asked me.

I stopped picking and sat back on my heels. "No."

"Well, they do. So tell that daddy of yours not to be shooting them."

"He doesn't hunt much."

She moved on her knees to the end of a row, so that her back was toward me. "Lou Jean," I said, "do you ever get sad?"

"Sure, honey. Everybody gets sad." Though she kept on picking, I knew I had her full attention. She was the only grown-up I knew who made me feel that way. "If you get sad, you can talk to me, you know."

I moved forward, careful not to crush the bean plants. In the near dark, it was easy to miss a few pods. "You know, Lou Jean, if you got sad, you could talk to me too."

When she didn't answer, I stopped picking and stared hard through the gloom. She too had stopped picking, but her hands still worked, snapping a bean over and over, throwing it not into the basket but onto the dirt in front of her knees. Behind her, the lost bobwhite still called, but no other answered, and I wished I hadn't said anything.

11

For the next week, things were peaceful. Mother's disposition was much improved. On the afternoons that Dad and Charles Dale drove off to softball practice, she was almost giddy. She'd watch the truck leave the drive, her head cocked as if the noise of the changing gears was a source of comfort, balm, maybe, for the fact that we'd joined the church without Charles Dale present.

Only after the truck turned onto Fifth and we heard it shift into fourth would she turn back into the room. Her hands would clap then, in a satisfied, industrious manner.

She seemed to always have something to do, somewhere to go, and I noticed, with growing resentment, that she never left the house without looking perfect or without glancing toward Lou Jean's as she walked to the car. She spent hours organizing her fellowship committee. She also spent a great deal of time choosing even more new clothes, not school clothes for me, but resort wear for a trip she and Dad had planned to Galveston, the annual meeting of the lending association he worked for.

The one advantage of all this busyness was that I was able to spend more time with Lou Jean. In the mornings we watered her garden, and in the afternoons we gathered the produce. During the day, we canned squash, tomatoes, and peas. I was careful not to mention sadness again, and she seemed cheerful enough, though I noticed that she always found reason to be inside when it was time for Dad and Charles Dale to leave. I would look up from plucking a tomato, watering the pintos, and find her gone.

Then, three days before my parents were to leave, Gran came down with the flu. When Dad came home from work, Mother gave him the news. She stood at the stove, frying bacon for supper. Dad sat down in a kitchen chair and planted his elbow on the table, motioning for me to do the same.

"I've asked you not to arm-wrestle at the table," said Mother. "I guess I'll just stay home."

"No," said Dad, ignoring her arm-wrestling warning. "It'll be fun for all of us to go."

"Nobody else is taking kids. They never do."

"So we'll hide her." Dad ignored the fact that my free hand was now gripping the leg of the table for more leverage. "She can come out only if she acts like she's not with us."

"Why can't I stay with the boys and Lou Jean?" I asked cautiously. When Mother didn't answer, I added, "You've already bought all those clothes."

She spun around so fast that Dad and I jumped, releasing hands. Bacon grease flew from the fork she held, splattering the kitchen floor, and her hair, made wild by the heat of cooking, seemed to spring away from her head. She pointed the meat fork at me. "Kayla Marie, that is out of the question. You are not, under any circumstances, to even mention it to anyone in that household, do you understand me?"

Before I could answer, Dad did. "Sarah Jo, you don't have to jump all over her. All she said was—"

"I'm not jumping all over her," she interrupted, redirecting the fork toward him. "I just want it made clear, that's all. I'll stay here and everything will be fine."

"No." His voice was even and slow. "Everything will not be fine. I thought we were going to have some time together."

"Well, we aren't." She bent and wiped up the grease with a paper towel. "Maybe we can go somewhere later in the summer." When she stood up, she smiled at me, but the smile looked as if it hurt her teeth, and her hair still stood away from her head. "Maybe you and I can run to San Antonio while Daddy's gone, and do some of your school clothes shopping. Maybe Charles Dale can go with us."

She turned away from his eyes and back to the skillet. Her shoulders rose and then fell, as if she took a deep breath. Makeup had settled into the crease at the side of her mouth, making it deeper. Her lips seemed sewn together in a fierce, unyielding seam. Gone was her ladylike look, and gone was her "new town, new look" look. In their place was a whole new look, with frizzed hair, cotton apron, hunched shoulders, and a closed face. As if she had finally climbed out of the pages of *Ladies' Home Journal*, taken a brief stroll through *Cosmopolitan*, and ended up in a U.S. history book, in the chapter on women of the Great Depression.

When the last of the bacon was out of the skillet, she turned off the burner, tossed the fork in the sink, and backed up against the counter. Crossing her arms, she stared back at Dad. The two of them remained this way for a full thirty seconds, and then my father rose from his chair, never taking his eyes from hers, and walked to the telephone.

He looked away long enough to find a number in the phone book, to dial, and then he again stared at Mother as he began to speak. "Lou Jean, this is Phil, next door. Yeah, I know, it has been a long time." Suddenly, he relaxed. His eyes slid from Mother's to the floor beneath the phone, he slumped one shoulder against the wall, and he crossed one ankle over the other. His voice rose both in volume and pitch.

"Well, you're all she's talked about, and she was thrilled that you helped her with those peaches. Yeah, you're right. She's a pretty good kid, except she cheats at arm wrestling." He laughed and looked at me. "Lou Jean says hello and to quit cheating your poor old father."

Mother clicked her tongue. The breath that followed was explosive. She pushed herself away from the counter, leaning into the room, the upper part of her body pointed like an antenna toward the phone. She might have been trying to hear both sides of the conversation. As if he believed she could, Dad changed topics. His tone became serious, and he stood straight again.

"I've got a favor to ask, Lou Jean. We're in kind of a bind here." He turned and faced my mother full on, and his eyes fastened themselves to hers in a way I'd never seen before. As if throwing down a challenge, a dare. "Sarah Jo and I were supposed to go out of town this weekend, and her mother's come down with the flu."

He was quiet then, for what seemed like a long time. I didn't have to watch him to know Lou Jean's reaction. I knew *her*, could almost guess the exact words she'd use in telling him how welcome I was, what good company I'd be for the boys. So it was my mother's face I watched, and, curiously, throughout the entire conversation, it never changed. Her hands changed, though. At first they lay atop her crossed arms. But the longer Dad listened to Lou Jean, the more Mother's fingers began to curl. When he shifted position, settling against the wall again, as if he planned to be there awhile, her fingers curled tighter, raking her arms and leaving red marks, like tails, behind them. And by the time he said good-bye, thanking Lou Jean for her kindness, Mother's hands were clenched. As Dad hung up the phone, she strode from the room, face still composed but fists now swinging at her side.

The next night, my father didn't come home for dinner. Though my mother said he was working late, at a meeting somewhere out of town, she didn't seem to hold much belief in her own words. In fact, she looked as angry as she had the night before.

In the way that she ripped the cardboard end from the box of fish sticks, in the way that she dumped them onto the cookie sheet, so wildly that their frozen forms slid across the metal and onto the floor, I knew that she didn't really believe what she was telling me. And in the way that she paused before picking them up, leaving them scattered across the beige-and-gold linoleum while she stared out the window at Lou Jean's house, I knew what she *did* believe.

We ate in silence at the kitchen table, and neither of us ate much. Mother seemed too upset to eat, and I just plain wasn't hungry for fish sticks gathered off the floor and slammed into the oven without even being brushed off. At least six or seven times during dinner, she left her chair and walked to the sink to peer out. She would perform some chore while there. Dip a cup in the sudsy water on one side of the sink, then drop it into the rinse water, walk back to the table, eat one or two bites. Then she would get up again, walk to the sink, lift the rinsed cup and place it on the dish drainer, walk back to the table. After another bite she would repeat the process, dropping a spatula or a spoon into the suds. The dishes were done by the time we were. I raked my uneaten dinner into the trash.

As I turned on the television in the living room, I heard her call me. Before I could answer, she was at the living-room door. "I've got a great idea." Her face was blotchy, and like the night before, her makeup was caked. Her hair was in her eyes, where it had been since she'd picked up the fish sticks. She went to the window and parted the blinds with one finger. "Why don't you go over and get Charles Dale?" she asked. "I'll make you guys banana splits."

"That's okay." I concentrated on changing the channel. I knew she wanted me in that house to make sure that Lou Jean was there and not with my father.

"Come on, it'll be fun." She walked up and grabbed the knob. "You go get Charles Dale. I'll find *Laugh-In*." When I didn't move, she chuckled and pulled me against her with her free arm. "I know you're not hungry. I looked in the trash."

When she released me, I headed for my room. "I'm tired," I said. "I'm just going to read." Still angry at the way she'd treated me, I had no desire to help. And what if she was right? Dad's voice had changed as he'd talked to Lou Jean. Become softer, lower, more personal, as if Mother and I were intruders at worst, strangers at best. As if he were alone with Lou Jean, or as if he *wished* he were, he'd talked in a voice steady, confident, and *connected*. By something stronger than forty feet of phone line.

❧

My mother had bought three new outfits to take to Galveston, all of them more *Cosmo* than *Ladies' Home Journal* or, thank God, Women of the Great Depression. The morning they left, she took a long time getting ready. My father had already carried the suitcases containing, I thought, all three new outfits, to the car. He had given me the phone number where they'd be, had checked to make sure burners were off, appliances unplugged, everything safe, and had called through the closed door several times before my mother finally came out.

I had not heard her speak to him since the night he'd called Lou Jean, and Dad had seemed quiet, attentive to me, and polite to Mother. Now he paced the living-room floor, and I, afraid that she might at the very last minute refuse to go, paced with him. Finally, she opened their bedroom door and walked out.

The outfit she wore stopped our pacing. It was red. Fire-engine red. Wanton-hussy lipstick red. Fresh-blood red. Pissed-off, wronged-woman red.

It was a two-piece suit, jacket and skirt, with a pillbox hat that matched, and it seemed familiar. The material looked hot, rough, and nubby.

Her cheeks were flaming and there were perspiration drops on her perfectly powdered nose. Scooped back under the hat to show the pearls in her ears, her hair was already starting to crimp.

"Let's go," she said to me, saying nothing to my father. I gathered my overnight bag and we walked outdoors, he closing the door behind us. As we walked down the steps, she turned toward Lou Jean's.

"You don't have to go with me."

"I am walking you over there, Kayla." Dad went straight to the car.

It wasn't yet nine o'clock, but the sky already had that hot white sheen that meant the day would be miserable. Dry flies sizzled in the mesquite trees, and grackles sat on the high wires with their mouths open, something they normally didn't do until the hottest months of August and September.

I walked beside Mother, who marched on her toes to keep her high heels from sinking into the carpet grass. It didn't matter what she wore; I was just glad she wasn't backing out. I had a whole weekend to spend at Lou Jean's, and I felt sympathy for every kid on the face of the earth who wasn't me. I even felt sorry for poor old Thad Howard, who was not, would never be, invited to spend the weekend at Lou Jean's, who would probably spend his weekend guarding the freezer to keep his own father from stealing his Popsicles.

I tried to open Lou Jean's door and go in like I always did, but Mother grabbed my hand and rang the doorbell. "Do you totally forget *all* your manners when you get over here?"

"Come in," Lou Jean said, pushing the screen door out for us and holding it.

"I can't," said Mother. Her hand gripped my shoulder and pressed down so hard that I couldn't go in either. She smiled. It was the same smile she'd used when telling Charles Dale how much she loved camping. "Lou Jean, you don't know how much we appreciate this. This has been such a hectic summer, and Phil and I just have not had one moment alone."

"Oh, that's fine," said Lou Jean, running her palm down the side of my head and ending with it cupped under my chin.

"We'll love having her. The boys are already planning things. But I need her first. We're going to put up pickles."

Mother's hand pressed hard enough to hurt, and I wondered if Lou Jean could tell. It was embarrassing, and I tried to push back, to raise up against her hand, but I couldn't. She kept smiling and lying, and the more she lied, the more she smiled, and the more she smiled, the more she pushed. "Your boys are so adorable. We'll be glad to reciprocate anytime."

"Oh," said Lou Jean, "I usually don't go anywhere that they can't go too, but thanks anyway." At this, my mother's hand dug in so hard that I almost cried out.

"Well." Her voice turned haughty, as if Lou Jean had said something to offend her, as if she meant my parents were negligent for going somewhere without me. "We don't either. We really don't get away very often." Then her hand floated off my shoulder, and she said, "But you know how it is, sometimes a couple just has to have some time alone."

Lou Jean dropped her hand from my chin. The look she gave Mother was stony. "Are you ready to go in, Kayla?"

Mother leaned down and kissed my cheek, telling me to be good, to mind Lou Jean, as if I were six years old. As Mother headed down the steps, I watched Dad. His eyes were focused through the windshield on some point out in front of the car. As she climbed in, he put the car in gear and started it forward, never looking left, never looking right. As if he feared hazards from either side and thought it safest to look only in one direction. As they turned the corner, the last thing I saw was the red pillbox hat, and I finally remembered why the suit looked familiar. Except for the color, it was exactly like the one Jackie Kennedy had worn to Dallas.

❧ 12 ❧

Lou Jean kicked off her flip-flops. With my bare feet mim-icking the soft tread of her own, I looked more like her. One of the surprises about Lou Jean, part of what created the fun-house atmosphere, was that she could just as easily have answered the door in a leotard and ballet tights, or a peasant blouse and faded jeans. She had no hard-and-fast rules for appropriate fashion, other than to wear what you chose.

In fact, she had few rules about anything, and the ones she had seemed backward sometimes, different from the way the rest of the world viewed them. In my mind, she was like some renegade from centuries before, from Zorro's time, standing high on a bluff, ebony braid sun burnished, white painter's smock whipping like a bright flag in a stiff wind, and in her hands the four corners of a blanket, held like a pouch. In the pouch, all the rules of the world, all the *normal* rules, the ones people thought you couldn't live without or shouldn't *think* about living without. In my vision she lifted the blanket, popped it up and open, her hands snapping apart as if to rip the blanket in half, and the rules launched into the wind, most of them blowing over the cliff and off to another land, never to trouble her again. The few remaining rules landed at her feet in all manner of disarray, upside down, sideways, out of position, none of them right, where she bent to pick them up, just as they were, so that even the rules she kept were different. Backward from the way the rest of the world read them, they made sense only to her.

Even the way she cut up apples was unusual. While my parents drove through the one tricolored traffic light and passed the PLEASE COME BACK TO ROSALITA sign, maybe talking to each other, maybe not, I watched Lou Jean slice apples for lunch. As if she'd never heard that apples should be quartered, the seeds removed, and, according to some folks, the peel removed, she whacked the apple horizontally, creating slices both round and red-skinned. "Why do you cut them like *that*?" I asked.

"You have to cut them like this. Or the stars won't show." She held one up. In its center, the holes, the cradles for the seeds, radiated out like the petals of a flower or the spokes of a wheel. Like a star.

"But it has pieces of seed in it," I said, grinning. My mother would be horrified.

"Which are good for you. Which aid in digestion." As if it were the most natural lunch in the world, she arranged the apple slices on a plate with cheddar cheese and the broken-up squares of a Hershey's bar. "Do you want to get the pickle crock out while I fix the sandwiches?"

On the dark shelves of the pantry, the closed boxes I had seen the first time I entered, still sat, tight-lipped and mysterious. All about the same size, small, giftshop, jewelry-store boxes, some of them highly decorated in bright colors with silver and gold trim. In anyone else's house they would clearly hold more than empty mason jars, rings, and lids, but in Lou Jean's, who knew? Reluctantly, I carried the crock back out into the light.

"What is in all those boxes?" I asked, setting the crock at one end of the table.

"I never did show you how to tell the future," Lou Jean answered, and to her, her answer must have made sense. "Call the boys for lunch, will you?"

An hour later, with lunch eaten and the boys outside, I layered cucumber spears, chile petins, garlic cloves, and carrots in the crock, with no more knowledge of the boxes' contents than I'd had when I asked. Lou Jean moved back and forth from the crock to the oven, spooning brine from a three-gallon menudo pan, checking a cake that was baking.

"Did you stay with Carmen when you were little?" I asked her.

She pulled the cake from the oven and set it on a cooling rack. "Almost every day after school. Sometimes Carmen picked me up. Sometimes your grandmother did."

I wondered what my mother must have thought of that, if it meant that she and Lou Jean had been forced to spend time together, and I wondered why Lou Jean didn't just go home from school with her own mother. "Was it because she had to work?"

Her look was puzzled, her head cocked. "Oh, you mean my mother?" Her head cocked again, and this time she held it there a long time before answering. Finally she said, "No. She didn't work. But she had things to do."

"What kinds of things?"

She poked the top of the cake with a toothpick. "I don't know. She never said."

"Did that bother you?"

"Getting to stay with Carmen and Rose? You've been with those two. How could anybody mind getting to stay with them?" Lou Jean tossed the toothpick in the trash, donned pot holders, and shook the cake, loosening it from the sides of the pan. When she set it back down, her face was red from the heat of baking. "Remember when I told you that the important things, the *really* important things I know, I learned from someone much older or younger? Those two are who I meant. They both know things most of us spend our whole lives rushing around trying to learn."

"Charles Dale says my grandmother is your best friend."

"She is."

"Isn't she kind of old?"

She lifted the pan, gave it one more shake, then turned it upside down. "Does she seem old to you?"

I shook my head. "She seems a lot younger than my mother." With a sound like a really tired person collapsing onto a bed, the cake fell out of the pan and plopped onto the rack.

Beside it, Lou Jean hovered. "Your grandmother made sure I had plenty of attention and love when my own mother was too busy. The best kind of friend, if you ask me." Gingerly, she touched the edges of the cake. "But you know, your mother's not so bad either. Sometimes she'll surprise you."

I reached for the last of the brine, pouring it into the crock, thinking how it must have been, the three of them, Lou Jean, Gran, and Mother riding in Gran's car after school, Mother hating Lou Jean. In my mind, Mother moved into a backseat corner, scrunched as far away from Gran's jokes and Lou Jean's cheerfulness as possible. "Do you think we could all do something together sometime? You and me and Gran and Carmen?"

The look on her face changed three times before she answered. First, it was sad, eyes half closed, as if she meant to admonish me for not wanting to spend time with my own mother, for not responding positively to her comment. When her eyes opened, though, a smile started at her lips. And, finally, the smile widened, and her eyes did too, to the point where her eyebrows were raised, like a mischievous child with the first inkling of some impish thought, about to say something she shouldn't. "Maybe," she said. "Maybe we can slip off and get together while your mother is busy sometime. Maybe while she's watching Charles Dale and your father play baseball."

The full crock, so heavy that it had taken both of us to lift it, rested on the pantry floor. In it, the pickles were covered in brine, weighted down by a heavy pottery plate, the crock itself covered by a clean layer of cheesecloth. "Now, Kayla," said Lou Jean, "we'll have to check those pickles every day or two. Spoon off the foam that forms around the edge of the crock. It's the spooning off that makes them crisp. No mushy pickles in this household." She grabbed Charles Dale, who had wandered in, hugged him, and kissed his ear. Charles Dale pretended to wipe off her kisses as she gave him more.

"So," he asked me when he was free, "when will your dad and mom be back?"

"Sunday night." I couldn't help noticing that Lou Jean went to the sink and washed her hands again.

"Hey," she said as she dried them, "should I empty a few of those boxes?"

I nodded, enthusiastically, and got up to do the lunch dishes, thinking her hands could use a break from the water. Charles Dale, making a disparaging wave toward the pantry, as if he knew what the boxes contained and could not be less interested, headed toward his room.

Out the window in front of me, the sky was darkening, the crepe myrtles scraping the stucco as the wind came up, and the kitchen was cozy with the smell of cake. Lou Jean moved around the kitchen, setting boxes on the table, filling a cherry red teakettle and setting it on the flame. About the time it whistled I was done with the dishes. The kitchen was dark now, clouds moving outside. The table's giant mesquite top was amber in the light of candles Lou Jean had set. Their glow reflected on china, a tea set, matching pot, cups, and saucers. "So, that's what was in those boxes," I said, moving closer.

"Yes, ma'am. Have a seat, please." She poured tea into a cup and set it in front of me. Bits of tea covered the bottom, and I turned up my nose. "Don't make that face. People who use tea bags don't know what they're missing." She slapped a book into one of my hands. Old, its deep blue cover frayed to brown in places, its title *Tea Leaf Divination*.

I took it and laughed. "We don't use tea bags. We use instant."

She sat down beside me, shaking her head in exaggerated pity, as if I'd said we drank dog pee. "Drink something good, for once," she said, pushing my cup closer and, at the same time, handing me a slice of cake.

Cautiously, I pulled the cake apart with a fork. I didn't want to be rude, but it looked so different from any cake I'd ever eaten. Dark and heavy. The kind of cake you'd eat in a castle. "What's in this?"

She leaned over the table, observing my dissection. "Orange slices. The kind you get at the dime store."

I was amazed. All that sugar. Chocolate for lunch, and candy in a cake. As if reading my mind, she said, "You can get away with it if you eat your apple seeds."

Charles Dale kept wandering in and out, slicing off a hunk of cake, getting milk to go with it, laughing at our tea party. As we talked and drank our tea, it was inconceivable that he could be the result of my father and Lou Jean's having an affair. She was too nice, too perfect, to do such a thing. And she had just said that my mother was okay, so how could she have done anything that would hurt her? I decided then and there that it wasn't true. It was a stupid rumor, told by a stupid kid, made more believable by the fact that Dad and Charles Dale looked alike.

And whatever I had heard Mother and Gran discussing, it had to do with something else. And it served me right, making me worry about something I had no reason to worry about, something that was none of my business. Served me right for being snoopy.

As I finished my tea, Lou Jean told me, "Leave a little, just enough to wet the bottom. Hold the cup in your left hand. Like this." I hooked my index finger through the handle, as she did. "Circle it three times away from you. To the left," I copied her as nearly as I could, as she swirled the tea, as she turned the cup upside down over her saucer and set it down cautiously, cupping its roundness with her palm. "Pick it up."

When I turned the cup over, I found that bits of leaf had stuck to its sides, some near the rim, others near the bottom. "What do you see?" she asked.

"I don't have a clue."

"Look closer. Don't think, just look." She scooted her chair toward mine so that she could look into my cup as well. She covered my hand with hers, relaxing my wrist so that the cup handle pointed down. "This is *now,*" she said, pointing to the edge of the cup immediately above the handle, the point due south. Then she moved her hand in a clockwise direction around the rim. "This is the future, going further and further into it. And sometimes, the things just to the right of the handle can be in the past. Look for what's coming toward you, what's going away, what *might* be behind you." She removed her hand, sitting back in her chair. She made a face at my frustration. "Just look at something, and decide what it looks like. The first thing that pops into your head."

Hearing the first drops of rain, I tried to concentrate on the cup. About a third of the way around it was what might look like a bush, a shrub of some kind. I held it up for Lou Jean to see. "Do you think it looks like a rosebush?"

"Doesn't matter what I think. What do *you* think?" Her face was impassive, offering no clues.

I sighed, deciding it was closer to being a bush than anything else I could think of.

"Look up *bush,*" she said. When I did, I saw that it meant a new friend.

"So I'm going to have a new friend before long?"

"I'd say in about a month," said Lou Jean, looking back into the cup. "Look again."

This time I found what looked like a bed, the covers piled up in the center, rumpled. It was located below the bush and was large so that it extended both toward me and away from me, as if whatever it meant, the thing it represented, would stay a long time. When I read the book and saw that the symbol meant worries and sleepless nights, I said, "Well, I don't like *that*."

Lou Jean laughed softly. "I guess not. But you know, a cup never shows you anything you can't handle."

"I want to look in your cup," I said. "What does yours say?" I leaned across the table toward her, and she held the cup so that I could see in it. Near the handle, to its left, was a pencil, its point unmistakable at one end, its eraser clear at the other. "A mistake," I read aloud. "A big mistake." I turned the cup back toward her. "Way over here by the handle—is it in the future or in the past?"

Charles Dale trekked back through just then, shaking his head, still making fun of what we were doing, and I looked to his mother for support, waiting for her to tell him off in her own funny way. She'd changed, though. Slouched down in her chair, she let her cup fall back into the saucer. As if she couldn't handle what the cup had given her. Charles Dale, not noticing her sadness, cut another slice of cake and wolfed a huge bite out of it. *The appetite of my father*, I thought. And then I thought of all those rules that Lou Jean had picked up backward. Maybe she *had* had an affair with my father. Maybe it was still going on, I thought, remembering that night Dad hadn't come home. Maybe *her* rules said it wasn't such a bad thing to do. And maybe Charles Dale, dropped shoulder, wide smile, gargantuan appetite, truly was my father's son. Illegitimate but real.

Just then, Lou Jean looked up and realized he was back in the room. She jumped up from her chair and put her arms around him, grabbing the giant piece of cake, pretending to wrestle it away. "Good God, child," she said, as he laughed and twisted free, "how many cakes should I have baked?" Herself again. As if just seeing him could make her happy, restore her good mood. She chased him out of the kitchen, toward the living room, calling to David, asking him if he wanted cake. Maybe, I thought, Charles Dale was like those apples, cut by Lou Jean's own rules and no one else's. Not into quarters or seeded, like the rules of the world *said* he should be, but into rounds. Where the stars could show.

Early the next morning I heard Lou Jean on the phone, laughing and whispering like David when he said naughty words. I had no idea who she whispered to or what she whispered about, until she loaded the boys and me into the backseat of her balloon-red station wagon and then drove straight to Carmen's house. The rain had passed, leaving the air cooler and filling Carmen's birdbath. Out she came, climbing into the front, and Lou Jean quickly drove away. When Carmen turned toward the three of us, her face was perfectly made up. Her lipstick left a tiny print on her palm as she blew kisses that covered all of us.

Nobody asked where we were going. Even David was too caught up with the excitement of going somewhere secret, with the party of it all, with the bright print of Carmen's shirt-waist dress, to ruin the mystery with questions. Somehow though, at least Charles Dale and I were sure we were headed out of town. He poked me and pointed as we came to the four-

way stop at the highway that led toward Uvalde and San
Antonio, towns large enough to rate our excitement. We were
both surprised when Lou Jean turned left instead of right, driving away from the cities and into the oldest and most ornate
neighborhood in town. An area I'd have to be blindfolded to
not recognize, where one dignified Victorian house followed
another, perfect white paint job after perfect white paint job.
Halfway down the street, like a harlot in the middle of the
choir, sat a hot pink house with lavender and purple shutters,
its grape-trimmed windows sneering and leering at its boringly
tasteful neighbors. "Where are we going?" asked David.

"Right there." I pointed to what my mother had often told
me "is making your grandfather roll over in his grave, right this
very minute."

"I'm going to check on your grandma," Carmen said to me,
her hand on the door handle. She climbed out, talking to herself. *Pobrecita.* Such a nice day to have to be sick." She walked
up the steps of the porch, pausing at a hanging basket, apparently not able to walk past it without breaking off a couple of
spent geranium blooms. Something about the way she saun-
tered said she wasn't very worried about Gran.

The front door flew open then and my grandmother came
out on the porch, handbag hanging on her shoulder, overalls
traded for an actual pantsuit, hair combed. The screen
slammed behind her and she brushed past Carmen. "Let's go,"
she said. "You can pick dead flowers later." Meekly, Carmen
followed her down the steps, then she climbed back in the
front seat and scooted to the middle, flanked by a woman who
washed her hands entirely too much and one who had at least
washed them today. She kept her eyes penitently down, proba-

bly drafting the confession she'd now have reason to make. Gran laid her arm along the back of the seat, turned across it and, pinning me with her eyes, said, "I'm sick. I feel awful. I'm too sick to stay by myself. We're taking me to Mexico, where I can get some first-class medical treatment. Got it?"

Fueled by the loudest voice in town, which alternately sang Hank Williams songs and bemoaned, "I'm sick. I feel awful," the car drove the twenty-five miles to Mexico, crossed the border, and parked on the plaza.

Thirty minutes later, less than twenty-four hours since expressing a desire to go somewhere with Lou Jean, Gran, and Carmen, I sat in the bar at El Moderno, my grandmother's favorite restaurant, a place I had only heard about. I held my first daiquiri and listened to the three of them carry on. Charles Dale and David were already out on the street, spending the five dollars Gran had handed each of us. "Bribe money. Keep your young mouths shut."

It made no difference that my daiquiri contained no alcohol. The fact that it looked the same as the other three, color pouring up through the strawberries as the glasses sat on a marble table hollowed to hold deep green lights, and that the same royal blue–jacketed waiter had delivered my glass as elegantly as the others while I sat waiting in a real leather chair with a leopard-skin back, was more than enough for me. The black lacquered walls around us, quietly illumined by spare and recessed white-gold lights, glowed like the walls in a dream, just enough to give me a sense of where I was without robbing any of the mystery. The bar itself, which seemed to stretch forever, was, according to my grandmother, carved from one huge ebony tree, brought all the way from Africa, and in the reflected glow of the mirrored wall behind it was the biggest and most beautiful chunk of wood I had ever seen.

With the boys gone and my daiquiri in hand, I felt as exotic and mature as Lou Jean, who looked at the other two over the top of her glass, straw between her lips and eyebrows raised as if imparting important knowledge. "Guess who's learning to read tea leaves?"

"She can do it," said Carmen, nodding in my direction. "It's in her blood."

"Just don't tell your mother," said Gran. "She already thinks we're a bunch of witches." She motioned for the waiter, waving the now empty plastic sword that had only a moment before held maraschino cherries and orange slices, evidently what she'd meant by the first-class medical treatment she could receive only in Mexico.

"*Witches,* or something that rhymes with it," said Lou Jean. She reached across the table and pulled a bowl of cayenned redskins away from Gran, who was hogging them. "These might not be good for your flu," she said.

"Sometimes you two ask for it," Carmen said, lifting an index finger away from the glass she held and pointing at them.

"What did you do?" I asked.

"Nothing," said Gran, looking at Lou Jean, the two of them giggling.

"Change the subject," said Carmen, then added to me, "They're hussies, that's all. Ignore them."

The last thing I wanted to do was ignore them. I wanted to ask a million questions. I wanted to know if my grandmother had faked sickness. And if she had faked it, did she do it so I would get to stay with Lou Jean. I wanted to know what Lou Jean and Gran had done together to aggravate my mother. As far as I knew, Gran had never done anything that *didn't* aggravate Mother, but what had she and Lou Jean done *together*? I was hoping the waiter would bring another round. My glass was still half full, but theirs were getting low, and, from my mother's litany of the ills of alcohol, I already knew that it was just the thing for loosening lips.

Just as the waiter started to the table, as I tried to decide which question I'd start with, Charles Dale burst through the door. The light that poured in around him cut through the peace and dark of the bar, as sharp and jagged as shattered glass. "David's gone. I stayed right with him, I promise, but then he was just gone."

Gran grabbed money out of her purse and pushed it into the waiter's hand. Carmen jumped up, knocking against the table and upsetting the ice still in her glass. I set down my unfinished drink and ran after Lou Jean, who was already headed for the street. "Where were you, sweetheart?" she asked Charles Dale, who was right with us, Gran and Carmen following.

The light on the street hurt my eyes. The glare that ricocheted from every surface, car hoods, the tin roof of the market, the street itself, made it too painful to look up and out, to scan for a little lost boy. "Right there," said Charles Dale, pointing to an outdoor stall that held frogs once alive and now stuffed into various positions, holding guitars, shooting pool, singing with open mouths.

Lou Jean ran up to the woman in the stall, flinging Spanish so fast I could only catch a few words. The woman pointed up a narrow street, away from the market and the central plaza, seeming to indicate where David had headed. By this time, Charles Dale was crying, and I grabbed his hand, squeezing it as we all took off in the direction the woman had pointed. As we poured into the traffic, horns honked and drivers shouted, and we wove in between bumpers and fenders, me wondering how a five-year-old could manage to get through all of these cars without getting hit.

The street we crossed onto was dimmer, shaded by taller buildings on either side, narrow enough for only one car at a time. Staying on the sidewalk, some of us on either side of the street, we ran, all of us shouting for David and peering into each open door we passed. Some were restaurants, some were shops. All of them were darker and cooler than the street we ran along and none of them held a little boy.

Before long, the street dead-ended into one even narrower and dustier. Lou Jean turned to the rest of us, her eyes red rimmed, her face flushed and hot. "Carmen," she said, and she was already moving to the right, away from the corner where we stood, "you and Rose go that way, toward the cathedral. I'll take Kayla and Charles Dale." As Gran and Carmen charged away from us and Charles Dale and I struggled to catch up with Lou Jean, she turned and yelled again, "If you see a cop, tell him. We'll meet you back at the market whenever." Her voice didn't break until she said the word *whenever*.

As we charged down the street, Charles Dale and Lou Jean on one side, me on the other, sticking our heads in every door we came to, the neighborhood changed. There were fewer shops and more houses, painted stucco walls surrounding courtyards, bougainvillea and passion vine climbing their heights. This made it harder to search, these tall walls and

closed gates. In the heat of the day, the courtyards were unoc-
cupied, and it took too much time to open the gates and go to
doors that most often remained unresponsive to our knocks.
After a few blocks of this, Lou Jean stopped, and the fear in her
eyes reminded me of some animal, wild and trapped. She
looked back the way we'd come, then ahead, up a street
becoming more and more residential. "Toward the plaza," was
all she said as she began to run, Charles Dale and I trying to
keep up, racing past houses and offices, dodging the thorns of
bougainvillea and roses.

We turned to the right again, onto a street with few houses
and more businesses. Three doors down, Lou Jean stopped so
suddenly that I ran into her back. She faced a darkened glass
door in a gray stucco building. There were no windows full of
curios, no outside racks of colorful goods, nothing that would
attract a five-year-old boy. It looked like a simple office building, now abandoned, and I wondered why Lou Jean had
stopped here. I looked above the door and saw the address,
123 CALLE NOGAL, but the letters above that weren't as clear.
AGOST . . . OCHO was all I could make out. More confused than
ever, I moved to Lou Jean's elbow. Charles Dale did the same,
grabbing his mother by the arm. "Mom," he said, "he
wouldn't be here. It's vacant." When she didn't respond, simply continued to stare at the building, the color gone from her
face and her eyes becoming more and more red, Charles Dale
moved toward the door, as if to look inside and reassure her.
But Lou Jean sprang behind him, catching him by the shirt, so
quickly and so roughly, that Charles Dale gave a surprised
"Hey . . ."

With a force, almost a violence, that seemed impossible in a body as slight and feminine as hers, she pulled her son back against her, clasped him from behind, her arms locked under his, around his chest. "No," she said fiercely, and held him to her, and her eyes stabbed at the building, as if battling it in some way. Over the sound of the traffic, the catcalls of the shop owners trying to attract our attention, I could hear Lou Jean's breathing. It seemed to stop every few moments, and as it did, her shoulders hunched forward as if to wrap themselves around Charles Dale's. Then, as if she were waking, her shoulders would surge backward, her breath resume. The sun reflecting from the street onto the backs of my legs was beginning to burn. The scent of Lou Jean's apple shampoo swirled with the rancid-meat smell of a taco wagon, making me nauseated and dizzy.

I don't know what we would have done, how long we would have stood there, Lou Jean locked in some kind of fear, Charles Dale locked in her strangled grip, me fighting back nausea and with no idea how to unlock either of them, if Gran and Carmen had not come around the same corner we had turned. Between them skipped David, his hands held tightly in theirs. Seeing us, they began to run, moving as fast as two old ladies dragging one small child could move. They reached us without Lou Jean even seeing, her eyes still clinging to that door, her arms still choking her son. Carmen pulled David up against his mother, tried to squeeze him in between her and Charles Dale, but Lou Jean's grip was so tight, the space between their two bodies so closed that Carmen gave up and instead lifted David. Holding him at eye level, she moved in front of the two locked figures, between them and the building.

Gran moved to Lou Jean's other side, took her arm and

shook her. "Lou Jean, you listen to me," she said. "He's fine. David's fine. He's right here. Here he is, sweetheart. Here he is." She kept talking, her voice getting slower, softer, a comforting decrescendo. Having no idea what we were doing but seeing Carmen's tiny arms start to tremble from the burden of holding David so high above her head, I moved to help her, sliding my arms under David's and lifting, holding him there as Carmen dropped her arms and started to cry, to talk to Lou Jean in Spanish.

The few words I understood were comforting, the same things I was hearing Gran say. Things like, "It's over. It's okay. He's okay." Though I knew Carmen must mean David, I heard her mention Charles Dale several times, understood her when she clearly said, "Charles Dale is right beside you, *mi hijita,"* and I wondered why. Her Spanish became too complex then, but as she and Gran continued to murmur in two separate languages, they finally found a way through to Lou Jean. Like someone who wakes from a dream just as she falls from the cliff, Lou Jean started, actually jumped, looked at each of us and then at the concrete she stood on, as if amazed to find it there. Releasing one of her arms from Charles Dale's midsection, she turned him so that he faced her, then grabbed David to her, held both boys against her as she finally, with what seemed a great effort, turned her back to the gray building and sobbed against the heads of her sons. With Gran on one side, Carmen on the other, she began walking toward the plaza, Charles Dale moving backward in her embrace, David carried on her hip. I walked behind and wondered what had just happened.

❧ 13 ❧

I hurt too much to sleep. I'd tossed all night, trying to find a comfortable position. My arms and legs ached. My body felt bruised, as if those Mexican cars had hit me as well as honked at me. At the first sign of light, I got up, and in the mirror of the bathroom I shared with the boys, examined my freakish face. Nose burned red. White half moons around the top of my eyes. Deep blue circles below. All the colors of the upcoming Fourth.

The sleeping house was uncomfortably quiet. It had been that way since we'd returned from Mexico the day before. David, exhausted by his escapade, had been asleep before dark. Charles Dale and I, no less tired, had soon followed. We'd left Lou Jean sitting on the front porch in the twilight, her eyes rimmed by circles that must have been contagious.

Quietly, I let myself out the back door. My sandals remained dry as I walked across the yards to our garage. Some mornings were like that here, so arid that there wasn't enough dew to wet the grass. I grabbed my bike, popped up the kickstand, and climbed on. The handlebars wobbled as my sore calves took their time responding. Despite the rain only two days before, the gardenia bush my mother had planted looked dead. Maybe some plants, gardenias and azaleas and things with lush green growth, weren't meant to grow here. Only colorless plants, so gray they seemed transparent, ceniza and guajillo and huisache, seemed to thrive. At Fifth Street, my first impulse was to turn right, the way into town and toward my grandmother's house and the shops. I had money in my overalls; I could bring back doughnuts for everyone. At the last minute, though, I turned left, ready for something new and maybe, just to be alone awhile. I'd yet to see the junior high, and I thought it was in this direction.

The road before me was perfectly straight, like a closed zipper connecting the gray fabric of brush country. After a while, though, there was a sharp plunge, and as I dropped off into it, the asphalt beneath my tires turned to concrete. My dad had explained these low water crossings, but it still seemed odd that this was a creek bed, and that the creek so seldom held water that it required no bridge. Instead, the road I traveled ran across the bed, asphalt replaced by steel and concrete to withstand the sudden and dangerous floods that Dad said could come with little more than a few inches of rain somewhere upstream. Where I now rode would then be under wild water that washed away cattle and coyotes and sometimes houses and flushed tarantulas out of their earthen lairs, sending them marching like furry brown armies, up the highways toward drier land.

Though my calves complained, I pedaled faster, up the steep incline and back onto the asphalt. I wondered if Lou Jean was up yet and wondered if I should have left a note. She needed no more worries. I had never seen illness like hers. It wasn't like a cold or flu, maladies that had a beginning point, when you started to feel bad, and an ending point, when you felt better, and that usually required a trip to the pharmacy for pink medicine. With Lou Jean, it was more like her spirit was sick.

On this part of the road, there were no houses. There were portable buildings and small mobile homes with signs that advertised frac services and drilling supply houses. Behind a chain link fence circling a trailer, beyond a sign that read SIKES OIL FIELD CONSTRUCTION, a mouthy black Doberman ran up and down. He barked and grabbed the fence, as if I was there to steal a dump truck, a maintainer, and a big pile of crushed rock.

I was also worried about what I'd read in my teacup, worried that even more worries were coming, and concerned about what I'd read in Lou Jean's. Was she afraid of making a mistake or was she upset about one she'd already made? Charles Dale was so much like my father, I had to admit.

Soon, even the businesses played out, and I'd yet to come to any school. Instead, I'd come to a place where the caliche beside the road changed to sand, soft as baby powder and marked by footprints, layers of them, all on top of each other, and all moving from the pasture beyond the fence, across the barditch and up to the highway. A *mojado* crossing, I knew from hearing Dad and Gran talk about the people who continually made their slow and painful way from Mexico, trying to find a life where they could make money to send home to families who couldn't travel with them. Often, they got no farther than the first highway they came to, where they were caught, or where, exhausted, starving, craving water, they simply gave up and sat until the next *Imigre* vehicle came by and took them to the immigration station. There, they got food, water, and a ride on a big green air-conditioned bus, back to the border, to go home empty-handed or to start their trek all over again. I made a big looping circle to the other side of the road, where stacked tracks moved off toward the pasture, under the fence and onward. I glanced out at the brush, then circled again, hoping whoever made the tracks was headed to east Texas, where trees held wild grapes and berries and creeks held water.

I pedaled on, tires on the smooth road, eyes on the ditch, thoughts mostly on Charles Dale. As much as I loved him, what if the things I'd heard Gran tell Mother were true? What if everybody in town, and more importantly, at school, knew what had happened between Dad and Lou Jean? All of a sudden the ditch was asphalt, a paved driveway painted with the image of a bobcat. I turned right and for a few minutes made a game of guiding my bike around the outside perimeter of the cat. Its lips were pulled back, revealing glossy fangs that dripped blood. Its eyes shone victorious. This was the first time I'd seen something in this town stack up favorably against Cameron, and I forgot all about Charles Dale. In Cameron the junior high driveway was made of antique brick. We'd never have been allowed to paint it with our mascot. Suddenly, I couldn't wait to see my new school.

I wheeled my bike away from the cat, careful to avoid its whiskers. One good thing about living in this place, I thought, was that people loved color. Maybe because so much of nature was gray in this part of the world, or maybe because of the proximity of Mexico—for whatever reason, people loved color enough to tile their kitchens and paint their driveways. I flew up the road, following painted pawprints that twisted and curved through a maze of mesquite trees and metal buildings, a bus barn, a maintenance shop, getting more and more excited, counting the pawprints I passed. Just as my legs began to burn and I thought I'd have to slow my pace, just as I passed the eighty-second print, I came around the edge of a huge garbage incinerator and saw the words ROSALITA JUNIOR HIGH SCHOOL.

Braking my bike, I stood and straddled it, excited, thrilled, and then sickened, because although the sign was colorful and fresh, the same paint as on the asphalt, it stood in front of a boring brick schoolhouse no bigger than the post office in Cameron. I leaned away from my bike, trying to see around the building, certain that there must be more. How could everything that was needed for junior high students be contained in such a tiny space? There was no gym, no separate cafeteria building, no band hall. There was only this squat ugly box with rows of windows and no sign of air-conditioning. A dusty brick square. Painted gray.

Wondering why my parents had done this to me, I headed for home. As I passed the bobcat I wondered how long it would stay fresh and new. How many days of school would go by before it too was covered in a layer of caliche and limestone dust? How could Dad say they wanted me to grow up in this colorless, derelict place, where the school looked like a death row designed for dwarves? Over my shoulder, I glanced back once more and saw what, in my misguided enthusiasm, I hadn't noticed before. The bus barn too was gray, as was the field house, the aluminum bleachers, the earth itself.

I rode faster, coming again to the footprints. I envied their makers. Hungry, thirsty, and tired though they might be, they were right this minute headed away from all this drab dry scrub.

I crossed the highway and rode down the wrong side of the road just to aggravate the dog. His spit darkened the fence, turning it an even uglier shade of guess what color. Maybe *this* was what had been wrong with Lou Jean in Mexico. It was possible to believe that someone could be made ill, emotionally and physically, by all this *gray*.

Ahead, in the ditch, was a *paisano*. Gray, of course. Threadbare and wiry. With her back to me and her speckled wings spread, she stood motionless, asking for it. I stopped pedaling. The asphalt was hot through my flip-flops as I scanned the pavement for a rock, a dislodged chunk of asphalt, anything to hurl at her ugly body.

Then I saw the other one. Beyond her, it moved back and forth, doing some sort of goofy roadrunner dance. Side step hop, side step hop. After a bit, it quit dancing and began circling, around and around, moving in front of its stationary companion, flapping its wings crazily.

At first I thought it was the sound of my flip-flops, a swishing as I slowly lifted one then the other, to cool my feet. Then I thought it was the bird, the flapping of her ugly wings. It took at least five minutes before I recognized what should have been unmistakeable. The buzz of a rattler. I froze, forgetting my scorching shoes. For all that Dad had said about snakes since we'd moved here, cautioning me over and over to "watch where you walk," I'd never asked what to do if I heard one but couldn't see it. As if to let me know, the snake struck, once twice three times, lifting its head from the circle of the roadrunners, flailing the one with the outstretched wing. Each time I flinched, now sorry for the bird I'd wanted to stone, but the snake hit only feathers, and as if realizing it had accomplished nothing, it finally dropped to the ground. The buzzing died down but didn't stop, and the circling bird continued, wild but in no way frenzied, as if she knew exactly what she was doing.

The snake turned with her, twisting the upper part of his body, trying to follow her movements, his buzzing growing furious again, but he didn't try to strike. He seemed hypnotized by her craziness and by the one bit of color in the whole countryside, a lurid patch of turquoise skin that flamed to red behind her unblinking eyes, and I was as captivated as he, as unblinking as she. He seemed to gather all his strength, then. His buzz grew so loud it drowned out even my heart. His head crept backward as if to prepare himself and this time, he struck *hard*. And when he did, the quieter bird moved in. She caught him just behind the head, her pointed bill driving all the way through him so that when she lifted her own head and her dancing companion moved to join her, turquoise and red now flashed back and forth between them like a shared signal, a communication all their own, like a dropped shoulder or wide smile. The impaled snake writhed in the air between them, still moving but very dead.

14

At noon on the Fourth, Charles Dale and I stood in the street in front of my house setting off Black Cats, me wearing a training bra that my mother had brought home only that morning and hoping that the thing wasn't as obvious to everyone else as it was to me. The catch dug into my back, and I could feel sweat collecting against the band that choked my rib cage. My chest looked as flat as it always had, and it seemed to me that bras, at least training bras, were unnecessary. Breasts were breasts. That's all they'd ever be, whether they were *trained* or not. The image of a man standing in a circus tent entered my mind. With great flourish, he snapped a whip, first at large Siberian tigers who responded immediately, jumping back and forth through flaming hoops, then at breasts, whose response was to do nothing. Who continued to sit motionless and unconcerned on their striped and colorful pedestals. I laughed right out loud, just as Thad Howard rode up on his clanking bicycle. He glared at me, thinking I was laughing at him, but said nothing. The sight of him, his perpetual sneer, made me nervous and made me want him gone. He was the last thing we needed.

Since returning from Galveston, my parents had rarely spoken to each other, and Lou Jean was still very sad. To make matters worse, Charles Dale seemed oblivious to the situation. He was his usual happy self, going to softball practice with my dad, examining bugs and leaves and worms. He had made me tell the snake story over and over. How could he not be worried about his mother? And why wouldn't Gran talk to me about the situation? When I'd asked her why a crumbling stucco building had been so disturbing to Lou Jean, she'd simply said, "Finding your child in danger can do awful things to a woman." Then she had changed the subject.

I resisted the urge to toss a firecracker into Thad's spokes, hoping he'd ride on, straight into hell, hopefully, though any place would do, and knowing he wasn't about to. He opened his smelly mouth, and I could see his bottom teeth, all facing different directions, some laid flat, like his father's Civil War soldiers after a battle. "Well, looky here," he said, "if it's not the Bobbseys." He sneered even wider, and his eyes moved down from my face. "Except one got a bra, so now I can tell you apart."

I lit an entire cluster then, at least eleven or twelve, and threw them underhand onto the street, right below his bony butt. He flew off the side of his bike, and it banged to the pavement just as the firecrackers went off. Charles Dale laughed so hard he had to sit on the curb.

"Bitch," said Thad, then turned to Charles Dale. "What are you laughing at, punk? You think your sister's so funny?" Anybody else on earth would have thought that remark odd, but an oblivious Charles Dale paid no notice.

"Shut up, Howard," I said, wanting him to be mad at me.

Though only hours before I had been mad at Charles Dale for ignoring his mother, for what appeared to me to be stealing my father, now I just wanted Thad to leave him alone. "And go home. You're killing innocent butterflies every time you exhale."

He didn't even look at me, he was so mad that Charles Dale was still laughing at him. "You think it's funny, you little bastard? Well, I think it's funny that you're a little bastard. Your own father didn't even claim you."

"Shut up, Howard. His dad was a hero. He died in the line of duty. The only way *your* dad could do that is if the refrigerator fell over on him." Then I ran to the curb, grabbed Charles Dale's arm, and pulled him up from where he sat. "Let's go," I told him. "It stinks out here."

"Yeah, go on, you little dumbass," Howard yelled, and by this time, the sneer was gone. His face was as red as mine. "Go inside and do it. Like your momma did with Twinsie's daddy. *Your* daddy, I mean."

Not even the deafest thirteen-year-old in history could have missed those screamed words. I looked at Charles Dale, who was staring at Thad, his forehead wrinkled down over his eyes as he tried to make sense of what he'd heard, the same way my father's forehead wrinkled, and I saw the exact moment when the wrinkles left.

It took me two steps to reach Thad. I grabbed the front of his shirt with both hands. "Shut up, you liar," I screamed, even as he was laughing so hard he couldn't pull me off, even as he was leaning around me, still yelling at Charles Dale. "Didn't you ever notice how you don't look anything like your hero dad or your slut mom? You look like *her* dad, dumbass, and you're too stupid to know it."

He was still laughing when I shoved him and let go, sent him flying backward over his downed bike, his feet hanging up in it, his body landing on the pavement on the other side. I landed on top of him and the bike, one knee braced on the crossbar, one knee in his stomach, and pounded his face, hoping only to see his nose go through his brain, using punches that followed through, the kind a father will teach his daughter if he believes he'll never have the chance to teach a son.

I punched him even after blood poured from his gray nose and from a cut on one of his floppy ears. I punched him until I was crying so hard I couldn't see his face. I punched him until someone kneeled down behind me and took my shoulders. "Kayla," Lou Jean said, "that's enough, sugar." She pulled me up, and I turned and held onto her, sobbing, my muscles still twitching and jumping with the excitement of the punching they'd done.

When my eyes cleared enough to see, I looked for Charles Dale and saw him standing on my lawn. When I had taken off for Thad, he had taken off for anywhere and had run straight into the arms of my mother, coming to investigate the sound of the bomb going off under the bicycle. Now she stood holding him, stroking his hair and talking to him in the same way his mother talked to me. Lou Jean walked me over to where they stood. The two women looked at each other, exchanged crying kids, and led each of us into our own house, leaving only one kid crying in the street.

When Charles Dale arrived the next day, we were still eating breakfast. My parents had yet to speak to each other that morning. If they had spoken to each other the night before, I hadn't heard them. After the fight, when Mother had marched me back in the house, Dad had stood at the front door, holding the screen open. He'd reached for me as I walked past, as if to draw me to him, but Mother had pushed me ahead of her, out of his range, and she had been the one who'd washed my face and changed my clothes. Her hands were unusually gentle, and her eyes were glossy. After I was dressed, she smoothed Jergens lotion on my red cheeks, so that when she pulled me against her, we smelled just alike. We could still hear Thad's howling, and finally we heard Dad's voice, "Go home, Thad." The front door slammed, the wails ended, and Mother released me. "What do you know," she muttered. "He *is* good for *something*."

The rest of the day and part of the night, I'd stayed in the mulberry tree, at the very top, where the leaves were thickest, where I had a clear view of the fireworks show orchestrated by the city, and where no one had a clear view of me. At dark, Dad had come into the backyard. From his lawn chair, he only saw the colored explosions after they'd climbed high into the sky. After they'd faded a bit. It pleased me that I saw them first, that the tree I hid in hid the fireworks from him. Now, though, it was his own face doing the hiding. He greeted Charles Dale with nothing more than his usual warmth. "Hey. There's the home-run king. I'm glad you're here." Mother took a deep breath and got to her feet. The look she gave Dad was mixed. In it was anger, the same anger she'd shown yesterday. She was fed up and tired. And I expected her to confront him then, to say, "Explain, buddy. It's past time." But also in her look was excitement and a certain hesitancy, like someone very near claiming something she's wanted a long time, wanting to grasp it quickly and decidedly, but afraid to reach. Saying nothing, she turned away from Dad, put her hands on Charles Dale's shoulders, and pushed him into a chair. Her bottom teeth clamped her upper lip, as if trying to contain something. I thought at first it must be words, the ones that went with her anger at Dad, then I saw that it was a smile, and I watched the corners of her mouth ease upward, too strong to be restrained by her bite. Her eyes sparkled with tears that showed only a moment, no longer than it took to slap more bread in the toaster. Then the tears were gone, along with all nervousness, all hesitancy. The hand that reached for the skillet, flipping it off the cold burner and on to the one now heating, was sure and certain, as if she always scrambled a fourth egg. As if each and every morning for the last thirteen years, she had served breakfast to one husband and two children, and the only thing unusual about this particular morning was that we had Cream of Wheat instead of oatmeal.

When I climbed out of my chair, they must have thought I was only going to the refrigerator for more juice, to pour Charles Dale a glass, because all of them smiled. The polite cheerful smiles of a family enjoying breakfast together. When I walked up to Charles Dale and stood there, one hand on the back of his chair, the other on the table edge, without bringing him any juice, their smiles faltered a bit, unsure. When I shoved his waiting plate halfway across the table, and asked him, "What are you doing here?" the smiles all died.

"Kayla?" said Mother, her voice shocked, at the same time that Charles Dale asked me, "What do you mean?" He looked not at me but at the space where his plate had been.

"I mean," I said, and I leaned down so that he *had* to look at me, "you have a home to eat breakfast in. You *have* a home. Why don't you use it?"

Mother left the stove and grabbed me by the shoulders. Her head leaned down from behind, inserted itself between Charles Dale and me. "That is enough," she said, pulling me backward, away from the table, then moving into the position where I had been. Charles Dale stood then and looked toward the door. Before he could move, though, Mother dropped my shoulders and took his, pushing him back down into his chair.

I turned and faced Dad, who examined his half-eaten egg as if surprised it was still on his plate. "Are you going to say if it's true or not?" I asked him. When he didn't answer, I leaned around Mother and asked Charles Dale, "Don't you want to know? Don't you want to know for *sure?*" He didn't answer me, but he raised his eyes to Dad's and left them there, where they were joined by Mother's and mine.

Dad picked up his napkin and began to roll it into a cigar, glancing up at the three of us from time to time. When he spoke, his voice was quiet, almost covered by the sound of the skillet. "I don't know," he said. "I don't know for *sure.*" He looked so serious then, so truly overwhelmed, that I might have believed him, if my mother hadn't whirled away from his words and stomped back to the stove. "Oh, for Christ's sake," she muttered, and I knew that Dad was lying. It took more than a scorched egg for her to use the Lord's name in vain.

Charles Dale moved into our house that day. Not officially. Not to sleep. He didn't bring his clothes, but he ate most meals with us. He showed up at seven every morning and went home only for a few minutes at noon and again late in the afternoon, always back in our door before the evening news was over. At nine o'clock, when I announced that I was going to bed, he never mentioned going home himself, just turned back to whatever conversation he was having with my father. I would hear him leave our house and slip into his own dark one after the ten-o'clock news ended.

Two days after the fireworks of the Fourth, I tried to talk to Charles Dale. We were in the backyard. I was practicing cartwheels and he was drawing in the dirt with a stick. "So," I said, as my hands hit the ground, "what do you think about everything?" Dirt showered down onto my head from the heels of my tennis shoes. I stood up and shook my hair, waiting for his answer.

Finally, he said, "Thirty-two."

"Thirty-two what?" I brushed dirt from my shoulders and picked grass from my ponytail.

"Thirty-two times yesterday, my mother washed her hands."

I dropped my hair, grass still in it, and knelt on the ground beside Charles Dale. "How do you know? You were over here most of the day."

"Thirty-two that I *counted*," he clarified. "I'm sure there were more." Though I watched him closely, he never looked at me. Just like the day he'd shown up at breakfast, I thought, and just like my dad.

The palms of my hands were red and itchy from pressing into the grass, and I rubbed them together, still watching him. Finally, he broke the stick in two, then tossed it. The pieces split paths in the air, one landing across the yard, the other flying back over his shoulder to land in front of me. "It's true," he continued, "what Thad said. My mother told me."

His voice was so sad that my own voice softened. "Maybe

that's why she washes her hands so much. Maybe she feels bad." His only answer was a shrug. Where the grass played out in front of him, he now circled one finger in the dirt. "What exactly did she say?" I pressed.

His finger stopped its aimless circles then and began forming letters. With the side of his hand, he wiped away what he'd written and started over. Instead of answering my question, he said, "You don't have to act like it's such a big deal," his voice hostile again. He bent away from me, hunched over his drawn-up knees toward what he scribbled. "Unless you're jealous."

"Why would I be jealous?" The red sand had stuck to the sweat of his legs, and his ears looked hot, the same color as the sand.

Before he could answer, my mother called from the back door. "Charles Dale, what's your favorite cookie? I'm making some for your softball refreshments."

"Chocolate chip. I *love* them." Then he turned and faced me, motioning with his head toward the kitchen door my mother had just reentered, a smug look on his face, as if to say, *There's your answer.*

"You mean because my mother's giving you attention?" He leaned back so I could see what he had written. It was his name. "Charles Dale Perry." He really looked at me then, for the first time since the fight with Thad. His eyes on me and not on what he did, his finger moved slowly across the dirt, pulling my eyes along with it, slicing through the word *Perry,* replacing it with *Sanders.*

I spent that afternoon at Lou Jean's. She was canning black-eyed peas. I kept wondering how Lou Jean would react to what Charles Dale had written in the dirt, if *he,* or what had made him, was the mistake that made her sad. I was quiet as we worked, but not as quiet as she. Although we worked side by side, although we were in her kitchen, there was no magic. The peas were still a little green and took forever to shell. My thumb was bruised and raw before we were halfway through the bushel. We said so little that we might as well have worked alone.

Lou Jean looked both older and smaller, as if her youth, her fun and vibrancy, were things with weight and size and were all now gone. With her head bent over the stainless steel colander, she seemed both warped and bowed, not like an old person, but like a tree too frail in a wind too strong.

Her movements too were smaller. Her smiles made it no farther than the corners of her mouth, her eyes did not widen as she talked, her lips formed words almost without opening. When David came in, complaining of a stomach-ache, she talked to him so quietly that I, only one chair away, could barely hear. She felt his head with one hand, the other still tightly clutching the colander to her middle. "You don't have any fever." With her free hand, she pulled him against her, then rose from her chair, and still clutching the colander, walked to a cabinet. The hands that managed to pour Milk of Magnesia and spoon it into David's mouth were oddly white, as if all the color had been washed out of them, but they were dotted with blisterlike spots. "Go lie down on the couch," she mumbled. "I'll come check on you in a little while."

I was shelling the last of the peas and Lou Jean was boiling water to blanch them when Charles Dale came in the kitchen door, carrying a plate of cookies. "Sarah Jo sent these." He glanced at his mother, who stood at the stove watching him, then set the cookies down on the table. "Peas, huh?" he asked, his head down, his hand on the back of a chair, only his eyes jumping from the bowl I held to the empty hulls in paper sacks on the floor and up to his mother, whose smile had widened for the first time all afternoon. She went to the sink to wash her hands.

"I can have them ready before you go to practice," she said, her voice lifting for the first time. "Would you rather have cornbread or hot biscuits?" She began to move around the kitchen in her normal sure way, grabbing a saucepan, filling it with shelled peas and water, reaching for the salt and black pepper.

Charles Dale's face changed. His eyes quit their nervous darting and locked against his mother's back. They seemed to be willing her to turn around, just as they had willed me to look over his shoulder that morning. And when he was sure of her full attention, when she faced him completely, smiling, waiting for his answer, he shoved the chair against the table and spun toward the door. "I hate fresh peas," he said. "Why can't you just buy them in a can like normal people?"

I watched him cross the yard, somebody I didn't even know, as foreign to me as my mother the day she came home in the blue sundress. And when I turned back around, Lou Jean had doubled over again, spotted hands clutching the filled saucepan to her middle, like a shield.

∽ 15 ∽

"Why would she send Lou Jean cookies?" I asked Gran. We were stopped at a red light, on an errand to buy more sugar for Mother.

"Just being neighborly?" she quipped. An old yellow pickup crept through the intersection, so slowly that I listened for its motor as it passed. Its pace reminded me of how Lou Jean had moved around her kitchen earlier that afternoon. Each step she took was labored. Each trip past the big black range, where the week before we'd stirred peach preserves and sung Ray Price songs, was slower than the last. Hand-washing, I realized, at least when done fifty or sixty times a day, must be hard work.

"It isn't a joke," I told Gran. "You should see her hands. She doesn't even let them dry before she washes them again. And Charles Dale should stay at home with her."

Gran made a quick right turn, jerked the car across the center stripe, leaned against her window to see around the pickup, then gunned the car past it. She'd yet to mention the night of the Fourth, when she'd shown up at our house to eat ice cream and watch the annual fireworks display and had found pyrotechnics far exceeding anything the Parks Department could offer. Enough hot words and gunpowder glances to explode our house *and* the one next door. From my perch in the mulberry tree, I had seen her drive up and go in the house, had heard Mother's raised voice telling her own version of the afternoon's events, and had then seen Gran leave, never calling to Dad, not stopping to tell him her latest dirty joke. Long after she was gone, Dad had sat in the backyard, unmoving, as if dead in his lawn chair. Even when I leaned far out over the alley and away from our house, trying to make the most of the weak pop and cheap flare of the city's meager offering, and the thin high branch I straddled croaked protest, Dad had said nothing. Like some brand-new ghost who could still see the world he'd just vacated, could still pass through it but could no longer interact, he'd sat mute.

Safely around the doddering pickup, Gran still didn't respond. Finally, I pressed her, "I thought you were Lou Jean's friend. I thought you were supposed to be her *best* friend." Gran hit the brakes as we met a city police car.

"I thought I was *your* best friend," she said, her voice tired and flip at the same time, so that I made my own voice as sarcastic as I could.

"I don't have a best friend. I'd like one. But instead, I have a *brother.* One who's only three months younger than I am." Gran glanced at me, only for a moment but long enough for the car to sway across the center stripe. Almost immediately, we heard the siren of the black-and-white as it whipped around and sped up to our bumper. Gran pulled over into the Catholic church parking lot and rolled down her window absentmindedly, her worried eyes focused on me and not the officer walking up to the car. "Sorry," I whispered.

The officer squatted by Gran's door, leaning his forearms on the open window, his face even with mine. He looked like a kid himself, his gray uniform shirt stained under the arms, the black hair at his temples wet and curling beneath his cap. He grinned at the back of Gran's head. "Are you going to *force* me to take your license away, old woman?"

"Shut up, Brady," she answered, still looking at me and not at him. "A yellow jacket flew in the window."

"That's interesting," he said. Behind him, the yellow pickup inched by. "I could have sworn your window was up. I'm not sure if it was up when you stomped on your brakes. But I'm sure it was up when you almost clipped my rear bumper." He looked across at me. "Are you Phil and Sarah Jo's daughter?"

I nodded.

"Well, do you think you can keep your grandmother in the right lane until you get your own license? I don't expect you to slow her down—the entire police force can't do that—but can you just keep her on the right side of the stripe?"

I nodded again.

"Good girl. Then when you get *your* license, we'll go on and take hers away. You won't mind chauffeuring her, will you?"

I started to nod again, then remembered to shake my head no instead.

He laughed and slapped the car door. "Better keep your window up, Rose."

He wasn't three steps away from us when she remarked, "You *are* the entire police force, you little asshole," her voice still absentminded, her eyes still on me. When I glanced nervously over my shoulder, Brady was still walking toward his car, either ignoring or not hearing Gran's comment. We sat there for what seemed like a very long time, long enough for even the yellow pickup to get somewhere, until finally, Gran asked me, "How are you doing with this?"

"I'm fine." Sweat poured from both of us. I lifted one knee and then the other, peeling the backs of my legs from the damp vinyl. "Except my legs are sticking to this stupid plastic. Can we turn on the air conditioner?"

"No," said Gran, but her eyes moved from my face to the rearview mirror.

I reached and tilted the rearview mirror toward me and watched Brady pull away. I rolled down my own window and stared out. "How come you're best friends with somebody my dad slept with?"

"How come *you're* so worried about somebody your mother hates?" When I didn't respond, she reached for the rearview mirror and adjusted it again. "You know," she said, "there's *always* a reason why people do the things they do."

"I know that." A yellow jacket, a *real* one, was buzzing around the side mirror. "Here's your yellow jacket. I just don't know why people won't tell me the reasons. Why I have to guess all the time. It *is* my business, you know."

"I never said it wasn't. What do you want to know? Ask me." She settled back against her car door and faced me, drawing her right knee up onto the seat between us, as if the Catholic church parking lot was the most natural place in the world for a child raised Baptist and a grandmother who thought most of the world's wrongs began with organized religion to have a heart-to-heart.

"Why did my dad sleep with Lou Jean?"

Gran's answer was quick. "You'll have to ask one of them. I wasn't there." The yellow jacket perched on the mirror, lifting one leg and then the other, as if admiring their shape.

"Why did my mother move us into the house next door to her?"

"You've asked me that one before," said Gran. She tilted her head and stared solemnly at the backs of her hands. "You know, sweetheart, just because someone is eighteen, or twenty-one, or even thirty-three, does not make her a grown-up." I looked at her hands to see what could generate such heresy. All I saw were brown spots, familiar, dear, but ordinary.

"You mean that Mother's still a child?"

Alternating hands, Gran rubbed at the spots with one thumb and then the other. Her voice was slow, either methodical or distracted. "No. But I suspect that she moved next door to Lou Jean simply to show off. And if that's the truth, well . . ."

"Well, what?"

"Well, then, it wasn't a very grown-up thing to do."

The yellow jacket began turning in circles on the glass. I thought then of how Mother had acted in the first days we'd lived here, buying first one new outfit and then another, wearing them to water flowers, to pick roses, anytime she was in view of Lou Jean's house. As if she really were showing off. Not only her new clothes but the fact that she still had a husband. Lou Jean's was dead. But, still, my mother was smarter than that, and more suspicious. She wouldn't take a chance on Dad and Lou Jean being so close together, just to show off. "I think she did it to steal Charles Dale," I said. "And it worked."

"No," said Gran, the word drawn out. "At least, I hope not." She stared past me at the yellow jacket.

"Well, that's what she's doing. And you should see Lou Jean's hands. When I first met her, she already washed them too much. But now . . ."

"Kayla, she's watched her thirteen-year-old son lose his father twice in one year. The first time to a land mine halfway around the world, and the second time to the truth, delivered by a neighborhood brat with big ears and a gossiping mother."

"I could kill Thad Howard," I said, wishing the Black Cats I'd tossed under his bike that day had landed down his throat, shutting his big mouth for good.

Gran leaned toward me. "Your parents should have told you. And Lou Jean should have told Charles Dale." She laid her arm along the seat and lifted my ponytail away from my neck. "Come on," she said. "You wanted answers. Ask me something I *know.*"

"Why did my dad allow us to move next door to Lou Jean?"

Gran's sigh was deep. "Another one I can't answer." She leaned her head back against the seat. "I've asked myself a hundred times. The best I can come up with is that he was worried about her."

"About Mom?" It didn't seem likely. She was not a person you worried about.

"She was pretty upset after she lost the last baby," Gran reminded me. "For your mom to stay in bed as long as she did is serious."

Gran had a point. "How did you and Lou Jean get to be such good friends? She's half your age."

"Well, it's simple. Lou Jean's mother was not what I'd call the most attentive mother in the world. She always had somewhere else to be. The beauty parlor. Bridge club. Lou Jean spent most of her time with a baby-sitter, usually Carmen Tamez, who actually . . . don't let this hurt your feelings, now . . ."—she covered her mouth and exaggerated her gaze, as if letting me in on some shocking secret—". . . is my best friend, and has been since we were in sixth grade." Then she went on, "Lou Jean was like a second child to Carmen, and to me too, I guess. And as she grew up, we three had more and more in common. We laugh at the same things, we *enjoy* the same things. We have fun together. Do you get what I'm saying?"

I got it, clearly. It was exactly why I wanted to spend every moment with Lou Jean. "Is that why my mother was always so jealous of her? Even before Dad, I mean?"

"Maybe part of it," said Gran. All the jokes were gone from her face. "It's odd, I know, and I'm sure it must have been hard for your mother. She likes *different* things. I loved her dearly—I *love* her dearly—but we're really different. Sometimes I wonder if she didn't have more in common with Yvonne, with Lou Jean's mother."

"Like they were switched at birth?" I asked. The idea was appealing.

Gran's grin was large. "Yeah," she said, "switched. I took home the bossy, grouchy one, and Yvonne got the prize." Then she immediately added, "You know I'm just joking."

"Yeah, right," I said sarcastically, but I couldn't help smiling as Gran punched my arm. "There's more that you aren't telling me," I said then. "I know that." I reached my arm out the window, slowly, extending my hand to where the yellow jacket dozed. "And I *will* find out." Laying my finger on the glass, I nudged the rust-brown legs, just a tiny pressure. Gran, beside me, offered no warning, just as Lou Jean never offered warnings when I handled boiling water or simple syrup in her kitchen. Mother would already have jerked my arm back in the car window, mouthing about responsibility for your actions and the price of medical treatment for wasp stings. The yellow jacket lifted its legs, first on one side and then the other, until it stood on my finger. *Charles Dale would love this,* I thought. *Not* the present Charles Dale, the one who had moved into my house the morning after we'd learned the truth, sending my triumphant mother into her baking frenzy and sending his own mother to the sink with endless bars of Lava, but the old Charles Dale. The one who believed that stinging things would not sting you if you showed them you meant no harm. Who had never killed a bug in his whole life. Who didn't even care if he sounded corny when he said things like "All creatures have worth. Even insects serve a purpose."

When the yellow jacket lifted off my finger and flew to an overhanging mesquite branch, I turned back to Gran. Her eyes were damp. "Think you're pretty smart, don't you?"

"Can we just *go*? I'm never going to get my legs unstuck from these seats."

Gran started the car, pulled out into the street, and immediately made a U-turn, heading us back the way we'd come. She flipped the air-conditioner switch to high. "I'll check on her when we get home, okay?"

Just as we passed city hall, Brady's car parked in the one and only space marked POLICE DEPARTMENT, I remembered. "We forgot the sugar."

I was back in Lou Jean's kitchen before dark, despite Mother's angry admonition to "stay at home, where you belong." It was

Gran who'd made her so angry. We had returned home with no sugar, and Gran had immediately gone next door. When she came back, she walked straight past Charles Dale and me and said, "Let's you and I go buy some sugar, Sarah Jo." Her voice was so cold and angry that Charles Dale and I both forgot the Dodgers game we were watching. Mother looked as surprised as we did but, saying nothing, plucked her purse from atop the television and followed Gran out the door. They'd come back with ten pounds of sugar and facial expressions so sour that a hundred pounds of sugar, spoon-fed, couldn't have improved them. Gran left just as Dad came in from work, and I started out the back door, meaning to sit in the mulberry tree for a while. It was then that Mother said, "Kayla Marie, you can keep yourself at home where you belong."

"I'm just going to the tree," I answered, slamming the screen behind me. I climbed only partway up, her words changing my plans, creating a resolve to be back on the ground and next door as soon as she wasn't watching. Stretched out on the lowest horizontal branch, looking up through the leaves, I didn't feel disloyal. How could you be disloyal to somebody who needed no one? Who mostly seemed to need *plans,* the plans she made or carried out, every moment of the day. Plans for Charles Dale to become part of our household. Plans for him and Dad to do things together. Plans for church activities. Plans crafty enough to mask how angry she'd been with Dad on the Fourth. As if she hadn't known the truth for years and as if *she* hadn't been the one who'd wanted us to move here, for whatever reason, in the first place.

I heard Mother's voice then, lighthearted and tricky, "Don't forget this box when you go. And don't spill the Kool-Aid that's in it." Knowing she was occupied getting Dad and Charles Dale off to softball practice, I jumped out of the tree and slipped next door.

Lou Jean sat at the kitchen table. Her braid was sloppy and loose, one strand of it caught on the back of her chair. She wore the same apron she'd worn that afternoon, and it was stained, stiffened with juice from the peas we wouldn't can. She didn't respond to my hello. The air-conditioner was off, the kitchen hotter than the backyard, and from the living room came the sound of television gunfire. Then, through the open window came the sound of my father's truck starting up and, above it, the sound of Charles Dale's laughing voice. "I hope the rest of the team likes chocolate chip. We've got about twelve dozen."

In Lou Jean's hands was a Big Red bottle, empty except for filmy white wisps of things, like bits of shredded tissue or stationery, which covered the bottom of the bottle and came up the sides more than an inch. As I slid into the chair nearest her, she remained silent, her full attention on the departing truck. "Do you want me to get you another soda?" I asked, and reached for the empty bottle. Lou Jean's hand suddenly sprang toward me, grabbing the bottle, pulling it from my grasp, anchoring it to the tabletop. Her head jerked forward, then snapped back, tethered by her braid to the chair back. She gave a startled "Ow," but her eyes never left the window.

Only when we could no longer hear the truck motor did her attention shift. Like a diver who has been at great depths, aware of the danger of surfacing too quickly, her focus moved from the open window to the floor below, then paused, moved again, from the floor to the leg of the table, and paused. When it finally reached the tabletop, it paused yet again, pacing itself, before coming to rest not on the bottle or on my fearful, wary face but on her hands. And I wondered if she could even see them. This afternoon they had been grayish white, but now, though a few white patches remained, they were mostly scarlet, a screaming, painful color. They looked scalded, as if she'd held them not under a running faucet but down into a pot of boiling water.

Ever so slowly, then, with a touch that seemed tender, Lou Jean reached with her right hand for her motionless left. She pulled it, curled on its side, into the palm of her right, adjusting it like a mother laying a sleeping child onto its bed. Then, as if grooming it, as a mother would lovingly smooth a turned-up collar, she began to work. Her thumb and index finger moved together, fastening on a fragment of dead skin, one of the few remaining white patches, no bigger than a dime. Carefully, delicately, working around its edges, she peeled it away. When it finally snapped free, she held it up for a moment, and the light from the silent window came through it, translucent and veined. Then she dropped it into the Big Red bottle, and it floated down to join the others, as fragile and useless as the unattached wing of an insect.

❧ 16 ❧

Mother sat in the light of the front window, reading her Bible. I walked straight up to her chair. "Lou Jean is really sick," I said, then listened as a car turned onto our street. I had called Gran before leaving Lou Jean's, and she had promised to come immediately.

The look Mother gave me was vacant, as if she couldn't be in Revelations and in our living room at the same time. "What did you say, honey?"

From her hair came a cookie smell, vanilla and brown sugar, too sweet, and I backed up a bit. "Lou Jean is sick," I repeated. "I just came from there. There's something bad wrong with her."

"Don't stand over me, Kayla," she said, though I had just moved back. She reached up with both hands to push against my forearms, seeming to come fully into the room then. "I thought I told you to stay home. What were you doing back over there?" She slid the palm of one hand down my arm. "You're hot and sweaty. Get your bath and then stay in your room until you can decide to mind me." She gripped both my wrists, squeezing them to emphasize her words.

I shook free of her, and her hands made a dull noise as they landed on the open Bible. "Listen to me," I said louder. "Lou Jean is sick. You're *making* her sick. You, and Dad, and Charles Dale." In my anger, I moved forward again, bumping against her chair. Mother jerked her knees to the side, then, away from me, and the Bible fell off her lap and landed splayed across my feet. As I bent to retrieve it, I felt a sudden rush of cool air and then a surprising pain, as she slapped the bare skin of my upper arm, then clenched it, her fingers circling me, her nails digging into my flesh as they'd never done before. She stood abruptly, pulling me up with her, the Bible still on my feet.

"If you think you're going to act like this, you can just think again," she said, starting toward the door and steering me ahead of her.

Trying to disentangle my feet, I kicked, and the Bible slid on its open pages, all the way across the room, landing prone against my father's recliner. Mother's fingers dug deeper into my arm as she pushed me into the hall and toward my room. "You can't just steal somebody's kid, you know," I told her. "You can't just show off because you still have a husband and hers is dead." Her fingers tightened before I'd finished the sentence. Her face, as clenched as her fingers, was eye level with my own, something else new to me. "Gran is Lou Jean's best friend," I kept on, wondering if she noticed too that I was as tall as she was and wondering at what point her nails would draw blood, "because she *wants* to be. People *want* to be around Lou Jean." I could smell my own sweat now. It mixed with the saccharine odor of Mother's hair, her clothes, and it produced a scent that was overpowering and poisonous yet provoking, goading. "Like *Dad*," I continued. Though I meant to add, *Like me, like everybody but you,*" though I meant to add a lot of things, I suddenly couldn't talk anymore. My throat and my teeth clamped shut. The smell of blood had finally joined the mixture of sugar and sweat, and I could no longer take it. All I could do was jerk away from her, blood speckling both our shirts, and run into the bathroom, kneeling at the toilet just in time.

My room was quiet and dark. In the two hours I'd spent there, sitting on the floor in front of my window, reviewing all the reasons I hated my mother, the air had cooled. My grandmother's car sat at the curb in front of Lou Jean's house, in plain view, a bold and shining sentinel. Moonlight funneled through its windows, hit the clear vinyl seat covers, and exploded, so that the interior seemed ignited, much brighter than the air outside it. I wondered if it might not help Lou Jean to go riding in that car, Gran at the wheel, telling stories, cracking jokes, Lou Jean's wounded hands held up to the windshield, moonlight coating them.

I hadn't seen my mother since she'd closed my bedroom door, leaving me with a wet washcloth, a glass of ginger ale, and instructions to not come out until morning. Although the house was silent, I suspected that she was back in her reading chair, the mistreated Bible back in her lap, dusted, consoled, and comforted after its traumatic trip across the floor. I *hoped* she was back in her chair—it faced the street in front of Lou Jean's, the spot now occupied by Gran's gallant Buick.

It both comforted and vindicated me to know that Gran was next door. I wished that Carmen's son Joe, evidently my mother's high school boyfriend, would show up. Since the day

I'd looked at the yearbook, I hadn't thought of him much, but now he seemed like the perfect solution, gorgeous enough to make Lou Jean not be sad and at the same time to make my mother furious. I imagined him turning off of Fifth in a 1953 Mercury, the kind I had seen in their high school annual, a sleek and souped-up black one with big silver teeth in its smiling grill. In my fantasy, he pulled up and parked on the street, dead even on the line between our two houses. The passenger door opened and his neat, trim legs, covered in brand-new jeans, stepped out. He stood there a moment, arms stretched above his head, his T-shirt white as a savior's robe, and every woman on the street, including my mother, stood just out of sight, bodies to the sides of windows, heads craned to see through the carefully opened slats of the venetian blinds. Every woman except Lou Jean, because, in my imagination, Lou Jean had already moved out of her kitchen, out of her house, and down the porch steps, so that by the time Joe shut his car door and walked onto her lawn, she had met him, the screen door slamming behind her, moving so quickly and so happily that the wind chimes sounded as she ran into his arms.

Through my window, I heard Dad's pickup pull into the drive. The motor shut off, doors opened and closed, Charles Dale and my father talked and laughed, though I couldn't understand their words. Next door, the porch light came on, and Gran stepped outside. "Charles Dale," she called, "you need to come in, sweetheart." To my father, once again, she said nothing.

Dad walked into my view and stood there, long after Charles Dale and Gran had gone inside. I knew that Mother, if she was still at the window, could see him too, but she didn't call to him. He faced Gran's car as if wondering why it was there, why she was at Lou Jean's so late at night. His hands were on his hips, making his shoulders seem very wide, just as the pads of his football uniform did, in the photo of him and Lou Jean's husband. For the first time, I wondered if her husband and Dad had been friends, if he knew the truth about Charles Dale, if he died believing he had two sons, or one. The fact that no one ever talked about him seemed strange to me. I didn't even know his name. I knew only that he'd played football, that he'd died in a war, and that even in shoulder and thigh pads, he was much smaller than my father.

Lou Jean's porch light snapped off, and Dad moved toward our house, as if ordered by whoever flipped the switch. I unrolled the washcloth and held it flat against the breeze coming in the window. Then I draped it across my hot arm. From the living room, I heard my parents' low voices, a few words clear. From my mother, *". . . fit, all-out hissy fit . . ."* And from Dad, *"upset . . . confused . . ."* I covered my ears. I was sick of hearing secrets.

The washcloth was already hot again. One last time, I held it to catch the breeze, then got up and went to bed, laying the cloth across my bruises. My parents come down the hall and toward their room, Mother's voice cheerful once more, questioning Dad about softball, about his and Charles Dale's practice. When my door opened a second later, I turned my face to the wall and locked my eyes shut. The air smelled like cookies again as steps came to my bed. The washcloth was lifted from my arm, and I heard it being fanned through the air before it was replaced. I waited until I was alone, then turned my open eyes back into my room, lifted the washcloth, and sailed it at the door.

The doorbell rang before daylight the next morning. I heard the clack of Mother's mules, the zip of her housecoat, and before she'd reached the front hall, the bell ringing again, continuous and demanding, someone's finger mashing the button as if intending to push it through the wall and into our house. I jumped out of bed and followed Mother, almost running into Dad, who pulled on his jeans as he walked. The bell paused for only a second, then rang a third time. Mother opened the door, then leaped back, bumping into Dad, who by now had caught up with her. I leaned around them to see what had made Mother jump. Standing within the door frame, the screen door resting against her back, was Carmen.

I pushed around my parents and went to greet her, wanting her to feel welcome, even at six in the morning. But she noticed neither me nor Dad. The look she gave Mother was singular. Mother looked confused and nervous and yet didn't say a word. Carmen put her hands down by her sides and pushed backward with her palms, against the screen door, backing out against it, onto the porch. "We need you next door," she said to my mother.

It was Mother's turn to back up. She pushed against Dad, and her voice sounded almost pleading. "Let me get some clothes on. Some makeup."

Carmen laughed out loud, then, loud enough that I looked across the street to the houses still asleep. It wasn't the mischievous, childlike laugh I was used to, the one she used with Gran, but a laugh that was derisive, cruel, and threatening, almost a growl. "Forget your makeup, Sarah Jo. Let's go." My mother followed Carmen meekly, as if she had no choice. If she

knew that Dad and I, me still in pajamas, both of us barefooted, walked behind her, she didn't show it. Her mules hung
and slipped on the wet grass and Dad cringed at the dew soaking his feet and pant legs. I rubbed the wakening pain of my
arm. Only Carmen seemed to have no trouble walking next
door, the back of her gray head covered in stiff, unyielding
waves that seemed welded out of iron. Gran's car sat unmoved
from last night. In the half-light of morning, it seemed tired,
deserted by its ally, the moon. Parked far behind it was Lou
Jean's mother's Cadillac. In between the two, like a referee,
was a brand new Mercury. Black and shining. And unfamiliar.

In my wonder at all the cars, I had fallen behind the others,
and as I hurried to catch up, I caught my foot in the grass. Dad
heard me and turned to help, grabbing my arm to keep me
from falling. When his fingers pressed the bruises, invisible in
the darkness, I cried out. Carmen, with her hand on the front
door, stopped and looked back at us. "I stubbed my toe." She
looked down at my bare feet.

Mother, on the porch beside Carmen, was the only one who
looked at my arm. "You need to be back home in bed," she
said, and her words were very slow, her voice worried and serious, as if she were really concerned about me. In the gloom of
the porch, she looked unusually pale, her shell-colored robe no
lighter than her skin, and I wondered how this was happening.
How could tiny, kindhearted Carmen have so much power
over my mother?

"No, she doesn't," said Carmen, "she needs to say good-
bye to Lou Jean. *Then* she can go back to bed."

"What do you mean, *good-bye?*" I climbed the steps ahead of
Dad and inserted myself between Mother and Carmen, forgetting my arm. "Where's she going?"

Carmen reached up and cupped my cheek, her tone more familiar. "She's going to the hospital, baby."

My throat got tight and her face grew wavy through tears.

"Kayla, she needs more help than you or I or your grand-mother can give her. And she won't be gone long. But she *has* to go." Then her voice changed again, back to the one that matched the battleship waves in her hair. "And she doesn't need any emotional hubbub. From *anybody.*" She looked past me, to Mother and Dad.

My dad nodded, and Mother simply said, "Yes, ma'am." Respectfully. Meekly. "Yes, ma'am," she said yet again, and fol-lowed Carmen in the front door.

After the dark of the front lawn, the glare of the living room was jolting. Lou Jean wasn't there, and neither were the boys. I took a peek at my arm and immediately clapped my other hand over it. Swollen and hot, the nail digs had dried into crusty crescents, drunken red moons that staggered down to my elbow, each one ringed by a purple bruise, like some evil cloudy nimbus.

On one end of the couch sat Gran; on the other sat Lou Jean's mother. Each had pushed herself into a corner of the sofa, and not even their knees inclined toward the middle. Lou Jean's mother's hair was as blond as my mother's, smoothed into a French twist, and as neat as the silk dress she wore. The deep teal of the fabric set off the gold in her hair and the gold at her ears. When she raised a hand and gave a small wave to us, a huge gold charm bracelet jangled down her wrist and caught on her sleeve.

"What did the doctor find out?" said Carmen, who walked immediately to Gran, leaving us standing just inside the door.

"He called," said Gran, "and they can take her today.

Yvonne's going to drive her up." Gran's eyes on Carmen looked as tired as her Buick. When they moved from Carmen to us, it seemed to take a moment for her to focus, as if she were sitting there half asleep, everything registering slowly. She must have been up all night.

Yvonne's eyes fluttered around the room, smiling at us, at Carmen, at everyone except Gran, as if fully rested. "Sarah," she said, and her voice reminded me of Mother's when she wore the raspberry dress, "I have a big favor to ask."

Mother's steps to the couch were tentative and subdued. She ran her hands down the front of her robe, and she glanced at Carmen before she spoke. "Of course Yvonne. What is it?"

"Sit down, Sarah Jo," said Gran. "All of you." Mother sat in the chair closest to Yvonne. Dad and I moved to a love seat.

A door opened upstairs, and a moment later, a white-haired man, wearing a suit and a tie, stood on the top stair and turned around, then slowly moved down a step, his back to us. Behind him, but guided by his hand, was Lou Jean. Like my mother, she wore a housecoat, but hers was solid white, the same color as the bandages, thick layered wraps of gauze that covered both her hands. On the third step down, the doctor paused and tenderly brushed both sides of Lou Jean's face, moving her hair out of her eyes. Her hands free for a moment, she reached her right hand to her left, as if to pick through the bandages. He gently took her arm again, separating her hands, and, little by little, they moved down toward us. Yvonne's voice went on, smooth and untroubled. Her words seemed to flow across her silken lap, gaining conviction and cheer as they went. She never once looked at her daughter, descending the stairs. She didn't notice the doctor pause to lift Lou Jean's long housecoat, to pull it out of the way of her feet. I strained against the edge of the love seat, wanting to be up and over there to help her but knowing what my arm would look like in the middle of the room. I pushed on my face with my free hand, mashing the tears back into my eyes, remembering Carmen's warning, and tried to concentrate on something else, on Yvonne's words. "I need you to keep the boys while Lou is gone. I know that Charles just loves spending time at your house, and I'm sure David will too." Lou Jean and the doctor had reached the bottom step, and still Yvonne talked as if they weren't even in the room, her eyes smiling at my mother, then me, then my father, then Carmen. She still didn't look at Gran. "I have no idea how long Lou will be away; we hope not long, of course."

Gran looked at Yvonne then. As angry as I had seen her with my mother, I had never seen *this* look. Almost involuntarily, my features arranged themselves the same way, my teeth clenched, my eyes squinted at Yvonne. I found that the tears stayed back then, and I wondered if Gran had discovered the same thing.

"I'm driving Lou to Austin today," Yvonne went on, "but then after Monday, I'll be gone for three weeks—I've had these plans for over a year." Her eyes flickered, a brief downward glance, then raised and happened to land on my face. After that, she didn't look at Gran *or* me.

When Mother failed to respond to this request, everyone's attention shifted to her. As if in a trance, as if she hadn't heard Yvonne and as if no one else were in that room, she stared at Lou Jean, led by the doctor to the sofa. Mother's face was even paler than it had been outside, and she leaned forward reflexively, as the doctor lowered Lou Jean to the cushions between Gran and Yvonne. Quickly, then, Mother glanced at Carmen.

She nodded her head ever so slightly, at Mother and then toward Lou Jean, and it seemed to me the nod was hard to understand. It might mean *Answer Yvonne's question. We're waiting.* And then again, it might mean *See what you've done? Proud of yourself?*

After settling Lou Jean, the doctor walked immediately to me and held out his hand for me to shake, saying with a smile, "I believe I remember delivering you." With my sore arm, I shook his hand, my free hand still covering the bruises. "Somebody needs to get this child some clothes," he said. "She's cold." Then he sat down in the one and only chair along the wall to my right. I pushed myself backward, further into the cushions. The night before, I would have given anything for someone to see my arm, to witness my mother's bizarre behavior. This morning, though, it seemed embarrassing and silly. As if I too had been to blame for what happened, and as if I, like Mother, should be old enough to know better.

Mother still hadn't spoken. Yvonne was becoming restless, anxious to have the safety of her year-old plans secured, and Gran seemed to be enjoying her frustration. She turned to Lou Jean and grinned, and Lou Jean actually grinned back, the first real spark of herself that I'd seen in days. Just for a moment, I wondered if Lou Jean might snap out of it, even now, at this last minute, and I looked at the doctor to see if he had noticed it, that change, that chance, on her face. He sat as mute as my mother. Gran lifted a hank of black hair from Lou Jean's face, laid it on the sofa back, behind her, and said softly, as if excluding everyone else in the room, "So. Is it okay with you if Sarah Jo keeps your boys while you're gone? Your mother seems to think Carmen and I are too old for the job."

There was an angry swish of silk then, as Yvonne uncrossed her legs, the heel of one teal pump firing against the wooden boards.

"I promise to make sure she does it right," Gran went on.

Yvonne recrossed her legs, kicking the front of the sofa with the same heel that had just stomped the floor. Lou Jean turned toward the noise, and as she did, her mother grabbed the hair that hung over her left shoulder, flinging it to the back of the sofa as Gran had, laying claim to her side of her daughter.

Lou Jean turned back to Gran, then, and the hair Yvonne had just lifted fell back where it had been. "No," she said simply, and her mother uncrossed her legs again, this time leaning forward to rest her arms on them, to look into her daughter's face. Lou Jean didn't seem to notice. She stared at the floor in front of her in exactly the same way I had found her staring at the Big Red bottle the day before, and, again, I wondered what she was seeing.

Then she redirected her gaze to my mother, who still sat motionless, her hands clasping the seat cushion under her legs, as if cold, her feet turned inward, the toes of her mules coated with wet grass and locked against each other under the hem of her robe. The only movement came from her eyes, quick repeated blinks. "But," said Lou Jean, her own eyes completely dry, "yes."

Dad spoke then, as if finally aware that Mother couldn't. "Lou Jean," he said quietly, leaning forward onto his knees, "we'd love to have them. We'll take good care of them for you."

When he spoke, when Mother heard his words directed to Lou Jean, she finally came alive. Like the night he'd talked to

Lou Jean on the telephone, prompting Mother to storm out of the kitchen, his words or the tone of his voice, or just the fact that he was talking to Lou Jean, again stirred something in her, some angry spark that now flared hot enough to dry her face and warm her hands. Jerking them out from under her legs, she pushed against the chair and stood. "Of course, we'll look after them," she said not to Lou Jean but to Yvonne. Then she looked at Gran. "And I don't need anyone to make sure I do it right."

The doctor sat back in his chair and looked at Carmen in a questioning way.

Mother walked to the door, and I noticed that her path went *behind* Carmen's chair, though it took extra steps to do so. Then she turned back toward us. "When the boys wake up," she said to Yvonne, "send them over. I know you'll have your hands full this morning."

Beside me, Dad suddenly stood. He walked straight to the sofa, bent forward, and lifted one of Lou Jean's gloved hands. Then he got down on both knees, so that his face was even with hers. The soles of his feet looked soft and pink. Vulnerable. His face, by contrast, looked tan and strong, without doubt or weakness. He gently pulled Lou Jean's hand to his chest, holding it there with both his own. "You," he said, "are going to get well." His voice was low, as if meant only for her, but so steady and charged that his words were clear to everyone. "And while you do that, your boys are going to be fine. I promise you that." Lou Jean's gaze left his face, wandering to her lap, to the floor, so that he shook her hand, tapped it gently against his chest. When he again had her attention, Dad continued. "And as soon as you're ready for a visit from those two, you call." Over their joined hands, his head nodded, as if to guarantee his words. "I'll make sure they get there." Slowly, Lou Jean nodded, and Dad laid her hand back in her lap, patted her knee, and stood up.

To her mother, he said, "Don't send the boys over until it's time to go."

To my mother, he said, "They need to be with their mother this morning."

As Mother turned abruptly, jerking open the door, he made his last comment to Gran: "I'll be at the office if you need me for anything."

Then he joined Mother at the door, and I hurried after his broad back, holding both my arms, as if anxious to get home to some warmer clothes, and marveling once again at the power Lou Jean gave my father. How he so quickly could change, simply by being in her presence. As if like me, and like Gran, he drew strength from any sort of connection with her, one as corporeal and sure as a phone line between houses, or one as flimsy and weak as layers of gauze.

❧ 17 ❧

By the time that Lou Jean rode off with her mother and the boys and I walked back into the house with mine, I no longer cared about mysteries, and I no longer cared about the past. If Lou Jean and my father had slept together while my mother was pregnant with me, producing a child who now alternated between being my friend and hating my guts, big deal. My parents' past, and their secret lives, were silly and meaningless, compared to now. Here and now, in the present, Lou Jean was on her way to a place called Glenwood Falls, a name that sounded like a nursing home, or someplace people went to and never came out of. In the present, she had not hugged a single child as she'd climbed into the car. Her voice had sounded broken, as if it came not from a human but from a baby doll whose chest had been stepped on, and she never said good-bye. Her only words to us were, "I left you something."

With all of us back in the house, Mother immediately began fixing lunch, bologna sandwiches, Chee-tos, and lime Kool-Aid, her idea, I suppose, of what to offer children who have just watched their mother hauled off to a psychiatric hospital.

She served all of it on G.I. Joe paper plates with matching cups, which I'm sure she had bought just for the occasion. Then she announced that no one would have to take a nap, and instead, that we would all play Candy Land, and why didn't we all have chocolate-chip cookies while we played. As soon as I could, I left the stupid game that everyone but David was too old to enjoy, making the excuse that I had to finish my library book before its due date, the next day. I carried the book out of the house, tossed it under the fig tree, and went through Lou Jean's kitchen door, into an empty house no longer spotless. Someone, Gran or Carmen, had done the breakfast dishes, but the floor was dirty, with stains that looked like drink spills around the mesquite table, and dust balls cornered against the refrigerator. Bits of dried cookie dough, red, white, and blue, cemented to a cabinet door, told how long it had been since Lou Jean had really cleaned her kitchen.

I grabbed a spoon and a bowl and went into the pantry to clear the pickle brine. Then I found the broom and dustpan and started on the floors. I had worked only a few moments when the back door flew open and Charles Dale ran in. He stopped when he saw what I was doing. "Do you want to go see what your mother left us?" I asked.

Instead of answering my question, he said, "My grandmother's maid is coming tomorrow," looking at the broom I held, not at me. His voice was cold.

"What if I just want to?" I answered, and he shrugged and left the room. I heard him go up the stairs and into David's bedroom, and in only a few minutes he came back out, calling down over the upstairs railing, "David wants his red Keds. Do you know where they are?"

I went to the dining-room door where he could see me, and I pointed to the closet at the end of the upstairs hall. "What are they doing in there?" Charles Dale shouted.

"They're too small for him. Your grandmother bought him new ones last week." Although I didn't add, *Which you, being his brother, might have noticed,* the old Charles Dale would have heard it in my voice, would not have had to be reminded in the first place. This new one only raced ahead, impatiently banging the closet door with his shoulder as he turned the knob.

By the time I'd climbed the stairs and followed him to the closet, he stood in the seat of an old armchair. Stuffing exploded through tears in the upholstery and mushroomed around his feet. Both arms reached above his head to the highest shelves, flinging cardboard boxes, old toys, and dust. "I don't know why he has to have them anyway," he fumed. "I'm going to be late for practice because of him."

"Because they're bright red," I said, aggravated now. "Not dull black, like his new ones. And *maybe* because your mother bought them for him." He ignored my comment, so I bent down and reached around his chair to a lower shelf, pulled out the new Keds box with the old Keds inside, and stood to hand it to him, banging my head on a toy microscope protruding from the shelf just above me.

"Here." I thrust the box at him, looking over my shoulder to push the microscope back into place. When he didn't take the box, I turned and found him motionless, the closet silent again. His quick exhale was ragged, and he sat down hard on the top of the chair back, so that the chair teetered for a moment. In his hands was a frog, long-dead and stuffed in a standing position. Its leathery green arms were outstretched, as if to an audience only it could see, its mouth open in mute frog song above its red bow tie, green brocade vest, and ugly brown cowboy boots. It was older, dustier, but otherwise exactly like the ones we'd seen in Mexico. Charles Dale suddenly began to scratch and scrape at the front of the frog's vest, dragging his fingernail across what I now realized was a red heart, carefully embroidered, satiny stitches dusty but still brilliant against the green brocade. "I hate Mexico," he said, and his eyes were red-rimmed, his face pale and sad. Softball practice and David's shoes forgotten.

"So do I," I said, hoping to reconnect with him and also remembering how frightened we had all been that day, David lost in the heat and traffic, Lou Jean falling apart in front of that vacant building. "I don't care if we never go back," I added.

"What do you know?" he said sharply, surprising me by laughing out loud, a laugh that seemed mean, more like the laugh of Thad Howard. The red around his eyes now spread to his cheeks, and his voice rose. "What could you even know about it?" With that, he began to slash at the vest, his fingers underneath it, twisting and prying, trying to rip it off the frog's body. When the stitches popped, he tore off the vest and threw it on the floor, then began to twist the frog, the lighter skin of its chest now exposed and naked, away from the darker skin of its head, trying to tear it apart. When that didn't work, he grabbed the frog by its wooden base and tried to smash it, its leathery head, its glass eyes, against an empty spot of shelf. But the frog held together, immune to his pounding, its sun-dried skin stronger than the vest it had worn, and the only damage was the flight of one green eye across the closet and out the door. Charles Dale threw the frog then, over his shoulder and behind us, and only the venetian blinds saved the glass of the window it struck. He jumped out of the chair, grabbed the frog again, and threw it once more, at me. Then he ran down the stairs, his hands empty. Long after I heard the back door slam, I sat in the cottony stuffing, holding a box of outgrown shoes and a one-eyed frog and wondered why, just when I'd decided to give up on mysteries, Charles Dale had to hand me another one.

By the time I'd finished sweeping and mopping, the sun was low enough to shine through a windshield and glint off the chrome of a rearview mirror as it pulls into a driveway and sits long enough for its owner to change clothes. To load bats, gloves, and boy, more quiet than normal, then leave. I was rinsing the mop bucket when I heard the screen open. Expecting David, I turned to caution him about the wet floor . . . and found Mother at the door. She hesitated, staring at the floor as if afraid to embark on it. The certainty she'd shown in the hours since Lou Jean's departure seemed to have left her, and it made me like her better, to see her made nervous by the prospect of entering Lou Jean's kitchen. Then she took off her shoes, and I realized her hesitation was only over whether to walk on the wet surface.

She pointed to the mop bucket I held. "Finishing your library book?" Ignoring her comment, I went into the pantry and put away the cleaning supplies, hearing her moving about the kitchen, hearing drawers being opened and closed. I returned to find her holding a butter knife, on her knees in front of a cabinet door, chipping away at dried cookie dough, as if she had a right to.

"I'll do it," I said, coming up to her quickly, and she surprised me by handing over the knife without arguing.

"Is it always like this?" She wiped a finger along the stovetop, the rough dried splotches of pea juice.

"Of course not." I gave the cookie dough an extra hard jab.

She walked across the kitchen and sat down at the table, and for a few minutes, the only sound came from my knife. "It is peaceful in here," she finally said. Then she laughed, and her laugh was nervous, like her face at the door. "David seems to like only really noisy programs. Ones with a lot of guns or a lot of fake laughter."

"Why are you here?"

"Why are *you* here?" she replied. "I seem to keep telling you to stay away from here, forgetting that you no longer mind me."

I didn't answer, and in a moment I heard her chair slide from the table and heard her bare feet come back across the floor. When she knelt down beside me, her eyes were as red as Charles Dale's had been earlier. "I wanted a chance to look at your arm," she said quietly.

I continued scraping cookie dough, one hand using the knife, the other catching the claylike bits as they fell.

In a moment, she said. "Charles Dale seemed upset earlier, after he'd been over here. Do you have any idea why?"

"No. He just got upset. When he was looking for David's shoes. He found a frog, like the ones you see in Mexico. He tried to tear it apart."

She stood again. "My knees are older than yours." Then she asked me, "You're sure you have no idea what upset him?" The softness was gone from her voice, replaced by an urgency. When I looked up, her eyes were no longer red.

"No," I said, more emphatically. "Something abut the frog. About Mexico."

"Probably she'd told him," said Mother. She spoke quietly, staring at the floor in front of her feet, but there was an edge to her voice, as if excited. "She probably has no better sense than to tell him."

I stopped chiseling cookie dough. "Tell him what?"

She answered without looking at me, her one word clipped. "Nothing."

"What?" I asked again, at the same time dislodging a huge chunk of cookie dough, the original red, white, and blue melted together, now only a disgusting gray.

She shrugged her shoulders, and her voice lowered again, and slowed. "Just that she made a really big mistake, a long time ago."

"I don't think she'd call Charles Dale a mistake," I said, chiseling harder.

"I didn't say *he* was the mistake." She scraped at the cookie dough with one pink fingernail. "Kayla, why do you and I have to make things tough for each other?" When I didn't answer, she said, "You know, it's not like I *try* to make you hate me. I *do* love you." She looked directly at me, and I thought for a moment she might bend down again, kneel beside me so that I could ask her, "How did it happen? Were you mean enough to Dad that you chased him to Lou Jean?" Instead, though, she moved away from me and lifted herself up to sit on the countertop.

"Lou Jean doesn't like people sitting on her countertops," I said.

"Why?" she asked, and she jumped back down again, wetting a paper towel and beginning to swab the cobalt tiles. "Is she afraid she'll have to pay the cleaning bill for their clothes?"

"Just like *that*," I yelled, standing up and throwing the knife into the sink, crossing the floor to the trash can to brush the dough clumps into it. "You say stuff like that, and then wonder why I'm mad at you. *You're* the reason there's dried food everywhere. You did this to her, and you don't even care. You smart off about it." I sat down in one of the chairs at the table, as far across the kitchen as I could be.

"What did she do to *me*, Kayla?" Her arms were folded across her chest, her feet crossed in front of her as she leaned back against the cabinet. "Do you even care about what she did to me?"

"I care."

"Well, it doesn't seem like it. It seems that you've decided *I'm* the wicked one, that I slept with *her* husband, that *I'm* the one who almost had an abortion."

"She didn't almost have an abortion," I yelled. "She loves Charles Dale."

"I never said she didn't."

"Well, don't say that. And haven't you decided that Charles Dale is your real child? Or should have been?"

She turned away from me, then, picked up the knife in the sink, and began scraping the dough from the blade. "You know, maybe I do have *some* claims to him. And it's possible for a woman to love more than one child, you know," she said quietly.

"I know," I answered just as quietly, my voice low enough so that she had to turn around and look straight at me to hear my words. "Lou Jean loves three."

✿ 18 ✿

Our kitchen looked like the site of some evil experiment. Every horizontal surface was occupied, as if someone had opened all the cabinets and drawers, and removed every pot, pan, and gadget. It might have looked as if we were moving again, everything we owned sitting out in the open, waiting to be wrapped in paper and stuffed in a box, if not for the fact that everything was dirty. Bowls, knives, cutting boards, the hand mixer, all were stacked in ugly leaning towers that dripped and streamed onto the counters. Even the rolling pin, which had not seen action since the day my mother learned you could buy frozen pie crusts, had been used. I picked it up from the floor where it lay in what looked like a full cup of spilled flour.

In the middle of all the mess, and looking just as disheveled, stood Mother. Under layers of makeup, ignited by the heat of the kitchen, her face looked polished, as if smeared with wax, then buffed. She stood at the kitchen counter cutting carrot curls into a bowl of ice. In the dampness coming from pots of pasta boiling on the stove, her hair was curled more than the carrots, and she looked pathetic. I was in no mood to feel sorry for her, however. It rankled me that she thought she had some right to Charles Dale. The way I saw it, she was still trying to steal Lou Jean's stuff.

"Nice of you to come home. Where's your library book?"

I stared back out of the house, remembering that the book was still under the fig tree, where I'd tossed it earlier, on my way to Lou Jean's.

"Wait," said Mother. "You can get it later. I need you now."

She looked like she needed *somebody*. Her eyes were as fevered as her skin. They skated the room, jittery, catching on one thing, then another. As if they needed to be too many places at once. They landed on a pile of place mats and linen napkins that sat on the kitchen table, then moved to the oven temperature gauge, the pots boiling on the stove, and, as a car came down the street, the window behind her. As if she'd just realized she'd tackled a job too large but was now too far into it to quit, she said, "I really want to cook a good dinner for tonight. I want it to be special, the boys' first night here." She walked closer, though she didn't touch me. "And I want us, you and I, to get along. I don't want to fight anymore."

A pot boiled over, red sauce screaming as it hit the burner. Mother jumped toward it, catching up the apron she wore and wadding it into a makeshift hot pad to pull the pot to safety. But the apron hem fell across another burner, glowing red, and I ran to help. I pushed the scorched fabric away, just as it started to smoke. "See?" Mother said, and laughed. "I told you I need help."

"Okay," I gave in. "What do you want me to do?"

"Set the table." She nodded toward the linens. "And wake David up. He fell asleep in front of the TV." She pulled off the ruined apron and threw it in the sink, running cold water on it. "Your dad and Charles Dale should be home any minute."

In the living room, David lay sprawled on the floor, his face pressed against the braided rug, his mouth open against the rough wool. I turned off the television and sat down on the floor bedside him. "David," I said, shaking his shoulder. When he didn't wake up, I shook it harder. "David, wake up. It's almost time to eat."

He reached out with one hand, then, and pushed against my arm. "Leave me alone." He turned his head away, exposing a cheek red and ridged, plowed into furrows by the rug. "Leave me *alone,*" he said more sharply, and slapped at me, his head still down, his eyes still closed. "I want my mom."

"Yeah, I know," I said. "You and the rest of the world." Instead of shaking him again, I sat and rubbed his back, thinking what Lou Jean would want me to do, and how she had stared at the bell tower. "David, your mom said she left us something, remember?" He didn't answer, and I wondered what she'd left. Letters, maybe, though I wasn't sure how she'd have written them, her hands wrapped in bandages. I pictured her dictating to Gran or Carmen, their fingers struggling to keep up with her words, their ears straining to understand her cracked voice. Maybe she'd left explanations, words to make Charles Dale feel better about what had happened all those years ago in Mexico. Words to make me understand why she'd slept with my father. Assurances about her coming home, quickly and whole again. I rubbed harder. "Don't you want to know what she left us?"

Dinner didn't last long Before the plates were filled, before even one drop of spaghetti sauce spilled on the plaid place mats, David asked, "When is my mommy coming home?"

My mother's answer was quick. "As soon as she's better, honey. Like I told you this afternoon."

"I like my spaghetti fat," he said, poking his food with one finger. He held his fork in the same hand that supported his head. Its tines threaded his thick black hair.

"He means macaroni," said Charles Dale.

"This kind's hard to eat," announced David.

"I'll cut it up for you," I offered.

"You can use your spoon," Mother told him as I chopped up his spaghetti.

"I know how to use a fork," David declared. "My mom taught me how." To illustrate, he forked a glob of spaghetti and lifted it to his mouth, dropping at least half. "This kind's no good," he said sadly, as if the red sauce that dripped down his bare thigh and onto the chair had betrayed him. "I told you."

Mother's chair screeched as she jumped up and went to the kitchen, returning with a wet cup towel. As she wiped his legs and swabbed at the stained cushion, David asked, "When can we go see my mommy?"

Mother's sigh was experimental, as if she wasn't sure how fast she could exhale without showing anger. "Your mother will be home before you know it, sweetheart." Her voice was cheerful as it trailed her back toward the kitchen. "She'll be home so soon, we probably won't have time to go see her."

"We're going to see your mother the very minute the doctors say we can, sport," said Dad. Almost at the kitchen door, her back to us, Mother stopped. She launched the wet cloth through the door, in the direction of the kitchen table, and chopped bits of spaghetti flew from it, midair. Mother turned around, and her face was white, with three red circles symmetrically placed. Two circled her eyes, one her clenched lips.

As she walked, very slowly, back to the table, David said, "I'm going to take my mom some spaghetti when I go. The real kind."

I jumped awake, hearing thunder, remembering that I'd never retrieved my library book. Quietly, I slipped down the hall and out the front door. At the side of the house, light came from our kitchen window, and I used it to duck under the branches of the fig tree and slip safely back out.

On my way to the house, I heard Mother's voice. "I will not have you going against my word in front of these children. *I* am the one who has to be here day in and day out, taking care of them the best way I know how. *I* will make the decisions that concern them." She stood under the light that hung over the kitchen sink, and her words were punctuated by the sound of dishes banging in and out of soapy water.

My father's voice was caustic. "*Your* word?" he asked. "Don't you want to go ahead and claim it as *God's* word? Quote some biblical passage that backs you up?"

"You leave the Bible out of this. As if you'd have any idea what's in it." She stuffed a handful of silverware into the drainer. Several pieces missed and clattered back into the sink. "She's such an angel," she said sarcastically. "She's such a fine example of a mother that she told her son she'd thought about aborting him. She *told* him. And you're going to haul him to Austin as soon as she's able, to see her? To see *that?*" She grabbed a large pot from the stove and slammed it into the water. Suds flew up around her.

"Well, it was just a matter of time," said Dad. "You would have made sure he knew, one way or the other."

Mother whirled toward him. "That is a lie. What I want is for him to have a normal, happy childhood."

"Like Kayla's having?" asked Dad. I reached for my arm, instinctively covering it.

"*Why* did I let you talk me into moving here?" Dad continued. "You promised you'd leave her alone. You'd provide an opportunity for the kids to know each other. You'd make sure Charles Dale was welcome in our home, but beyond that, you'd do *nothing*. Why was I such an idiot?"

"I don't get it. *She* sleeps with you while you're married to me, *she* gets pregnant, *she* cons somebody into marrying her, taking in her and her child, *your* child. I never cheat on you, I never run around, I certainly never get pregnant by somebody else, but *I* am the villain."

Dad's voice was so quiet I had to lean forward to hear it, dropping the hand from my arm. "You know as well as I do she didn't con *anybody* into marrying her. You know why he married her."

"It was the Christian thing to do, whether you admit it or not," said Mother, and she turned back to her soaking pan.

"Right." Dad's voice was even more sarcastic. Then he said very pointedly, his words still quiet but maximized, each one separate and exaggerated, "And that's why her boys are in this house right now, isn't it? Because it's the *Christian* thing to do." When Mother didn't answer, Dad said, his words slower and even more exaggerated than before, "There were never any saints in that house, any more than there are any in this one."

"You're not used to this, are you?" whispered someone close beside me. I jumped backward, sitting abruptly to avoid the branches of the fig. In the process, I dropped my book. Charles Dale bent and picked it up, then held it. He was looking at me in a strange way, as if seeing something he'd never noticed before. "You're just like me," he finally said.

"What's *that* supposed to mean?" I whispered as loud as I dared, still angry with him for the way he'd treated his mother, for the way he'd been treating me.

He pointed behind me to the tree. "I used to come out here too." Then he sat down beside me, his legs crossed, my library book on his knees. Mother's voice had become a scream as she accused Dad of lying, of cheating, of wanting to take the boys to see Lou Jean just so *he* could see her.

"Your parents argued like this?"

"No," he said. "Worse."

"What did they argue about?" I hoped it wasn't my father.

"Everything. He wasn't very nice to her." Lightning popped, and in it, Charles Dale's face looked like stone, a carved scowling sculpture.

"Then why did he marry her?" The sound of flooding water came through the window as Mother jerked the stopper out of the drain and hurled it down on the countertop.

He shrugged. "My grandmother said his parents were as poor as church mice." Charles Dale opened my book, then closed it, opened and closed it again, quietly, with no noise. I expected him to chastise me for reading something as uneducational as *Cherry Ames, Student Nurse,* but he only said, "And my mother had enough money to take care of me and him." In the next flash of lightning, he saw the bruises on my arms. "What happened to you?" he whispered.

"So why'd your mother marry *him?*" I asked.

For a moment, he only stared at me. I thought he was going to be angry with me again. He looked at me as if my question was ridiculous. "You heard your mother. She needed a quick husband." He stood up brusquely. "We'd better go in before they quit fighting and realize we're gone."

Lightning popped again, as if to illustrate how visible we were, and I thought of the woods behind our house in Cameron, of all the places to hide there. What good was a tree you couldn't sit under without avoiding its branches? Everything here either stung or pricked. Carefully crawling out, I asked, "Did you ever see real trees?"

Even without lightning, I could see the confusion on his face.

"*Real* trees," I said. "The kind that grow tall instead of flat. That don't give you rashes. Dogwoods and redbuds that grow close together, not spread out like they're afraid to touch each other."

"No," he said, and he sounded sad. "I never did."

We walked away from the window and toward the front porch. "Charles Dale," I asked, "what was your father's name?"

"David," he answered, "Senior."

Our lawn looked as if it had been attacked. Downed branches covered the grass. The ones remaining on the trees were mangled, hanging by thin veinlike threads of wood and bark, their leaves shredded and chewed. "What did this?" I asked Charles Dale.

He turned back to look at me, surprise on his face. "Wind," he said, with a nod, like a reminder. "Hail. You didn't hear it?"

I shook my head and walked down the steps to join him on the sidewalk. We held plastic bowls of cereal, which we had poured ourselves, in a kitchen still full of dirty dishes, pots, and pans. Standing in the middle of the disorder, Mother had watched us fill our bowls. Her hair was uncombed. The house-dress she wore was one I hadn't seen in years, purchased long ago in the Mature Woman's Department at a Cameron store. Green and white seersucker with a fat green zipper that was now jammed, caught on the fabric just below her breasts. Falling through the gap created by the snag was a pink flannel nightgown. The white satin ribbon at its throat, meant to be a bow, was clenched in a double knot.

"Your mom looks awful," said Charles Dale. He finished his cereal and drank pink-tinged milk from the bowl. Then he left it on the bottom step and began dragging broken branches, some of them really large, to the curb. Like huge brooms, the branches he dragged swept torn leaves and twigs, leaving clear green paths among the debris. I left my bowl unfinished and went to help him.

Righting a lawn chair that lay on its side against the Arizona ash, I found a large gash on the trunk of the tree. "We'll have to doctor that," Charles Dale said. "So the bugs won't get in it." He ran his hand back and forth over the cut. "Do you have any white paint?"

"I think so," I said, and went immediately to the garage, glad that he seemed to like me again, to be talking to me in our old way. I wasn't sure what had changed him, only that he had been different since we'd watched my parents fight last night, nice to me *then*, and, so far, nice to me this morning. Still, I was wearing a shirt with sleeves. I knew at some point he'd say something again about my arm, but I just wasn't ready to deal with it yet. In the garage I found a small amount of white paint in an old can and shook it hard. Pulling out drawers in my dad's worktable, searching for a brush, I kept hearing screeching noises, soft rodentlike sounds that made me open the drawers cautiously. I grabbed the first brush I saw, picked up the can of paint, and backed out of the garage, but the noises followed me out into the yard. On the back steps sat my mother, her head down on her arms. The sleeves of her housedress were pushed up above her elbows, so that she cried onto pink flannel. I couldn't remember ever hearing my mother cry, and it seemed to me that she needed practice. Her sobs didn't sound like other people's. They were restrained, caught, as if, like a mouse, they really were trapped in some dark drawer.

"Mom?"

She jumped, her head and arms coming up so fast that she knocked the brush out of my hands. "Kayla," she said, "you scared me." She looked away and dug an old Kleenex from the pocket of the housedress, then blew her nose. "I'm sorry, sweetheart," she said. Then she said again, defensively, "You just *scared* me," as if my startling her was the only reason for her tears. As if she hadn't been crying before I showed up.

She wiped her eyes with her sleeve, then nodded toward the paint and brush. "What's that?" she asked.

"For the tree in the front yard. It got cut in the storm. Charles Dale said we have to paint it so the insects won't eat it."

"No," she said, standing up and turning back toward the door. She wiped her eyes once more, then dusted the back of her housedress. "You'll just get paint all over you and make another mess for me to clean up. Let your father take care of it when he gets home."

Her no was surprising, since she'd done nothing but enthuse over Charles Dale's ideas since the first time she'd met him. "But Charles Dale says—" I started, thinking she must not have heard his name.

She interrupted me. "I don't care what . . ." Then she stopped and looked over my head. "Charles Dale, sweetheart, I'm not sure paint is what the tree needs. You two just go on and play. We'll get Phil to take care of the tree." She opened the back door, saying, "I need to get David up. Does he usually sleep this late?" Before Charles Dale could reply, though, she was through the door, the screen closing tight on the tail of her housedress. She jerked it out, muttering to herself, and was gone.

"She really *does* look awful," said Charles Dale as we walked back around to the ash tree. He picked up a smashed bird's nest that we hadn't noticed before. "And she doesn't know *anything* about trees."

David had just vomited for the third time in as many hours. In between retching, he screamed at us about how much his stomach hurt. "He's constipated," Charles Dale said to my parents. "He eats too much cheese. Once, it got so bad, he had to go to the emergency room." He shrugged as if he were simply delivering a well-known fact, and what he said was the truth. In the week they had stayed with us, David had eaten plenty, but only a very few things. Bologna sandwiches. Macaroni. Ice cream. Chips. And cheese. Lots of it.

"I'll get the Milk of Magnesia," said Mother, heading for the bathroom.

"It won't do any good," Charles Dale called to her, but she ignored him. Now that he lived here, she didn't seem to listen to him as much.

In a moment, she was back in the guest room shared by the

boys. Though she put on makeup and a dress before Dad came home from work each day, she was now, in the middle of the night, back in green seersucker and pink flannel, the gown knotted tight. On two separate nights, when I'd gotten up for a drink of water, I'd found her asleep on the sofa, her open Bible facedown on her stomach.

"That won't work," said Charles Dale again. David flopped over on his bed, turning his back to Mother and her spoon. "Enema's the only thing that works. But he hates it."

"I can imagine," said Mother, pouring white liquid. "Come on, David," she said. "Look, sweetie. It's mint favored." Facing the wall, his eyes and lips clamped tight, David answered her with a backward slapping motion, hitting her arm and spilling Milk of Magnesia all over the bed and the housedress. "Listen here, mister," she said, dropping the spoon on the nightstand, grabbing David's shoulder, then reaching under his arms to sit him up against the headboard. He slapped at her hands, his eyes still shut tight, and screamed even louder, kicking his legs now.

Dad pushed in front of Mother. He sat down on the mint-smelling sheets and in one smooth motion lifted David onto his lap, rocking back and forth, one hand on David's pajama-covered butt, one on his head as it leaned against Dad's shoulder. The kicks slowed, the screams retreated to moans, as they rocked. "You feel pretty awful, don't you, fellow?" Dad finally said. David stopped moaning long enough to nod. "And Charles Dale says an enema works. You don't like them, but they work?"

"I will not give that child an enema," said Mother. She walked across the room, her arms folded in front of her, as if the space between the twin beds was too tight for the three of them. "It is a disgusting practice. Milk of Magnesia always worked for Kayla." She looked at me as if for confirmation.

Dad continued to rock, responding to Mother's words as if he talked to David and not her. "Well, though," he said, "you're not Kayla, are you?" David shook his head, eyes still closed. "You're David, right? At least you were the last time I looked?" David nodded. "Well, then, what would make an enema better? I mean, *nothing* can make an enema better, but what is it that you could *think* about during the enema, something we might go buy tomorrow, that might help us get through the enema tonight?"

David didn't answer, but his moans stopped. Dad kept rocking. In a moment, he asked again, "Is there *anything?*"

"New skates," mumbled David against Dad's chest. "Mine aren't red."

"Good God," exploded Mother, pushing past Charles Dale and me and stomping down the hall, going into the bedroom and slamming the door. Dad lifted a silent David and carried him into the bathroom.

I started back to my room, then realized that Charles Dale hadn't moved, that he still leaned against the door frame, making no effort to go back to bed When I walked back up to him, he was crying. Soft, quiet tears that he let drop on the floor between us. "What's wrong?" I wanted to take his hand but hesitated, remembering his reaction the last time I'd tried to comfort him.

"That's the way my father always held him." I got up my nerve to pat his shoulder. He didn't push my hand away, but in a moment he walked to his bed and climbed in. And I walked back to my own room, hoping that they gave enemas in heaven. Hoping that at that very moment, David Senior was getting a big one.

19

"Oh, my God, they've killed you."

Gran's voice came from directly overhead, and I sat up quickly, rubbing my back, disoriented. I hadn't heard her car or her footsteps. "I guess I fell asleep," I said.

"I guess so," she said. "On the front porch. Didn't you sleep last night?"

"Not really," I admitted. By the time David was back in bed, there hadn't been much night left, and Dad had spent it in the living room, turning the television on and off, getting in and out of his squeaking recliner.

"Hmmm. So how's it going?"

I shrugged. "Charles Dale is kind of sad. And Dad had to give David an enema." I lay back down and closed my eyes. "I wish Mom would find something else to wear."

She grabbed my arm and tugged on it until I sat and then stood. "This won't do." Her agility was surprising. In one motion she pulled open the door and shoved me ahead of her and through it. "Let's go," she said, as if she expected me to take the lead, but then, abruptly, she marched around me, straight to the kitchen.

Leaning against the counter, Mother waited for the coffee to perk, her facial expression matching her outfit. When she saw Gran pull out a chair at one end of the kitchen table, she opened a cabinet and took down another mug, and when the coffee was done, she filled the mugs and walked to the table, handing Gran a mug before she sat down between us. When she finally spoke, it was to me and not Gran. "Do you want a cup?"

I stared at her, thinking I must still be disoriented from my sleep. She normally acted as if coffee had a legal drinking age, the same as alcohol. Slowly, so as not to jolt her into changing her mind, I moved out of my chair and to the pot. I poured myself a cup, then took it, along with a knife, back to the table. Gran reached for the knife, opened the package she'd brought, and cut several slices of pound cake, letting them fall against the aluminum foil, then shoved the whole thing to the center of the table.

She stared at Mother, who picked up the creamer and handed it to me. "Use a lot," she said. She had added none at all to her own cup.

Gran chewed on cake. "You look like hell." She nodded toward me. "So does she."

"Thank you, Mother."

"I mean it, Sarah Jo. If you're trying to catch up with Lou Jean, you're doing a good job."

My mother's face turned furious. "Why is everything a joke?"

"Why are you still in that *joke* outfit? It's ten o'clock in the morning, for God's sake."

"I am *exhausted,*" Mother's clenched teeth strained the words.

"Well, you know," said Gran, as if her only goal was to make Mother madder, "filling Lou Jean's shoes is hard work. You're finding out."

Mother's eyes grew red, and though she unclenched her teeth, her words were slow, and very quiet: "I hate you."

"*Now* do you want to tell me why you moved here?" asked Gran. When Mother's only answer was her glare, Gran looked at me. "Go wake up the boys," she said. "Pack enough clothes for a couple of days."

I jumped up, leaving my unfinished coffee, hurrying ahead of the eruption I knew was coming. When I'd made it to the door without hearing an explosion, I looked back. Mother's face was calm, her mouth relaxed and unclenched. The jaw that only a moment before had jutted toward Gran like a shield now seemed to settle, as if gratefully, into the ruffles of her nightgown. Like a head onto a pillow. She didn't argue. She reached for a slice of cake.

The boys and I were packed and out on the sidewalk, about to climb in the car, before Gran managed to make Mother angry again. Walking by the bruised and gored ash tree, Gran paused. Stroking the gash, she looked back at Mother. "You know, sweetie, if you'll smear this with some white paint, it will keep the insects from getting into it."

There were only two rules at Gran's house. No chewing with your mouth open. No whining. Everything else, even offenses considered serious at home, was tolerated, if not applauded. While Gran fried chicken and made gravy and biscuits, David climbed to the top of her stairs. On a bottom that should have been too sore for such adventure, he proceeded to bump his way down the entire flight, sliding off each stair to land on the one below it. In response to my look, he said, "Climbing over moon rocks. Can't use your feet."

Charles Dale, his mood suddenly buoyant, decided to teach himself to play the piano. Standing before it, he began what my mother always called "banging," striking the keys so hard and so loud that Gran ran in from the kitchen, making me think we were about to see the enactment of a third rule. Instead, though, she veered to the bathroom and came back out with a jar of Vaseline. She smeared a big glop on Charles Dale's hair, used her fingers to comb it away from his face, and pushed up a fat pompadour. "Get after it, Jerry Lee," she said, then went back to her cooking, dancing in front of me, shaking her butt as she paused.

I wished that Lou Jean could see and hear the boys right this very minute. She might need earplugs, she might get a headache from the noise, but she couldn't possibly be sad. While David's butt kept time to Charles Dale's banging, I wandered, room to room, not because I looked for anything specific but because I never knew what I might find. Gran never threw anything away, so her house was like a time machine. And she didn't care if you opened drawers or looked under beds, sometimes as excited and surprised by my finds as I was. I walked into her bedroom and opened her closet, releasing its smell of lavender and leather.

My grandfather had loved coats. In a part of Texas where a coat is needed only a few days a year, he'd still found excuses to buy them, annual trips to Colorado, two longer trips to Alaska. Seven coats, in various combinations of calf hide, wool, sheepskin, and down, hung at the back of the closet. Around each hanger was tied a muslin packet of lavender, grown and dried by Gran, replaced each and every summer, as if the coats, twelve years unworn, might someday be worn again, or were at least still too important to be moth food.

I took down a wool one, red and black, in a huge checked pattern, with collar and cuffs made of tan leather. The silk lining was cool against my arms and legs as I slipped it on over my shorts. On a shelf behind the coats I found an ancient pair of cowboy boots, Gran's initials tooled in leather the color of a fawn beneath his spots. Inside the left boot was a satin label of emerald green. BEN'S WESTERN WEAR, COTULLA, TEXAS. I kicked off my flip-flops, pulled on the boots, and, dressed properly, moved to a familiar spot, my grandfather's chest, still stuffed full of the black-and-white photographs he'd loved to make. Each time I looked at them, I found new ones, ones I hadn't seen before. I pushed up my sleeve and reached far back into the drawer, pulled out a small clump of photos, and clomped toward the living room. The coat hem bounced against my boot tops.

Charles Dale had now begun to sing, "Well, since my baby left me," and I knew that I couldn't sit in the living room with the noise, without at least reminding him that he was supposed to be Jerry Lee, not Elvis. His misplaced lyrics, the howls of the tortured piano keys, and David's butt-thumping made me want to find a quieter place. I opened the door to Mother's old room and moved inside, where I knew the air conditioner would be running full tilt. As if Gran expected someone to use the room—or was simply unconcerned about the electric bill.

The boys' racket retreated. The white satin drapes were closed, and the blue of the walls made the light seem more like dusk than noon. The air, whether from perfume bottles that still stood on the makeup table or from dried corsages pinned to a bulletin board, smelled like some flower that bloomed only at night, safe from the heat of day. Sweeter and more fragile than the lavender that sprang from my grandfather's coat. Beside Mother's white canopied bed was a milk-glass lamp, its base convoluted and richly patterned, its shade rimmed with ruffles. I switched it on, then climbed onto the yellow chenille spread. Against its rose-patterned tufts, propped against my boots, I laid the photos.

All of them were black and white, taken on homecoming night, 1952, my parents' senior year. Their glossy finish seemed unmarred by years, fresh and bright, as if my grandfather's chest had saved them not only from being scratched or bent but also from their own aging. In the first one, my mother rode on the trunk of a convertible. She wore a white net gown, its huge belled skirt shaped like the lampshade beside me, and she smiled and waved at Granddad's camera, stadium lights caught in her gloved hand. Her legs were concealed beneath waves of ruffles that surged around her and out to the fenders of the car. In the distance, indistinguishable, were two other girls, each in a separate convertible, and past them, a stadium full of dotlike faces. In the second photo, my mother stepped out of the car and reached for the waiting arm of my father. Wearing his football uniform, he smiled too. And in the third, Mother and Dad stood on the football field, both still smiling, though their smiles had changed and now were expectant. Nervous. As if they knew that something good *might* be forthcoming, and also knew that if it didn't come, they'd be expected to perform as if it *had*.

In the fourth, they were no longer alone, and though Dad still wore his smile, now more nervous than ever, Mother's smile was gone and she no longer looked at the camera but, instead, at the ground in front of her. Down the field from them stood a couple I didn't recognize, and between that nameless couple and my parents stood the just-crowned homecoming queen and her date.

Lou Jean's dress was satin, and even in the colorless photo, it looked red. Between the buoyant skirts of the girls on either side, Lou Jean's was slim as glass, bright, and fitted to her curves in the most uncomplicated way. Between the birthday-cake dresses that bordered it, Lou Jean's was a champagne flute. Her crown sat straight and true, as if it knew where it belonged, and she smiled for the camera, a familiar smile, as if at someone she really liked. One arm held a dozen roses. The other held the extended arm of an unsmiling Joey, who stared at my mother as if his heart would break.

David was asleep and Charles Dale was too full of chicken to assault the piano. He and Carmen, who'd shown up in time for lunch, sat across the table from Gran and me. I hadn't eaten much, my thoughts on the photo still lying with its companions on Mother's bed. I had been so sure that Joey, tired of the carping Mother must have done, even back in high school, had been the one to break up. And now I had to wonder. If *she* had ended their relationship, if he'd been in love with her even after they broke up, loved her enough to look miserable while in the company of the most gorgeous girl in town, the newly crowned homecoming queen, then what had happened? Why had Mother ended up with Dad rather than Joey? "So," said Gran, "What are we going to do with our afternoon?"

"*Not* play the piano," I said, looking at Charles Dale. On his chest was a large spot of grease, where he'd absentmindedly wiped his hand after running admiring fingers through his pompadour.

"*Not* read *Cherry Ames*," he retorted, and his teasing smile was so much like Dad's. I hoped that Carmen would go home soon. I didn't want her to see the photo, with Joey's sad eyes on the exact patch of dry October turf that Mother's clung to. After all, Mother wasn't exactly her favorite person. And I thought that I might ask Gran about it. Ask how it was that Mother and Joey had broken up, and how Mother and Dad had gotten together.

From the living room came the sound of the front door opening, and almost immediately, Dad stood in the doorway. So much for questions, I thought, as Gran and Carmen rocketed out of their chairs, getting another plate, reheating the gravy. Dad sank into a chair at the table, looked at me, at my boots, and at Charles Dale, his greased hair and shirt, and said, "I'm not very hungry."

"We don't look *that* bad," I said.

"You sick?" Gran asked, pointing at him with one of the green onions she stood cleaning. She dropped it with its mates onto the relish tray, then held the whole thing, an odorous invitation, in front of Dad. "The gravy will be ready in a sec." When he shook his head, pushing toward the tray with his flat palm, she set it down again, her voice now more concerned than playful. "You really are sick."

"I need to talk to Kayla," he said solemnly. "Alone." Gran reached behind her, pulled a chair to the table, and sank into it, as if some meaning to Dad's words had registered but his actual words had not.

It was Carmen who stood, pulling Charles Dale from his seat. "You need a clean shirt, *mi hijo.*" She pushed him ahead of her. "Rose," she said, and it wasn't a question.

Gran stood and trailed them, then stopped at the door. "Phil? Sarah Jo's . . . ?"

"She's fine." He pushed his empty plate away and it bumped against the relish tray, the chicken platter, rearranging everything. He nodded toward my boots. "Nice footwear." His own feet wore tennis shoes, unusual for twelve noon on a weekday.

"Did you already go home and change?"

He nodded again. "Halfway through the morning, I decided to take the day off. Your mom and I needed some time together."

"Was she still in her robe when you got there?"

"Yeah, she was." His voice was sad. "I'm sorry about that."

"It's not your fault. She's the one who's acting so weird." The onions smelled too strong. I rose and carried the relish tray to the counter. "She's always grouchy." When I set down the tray, an olive rolled on the floor, so that I bent to find it. "And she's too bossy."

"Kayla. Come sit down. Leave the olive."

Dad's face looked as tired as Mom's had that morning. He leaned forward onto the table. "Your mom and I aren't getting along very well right now." With his thumb and forefinger, he lifted the edge of his clean plate, turning it in slow circles on the table. "I don't seem to know the right thing to do with her. I seem to pretty much do everything wrong."

"That's just Mom," I said. Now the leftover gravy bothered me. Stone cold, it had formed a brown wrinkled skin. Like someone old, who'd spent too many years working in the sun. I picked it up and carried it to the sink. "You know that, Dad. She's just like that." I was also bothered by Dad's face. For the first time in my life, it didn't match his clothes, as if, overnight, it had grown too old for the jeans and Converse he wore. "She's just tired," I continued. "Everybody is." I came back to the table and sat down, reached for the plate he spun, trying to make a game of stopping the circles he made, of making the circles go the other way. "You two love each other."

He let go of the plate. "Kayla. Loving each other doesn't necessarily mean that you're happy together."

Before I could ask what he meant, he said, "I'm going to stay at the river camp for a while."

Like the day I'd punched Thad Howard, I could hear my heart. I thought if I looked down, I'd see it moving, pounding against my chest, like someone fighting to get out. "Did Mom know before today?"

Dad looked at me for the first time. "No."

"So you took the day off, just to tell her you're moving out?"

"No. I wanted to talk to her about it."

"Well, you can't have talked very long. We haven't been here three hours."

He started the plate spinning again. "We talked long enough."

"Is it what Mom wants too?" He didn't answer. "It isn't, is it? It's just what you want. Mom would never want a divorce.

"We never should have moved here," I said. "It messed everything up." I could still smell the onions. They, and the jelled gravy and the spinning plate and the sight of the chicken platter, grease pooled under the leftovers, were all making me dizzy, as nauseated as I'd been on the street in Mexico. "Lou Jean wouldn't be sick right now if we hadn't moved here." I laid my head down on my knees, and my words were muffled. "And you and Mom would be getting along just fine."

"Come on, Kayla," said Dad. His voice grew edgy, louder than usual, a voice that matched his face. "We didn't get along in Cameron."

"You didn't fight like you do here." I wanted to lift my head, to make my voice louder, but I was afraid to. "You're different here. You even *look* different."

"We didn't fight in Cameron because *I* didn't. Because I wouldn't."

"But after Mom lost the baby," I reminded him, "you didn't fight as much. You got along better."

"No, sweetheart, we didn't," said Dad. His eyes closed and his head shook back and forth with his words. When his eyes opened again, his voice was lower. "She went through so much . . ." He stood and walked to the sink, took down a glass, filled it with water. "But I can't give in anymore, Kayla, because, the older I get, the more giving in feels like giving up."

We sat quietly then, me wondering if maybe he just needed a vacation, as he said, "a little time at the river camp." He certainly looked like someone who needed a vacation, a trip to somewhere calm and restful, maybe Galveston and maybe somewhere else. Without a traveling companion who wore a nubby suit too hot for the climate, spiked heels too pointed for the ground, and a frown that the entire Gulf of Mexico couldn't wash away. Maybe he only needed a little time alone. But what happened if he so enjoyed being solitary that he wanted to stay that way? And what happened if he grew tired of being alone and decided to seek out more suitable company, someone who herself wore jeans and tennis shoes, who, I'd be willing to bet, had not owned a pillbox hat in her entire life?

I sat up. If I leaned one elbow on the table and balanced my head in my hand, the nausea receded enough to talk. "Did Lou Jean almost get an abortion?" I hated it that there was no kindness, no concern in my voice. My words sounded like a judgment, the tone like Mother's. "I think it's awful that she'd do that."

Dad drained his glass, filled it again, then set it, full, in the sink. He nodded.

"I think it's awful that she'd do that," I said again. "It's mean."

"It's also mean to judge people when you have no idea what they've been through."

"So why didn't she?"

He shook his head very slowly, tiny palsied shakes, like someone having a dream both frightening and uncontrollable, and I realized that he wasn't looking at me but over my head. "Do you want to answer that one?" he asked, and I turned to find Mother standing in the doorway, her hair done, makeup on her face, housecoat abandoned for slacks and blouse.

"Because," she said. "For once in her life, she acted like a Christian."

My mother's room was brighter than it had been at noon, the sun now low enough to slide through the windows. Mother and Dad had spent most of the afternoon on Gran's shaded porch, talking quietly, but at the end of the day, Mom had gotten in her car and driven off alone, and Dad had taken Charles

Dale and David to the Western Auto to buy skates. And I was more confused than ever. I didn't want my father to be miserable, but I couldn't imagine a life in which he didn't live with us. The last thing I wanted was to be mean to Lou Jean, to judge someone so good to me, someone I loved so much, but what if Dad loved her just as much as I did? Or more frightening, what if he loved her more than he loved me?

The photos were still strewn across the bed. I looked at each of them again, as if they might have changed during lunch or the hours afterward. They were all the same, though. Lou Jean still glowed and Mother still glowered, and I wondered if there had ever been or would ever be a time in which both of them were happy simultaneously. When Mother's happiness didn't come at the expense of Lou Jean's health, and when Lou Jean's well-being wasn't a threat to Mother's joy. And maybe a threat to mine.

❧ 20 ❧

Charles Dale had a friend visit the next day. Among gerani-ums and petunias beginning to show the wear of summer, I watched as he and Gran drove off to collect the company. David, worn out from skating cramped circles around the back patio, was still asleep. Charles Dale had never mentioned this guy, and I was surprised the night before when he'd asked Gran if Murray could come over. Murray Ball, he'd said reverently, as if the guy were someone special, and as if he didn't notice the ridiculousness of such a name.

"How come you never invited him over before?" I'd asked.

"He spent the summer in Victoria with his father. I think you'll like him." The way he'd said it let me know he'd already heard Dad's news.

I got up from my rocker and walked around, plucking dead blossoms and chunking them over the porch railing. If he thought I wanted to be fixed up with some other kid from a broken home, he was an idiot. I'd probably laugh out loud when he introduced us. With such a name, the guy had to be an absolute dope, and if he wasn't, his parents were, for sure. He'd climb out of the car holding a butterfly collection, perfectly dead bodies glued to the heads of pins. He and Charles Dale would spend the day drooling over them, taking turns reading from some dog-eared field guide, while I spent the day stuck with David, who was really beginning to get on my nerves. After they'd returned the night before, Dad had spent hours holding David's hands, leading him around the patio, hours that once upon a time, he'd have spent with me.

"Listen for David," Gran had said before she drove off. "He might be scared, waking up in a strange place." I walked on tiptoes into the house and to the guest room the boys were sharing. Sprawled on his stomach, David lay half on, half off one of the twin beds. His right arm hung down, fingers dangling. His right leg, pajama caught on the mattress, hung bare, almost to the floor. One small shift in the wrong direction, one small scare, and his entire body would fall onto the floor. I walked closer, quietly stepping over his Keds, still tied, and his skates, already pocked from their trips around the brick patio. His face was turned toward me. Within a mass of black hair, jagged chunks cut yesterday to free a wad of chewing gum, his skin was very fair, much lighter than Charles Dale's. With his eyes closed and his mouth shut, he didn't look bratty, just young. I lifted his right side and pushed him back onto the mattress. When he batted my hands away, I said, "So go on and fall." When his only answer was to stick his thumb in his mouth and draw his knees up close to his chin, I added, "Big baby," and I picked up his skates and left.

I had started through the house, meaning to hide them in the garage, when I heard car doors slam out front. I ran into the bathroom, opened the dirty clothes hamper, and stuffed them under several wet towels. By the time I made it to the front door, Gran's hand was on the knob, her other arm hold-ing a bag of groceries. "You look like you've been shot out of a cannon," she said. "What's going on?"

"Nothing," I lied, holding the door open for her. "David's still asleep." I ducked past her and out onto the porch, and walked face first into Murray Ball. "Ow," I said, backing away, rubbing my nose.

"Watch out, woman," he said, rubbing his own nose, which was at least two inches lower than mine. "You have a very hard chin," he added, the words coming from lips that barely moved.

"This is Murray," said Charles Dale, who towered over him. "He's practicing to be a ventriloquist."

"Oh." He carried no butterfly collection, and he didn't look at all like an egghead. Short but perfectly built, with long legs and really wide shoulders, he was dressed not like a kid but like the coolest of men. He wore a white oxford cloth shirt, button-down, tucked into deep blue Levis, no belt, and on his feet were light brown penny loafers, no socks. His hair, as black as David's but much longer, was combed back, sleek and shining with something clean, definitely not Vaseline. And he smelled like a tangerine, at the moment when your thumbnail pierces the rind.

"Can she say more than *ow* and *oh*?" he asked Charles Dale.

Charles Dale grinned. "On a good day." I wanted to slap him but hated to raise my arm. The T-shirt I wore had a hole in the side. Backing my way into the house, I turned and ran to the bathroom, where my duffel waited with clean, rent-free clothing. Gran stood in front of the dirty clothes hamper, star-ing down into it as if it held answers. In her left arm was a mound of wet towels. In her right was a pair of skates.

She turned when she heard me, holding up the skates. "I

don't suppose you could tell me how these got in here." Her face was mixed, partly ready to laugh, partly sad.

Betting on the part ready to laugh, I told the truth. "He deserves it. He's a brat."

Good thing I wasn't betting money. "He *is* a brat. But your joining him isn't going to help any of us." I took the skates without looking at her. "Put them back where you found them," she said, and walked around me and past Charles Dale and Murray Ball, who stood in the doorway. I pushed past them, holding the skates over the tear in my blouse and wishing I had something to hold over my red face.

Above Gran's sofa hung a large oval mirror, flanked by framed pictures of Blue Boy and Pinkie. From where I sat, the mirror reflected Murray playing the electric guitar, what he'd brought in place of a butterfly collection. By the time I had returned David's skates to his room and changed my blouse, Murray and Charles Dale were already singing, Murray's amplifier plugged into the socket by the piano, which Charles Dale had wisely chosen to abandon. Murray's voice was low, and though he was much smaller than Charles Dale, he seemed older. Not just the way he dressed but also his body. He was short in the way that Bobby Darin and Sammy Davis Jr. were short, a *cool* sort of short. As if his growth had been stunted by expensive Scotch, Cuban cigars, and late-night parties with gorgeous women.

"What do you want me to sing next?" Staring at the patch of bare skin between his loafer and the hem of his jeans, amazed at how smooth it looked, not like the feet of most boys, I didn't realize he'd spoken to me. "Kayla?" he asked.

"Oh," I stammered, and he and Charles Dale laughed.

"Are you *sure* she talks?"

Charles Dale shrugged. "She used to."

"How about Sunny and the Sunliners? Have you heard of them?" I shook my head no. "Didn't think so." His voice was sympathetic rather than smug. "You probably didn't have any good music in east Texas."

"No," I agreed, as if it were a shortage I'd pondered with great sadness. Charles Dale's smirk, I ignored. Murray began a song about a guy begging to be put in jail, locked away by a judge for failing to love someone truly. I tried to listen, but my eyes kept straying, from the mirror, where his gleaming hair made Blue Boy and Pinkie look old, to that patch on his foot. It was so smooth, and so was he, as if playing and singing before strangers was something he did every day. I wondered how he acted at school, if he was this comfortable with teachers, with grown-ups, and if there was anyone who made him as nervous as he made me. And I wondered if he knew that we already had something in common.

The boys and I went home on Sunday to a house very different from the one we'd left. Knowing that Dad had moved out, I expected Mom to be worse than ever, moping around in her ugly nightgown, but she was cheerful, full of energy, glad to see us. Wearing the sailor outfit, she came out to meet the car, smiling, welcoming, opening car doors. "Well, looks like *somebody* got some rest," Gran commented. She herself had had none. She had made it her mission to get David weaned off cheese and had offered him fruit at every opportunity. David, not accustomed to a digestive system that actually functioned, kept underestimating how quickly he needed to get to the bathroom. Between his accidents and Charles Dale's self-taught piano instruction, Gran indeed hadn't rested much.

Except for the smell of burning cookies, the inside of our house was perfectly clean. "Oh, gosh," said Mother, running for the stove, pulling out a pan of what looked like perfectly spaced charcoal briquets, smoking on top and ready for steaks. "I keep *doing* that," she laughed, sliding the pan into a dry sink. "Oh, well, there's more dough in the fridge."

"So, tell me," she said, turning to put her arms around me. "How was it? Did you have a good time?" I nodded, wary of her good mood and of the way her arms felt. Tight around my midriff, they vibrated, the skin twitchy, as if it couldn't contain all the busyness and enthusiasm.

She released me and opened the refrigerator. "Are you hungry? Your dad's gone to get hamburgers."

"Dad's here?" I asked, surprised.

"Well, of course," she answered, pulling out more cookie dough. She walked past me with her eyes on the oven. "He's only tired, Kayla. Having two extra kids all of a sudden. He's merely staying at the camp until he's more rested. He'll still be here a lot of the time." Her voice was like the one she used when out of doors, in hearing distance of Lou Jean's house, but with something added, a new tone, piercing and loud, like a circular saw just as it enters a block of wood. "I guess you and I are on enema detail now." When we heard Dad's truck, she said, "Don't look so worried. This isn't permanent."

But Dad's face looked different. He looked wary and angry at the same time. And no wonder. We hadn't been at the dinner table more than two minutes when David announced that he was going to see Lou Jean. As Mother cut his hamburger in half, he told her, "I'm going to see my mother this Saturday. Phil said we could."

Mother laid her knife by her plate and picked up her own hamburger, Dad's eyes following each move. "That's wonderful," she said.

"She's the most perfect mom in the world," David continued. "I'm going to kiss her face." Mother picked up her knife and cut her own burger in two.

David turned and looked at her soberly, as if imparting great and serious wisdom. "You've *tried* to be our mom while she's gone, but you just *can't* be our mom. *She* is." He stuffed two French fries in his mouth, then said around them, "But you tried."

Mother brought her hamburger up to a smile that was tight. She took a tiny bite. Dad's own hamburger was untouched. The look of anger he'd given Mom as he'd carried in the hamburgers was changing. Now he seemed almost sympathetic.

"Hey, David," he said. "Why don't you eat more and talk less, and when we're done, we'll go practice your skating?"

Great, I thought, *more skating time with David*.

"Okay," David answered, cramming in still more French fries. "Just one more thing. I'm going to take my mom some cookies when I go."

Mom laid down her hamburger and turned to him, and the rest of us stopped chewing. "I think your mother would like that," she told him. She took in all our faces, the blank look on David's, concern on the other three. Then she tried a smile. "But I'm not feeling so well. Do you think you guys can bake them yourselves?"

❧ 21 ❧

On Wednesday night, Mother and Dad had a date. It was Mother's idea, something she'd begun planning on Monday morning, a way to "recapture what we had," she told me. She passed the time between Monday and Wednesday in a fevered state, rushing to do things she believed would make Dad want to come home, and it struck me as odd that she would try to recapture an earlier part of her marriage by doing things she'd never done before. Washing and drying Dad's white shirts, which, for as long as I could remember, had been sent to the laundry. Baking—and burning—cookies at a frenzied pace, making me yearn for the simple days, when we purchased cookies at the grocery, when I was allowed to wander down the aisle and choose what I wanted. She cleaned house from morning to night and talked on the phone incessantly, planning the first big event for her Christian Youth Fellowship, scheduled for the Friday night of Labor Day weekend, immediately following the first home football game. The phone rang continually, with calls from members of her church committee or from the preacher himself. Vases holding fresh flowers sat on every level surface, and David's crayons barely hit the sofa before she'd gathered them up and replaced them in their box.

The problem, though, was that she never finished one task before conjuring another. Cookies burned while she ironed, shirts scorched while she talked on the phone, and the Pledge and the dust rag never left the coffee table, because just as she went to put them away, she smelled cookies burning.

Three hours before her date, I found her standing in the kitchen, shoulders slouched forward under hair that dripped water, her juice-can rollers strewn across the table in front of her. Her back was to me. The mixer sat on the counter, maniacally whirling cookie dough, the drone loud enough to drown out my steps. Her sob, though, reached across the room, and her right arm, holding the ice pick, rose and then slashed down. I hurried to the table. "Don't do that," she yelled. "You scared me."

Her face was misshapen, her features contorted with the effort of holding back tears. Her breath caught on the way in. "Damn things," she said. "They just won't ventilate." She brought her arm down again and this time, managed to poke a hole in the can she held. The next time, though, the can crumpled in the middle, its two ends clashing before it flew out of her hand and across the table like a cue ball, knocking several others out of its path and onto the floor. She burst into tears.

I walked to the mixer and turned it off, then returned, and she let me take the ice pick from her hand. "I just wanted it to be smooth," she said, still crying.

"It looks good curly. Just go dry it, and I'll finish the cookies." Her shoulders still shaking, she walked out of the room. I gathered the juice cans and chunked them in the garbage.

On the counter sat a cookie jar shaped like a mouse. I lifted its head and discovered it full. Not surprised, I reached into a cabinet for the Tupperware storage containers Mother had bought at a Cameron party and never used. I opened all four of them before finding one, the smallest, that wasn't already filled with cookies. It frightened me that we had so many cookies. I wanted Dad to come home as much as Mother did, but I didn't see how two thousand chocolate-chip cookies would bring him back, and I wondered if cookie baking could become the same as hand-washing. Mother had seemed more needy in the last few days. Dad's leaving had changed her normal bossiness into something more desperate, something like illness, and I promised myself I'd try harder to get along with her, to compliment her, to help her, even if I couldn't understand her.

Two hours later, I scooped the last of the cookies onto the turkey platter. I covered them with foil, leaned against the counter, and stared out the window at the peace that was Lou Jean's house, even without her in it.

"You miss her, don't you?"

Mother was dressed for her date. Her makeup was perfect, she wore her pearl earrings, and she'd managed to dry her hair without frizzing it. She wore another new dress, bright white voile sprigged with yellow and green daisies. The sleeves were puffed, tiny caps banded with white velvet ribbons tied into bows. I tried not to stare at the hem, which stopped at least six inches above her knees, or to think about the fact that I still had no new school clothes.

"You look nice," I said, honoring my promise.

"You can't wait for her to get well and come home, can

you?" The crystal and raspberries were gone from her voice, and so was the desperation. She walked up, and like me, gripped the countertop in front of her, leaning her body against her hands and toward me at the same time. "Don't you care that he may leave us? Or do you even get it?" Her face was so close that it blurred. "Has it not occurred to you that you are being used?"

I leaned away from her. "She doesn't say bad things about you. Why can't you just leave her out of it?"

"Because she's using you. And you can't see it."

"What do you mean?"

Suddenly, Mother was right in front of me, patience run out, right hand snapping fingers two inches from my face, her mouth only an inch further. "I *mean* she's using you to get what she wants, Kayla." She snapped her fingers again for emphasis. "For God's sake, wake up!" Her words smelled like Listerine, acidic and bitter. "It's the oldest trick in the book. Win the child, win the father."

I looked at all the hundreds of cookies. Dozens and dozens and dozens, and I remembered her voice: *Charles Dale, what's your favorite cookie?* The tone she had used on the day Lou Jean had become so ill.

I lifted the head from the mouse, took out a cookie, and shoved it into her hand. "You've got the rule wrong," I said. "Isn't it win the child, *keep* the father?"

"What's that supposed to mean?"

"Nothing. Just that *my* favorite cookie is oatmeal, and Charles Dale's is chocolate chip. Guess which kind we have two thousand of?"

✎

An hour later, she sat on the sofa with David, watching car-
toons and waiting for Dad. Across the room, I sat beside
Charles Dale on a low Victorian love seat that Mother had
wheedled Dad into buying. Its cloth was fussy, ornate, and
uncomfortable, exactly what Mother would choose. Tears kept
coming to my eyes. I was angrier with her than I'd been all
summer, but I was also unsure. The idea that Lou Jean had
been nice to me only because she wanted my dad was so clearly
something that Mother would invent. Something she was not
above fabricating to make me hate Lou Jean. But what if
Mother was right? At this point, anything seemed possible.

I had begun the summer believing that we were moving to
my parents' hometown because both of them wanted to, and
that we had bought this house because my mother and father
really liked it, this particular combination of wood and brick
and carpet and paint. I had met Lou Jean and decided that she
was the most wonderful person I had ever known and, just like
her oldest son, was incapable of harming anyone or anything. I
had never questioned the fact that my mother and father would
be together until old age, until one of them died. It was something I never thought about, too outlandish to even be near
my thoughts. It was almost as otherworldly as the idea that my
mother would put puncture marks and bruises on my arm.

Now, I knew that we had moved here, to this town and to
this house, because one of my parents, though I couldn't have
declared which one, wanted to be next door to Lou Jean. That
it had nothing to do with the makeup, the physical characteris-
tics of our house, and everything to do with the neighbor who
had been the closest but who now was the most distant.

I also knew that Lou Jean was capable of hurting people.

Rules or no rules, she had slept with my father, and callous or not callous, my mother must have been hurt. Lou Jean also had come close to aborting her own baby and now suffered for it in ways that made me squinch my eyes to keep from remembering. Of everyone she had hurt, it seemed to me she had hurt *herself* most.

And Charles Dale? As kind as he was to cats and cowkillers and coral snakes and kid brothers, he wasn't kind to me. And he wasn't kind to his mother. It was at least in part because of him that she was where she was. My father had moved out, and my parents had little chance of remaining married until their next anniversary, much less old age. And though my bruises had faded, tiny white crescents remained, testimony to the fact that I didn't know my mother any more than I knew anyone else who lived in our house. I knew Thad Howard—could have guaranteed his behavior—better than I knew my own family.

Something else I knew: I would have to depend on myself, just as Charles Dale would have to depend on himself. We had gotten along better the last few days. *Maybe* we could begin to depend on each other. Because my father, my mother, Lou Jean, the adults we should have been able to depend on, were too caught by their own sticky traps to help us. We were too young to pull them out, and they were too weak to pull themselves out.

How weak Lou Jean must have been to decide to abort her child. Did she make the decision on her own or did she have help from someone? If Mother could send Lou Jean to a psychiatric hospital now, with Charles Dale well and strong, thirteen years of vigorous and sure growth behind him, a happy lifetime ahead, what had she been able to do then? With a wedding license and the bulge of me inside her, undisputed claims to Dad, undeniable proof of ownership—and Charles Dale so tiny in Lou Jean that he was still invisible, small enough to be sucked out and denied—what damage must Mother have been able to do?

I knew something else at this moment: I knew that Mother had no idea how to sit in a miniskirt. With David leaning against her, she laughed as if *Popeye* and *Captain Gus* were the funniest things on television. Popeye opened yet another can of life-saving spinach, and David giggled and settled in closer to Mother, and she allowed his closeness, relaxing more and more into the couch cushions, unaware of the sight she created. I poked Charles Dale.

Mother's knees leaned discreetly to one side, her legs crossed only at the ankles, observing the very rules of proper posture she had always preached to me, and yet something was very wrong. Applied to her new wardrobe, her old rules were ineffective.

Her skinny thighs came nowhere close to meeting and left a gap that was anything but ladylike. Captain Gus came to the part of his show where he read the letters from his little mateys, telling who had measles and who had broken an arm while skating, wishing everybody happy birthdays and speedy recoveries, and Mother relaxed further into the cushions. Her hem had risen almost to the top of her legs, revealing a large white patch of panty. I poked Charles Dale again, harder this time, and when he didn't respond, looked at him out of the corner of one eye. He was way ahead of me—fixed on Mother's underwear with a gaze strong enough to support an entire truckload of spinach.

It took a full twenty seconds for Mother to realize what Charles Dale stared at. I counted as I watched her face change. First she smiled at him, thinking he was looking at her, at her face, anyway, noticing her makeup, admiring her new dress, beaming his appreciation for all the cookies she'd baked, all the lovely things she'd done for him. When she realized that her smile was getting no response, that Charles Dale's eyes were focused on something lower than her frosted lipstick and puffed sleeves, she looked downward, trying to see what he saw. Had she cut her knee while shaving? Was there a new Kool-Aid stain on the front of the sofa? She bent forward, saw nothing, then settled back against the cushion, her smile now replaced by a look of bewilderment. Charles Dale, entranced, never registered her body shift. The line of his gaze had become all but visible and was in fact what Mother's own eyes finally tracked to find the object of his awe. And by the time she realized what he was looking at, her skirt had reached the highest point possible to still technically be a skirt, and even *she* could see what now was a broad gleaming white display, a fairly close representation of a longhorn steer, its face between her thighs, its horns extended out across their tops.

She jumped up so quickly that she forgot her ankles were still crossed and sent David backward into the space he'd had no warning she would vacate. Struggling for balance, she looked at Charles Dale only a moment more, before shifting her glare to me, as if I were responsible for the whole thing, as if I hadn't spent the afternoon baking cookies, saving her from an ice-pick wound. The grin I'd dropped when she first looked up jumped right back on my face and stayed longer than she did. When she spun on her still-crossed ankles and strode out of the room, I was still grinning. The next thing we heard was the crash of her bedroom door as it flung open against the wall, and the slam as it closed again. "I bet on the blue sundress," I said to Charles Dale. He was still mute.

By the time she came back, wearing not the sundress but the sailor outfit, and looking like she might march us down the plank at any moment, Dad had come in the front door, holding a beer bottle. "I thought you were wearing your new dress," he said.

By way of answer, she turned her back to him, speaking instead to Charles Dale and me. "You make your sandwiches. You clean up the kitchen, you watch TV for one hour, and you go to bed. I don't want to see a single light or a single dirty dish when I get home. Do you understand me?" She waited for us to nod, which he did and I didn't. She narrowed her eyes at me, then whirled back to Dad, giving a warning look to the beer in his hand. "I guess I'm driving." Dad set his beer down pointedly, I thought, placing it on the bare table and not a coaster. He glared at her back as she went out the door ahead of him.

Charles Dale looked ill, traumatized. He looked as if he needed some cheering up, and a big fat bologna sandwich. I was right. We kids were going to have to rely on each other. Getting to my feet, standing before him, I leaned down and slapped him on the back. In my cheeriest voice I said, "Way to go, cowboy."

An hour later I made my way to Lou Jean's, knowing I would be in even bigger trouble if caught but irked by the idea of starting a television program I couldn't stay up to finish. In the pantry, I cleared the pickle brine, noticing that there was less foam, resolving to mention the pickles to Lou Jean on Saturday, wondering how to say "Will you be home before they're ready?" without saying it. I rinsed the bowl and spoon, then wandered through the spotless rooms. Yvonne's maid came twice a week to clean a house no one dirtied. In the downstairs bathroom, I found a tube of lipstick. Rolling it up brought the smell of Lou Jean, and I leaned into the mirror, applying it to my own mouth. Coming out of the bathroom, I noticed light shining down from Lou Jean's room upstairs. Realizing the maid must have left it on, I climbed to turn it off, and the stairs creaked under my feet, a sad sound that I'd never noticed, not even on the day I'd watched the doctor bring Lou Jean down. As if even the stairs, the wood and paint of her house, missed her.

The upstairs hall was dark, and I crossed it quickly, listening for cars, worried now about the time. The light switch just inside the bedroom door was turned off, but light came from somewhere. As I walked through the room, flashes of color caught my eye, bright colored flecks that I didn't realize were glass until they crunched beneath my steps.

On the bedside table, Lou Jean's dragonfly lamp lay on its side, the stained-glass shade shattered, the light from the bare bulb throwing sharp slitted shadows across the rumpled bed-spread and sheets, illuminating a scrawl on the wall. Across the plaster, over the headboard, was the word DAM. Written over and over, it's capital letters looked angry and red. Bloodred.

The top drawer of Lou Jean's makeup table had been pulled out and hung dangerously by its back edge. The rest of the room seemed undisturbed, until I looked at the closet door. At first, it seemed flush with the wall, normal, closed and latched.

But as I moved toward the center of the room, I looked down to avoid tracking glass onto the Oriental rug, and when I glanced back up, the door no longer seemed solidly shut. Up closer, it now appeared open, its edge not quite meeting its frame, as if in that split second when I'd looked down, without my attention, it had opened. I ran for the door, forgetting the carpet and the glass until I felt a sting on the back of my right ankle. I didn't stop until I'd reached the kitchen. In the company of the pilot light, listening for any step on the stairs, I rubbed my stinging calf, and my hand came away wet. I wiped the blood onto my shorts and ran out the door and home.

Ten minutes later, I stood on the grass between my house and Lou Jean's. The glass burned in my leg; I could feel the little chip under my skin but couldn't pull it out. On the ground at my feet, Charles Dale sobbed, and I wished I had followed my instincts. It had been so tempting, back inside the safety of my own house, to simply stay there. The smells of last night's burned meatloaf and today's scorched laundry suddenly welcome, I had wanted nothing more than to clean my leg, put on a Band-Aid, and be asleep before Mother got home. But leaving Lou Jean's room the way it was, without getting help, felt too much like leaving *her* injured and without help. I kept thinking of the sad sound of the stairs. And so I had dragged Charles Dale out of bed and across the dark lawns, my free hand holding a flashlight. Over his protests, his worries that my parents would drive up and find us outside, I'd not heard the water sprinkler until a blast of water hit both of us.

As we fled, our feet had tangled and we had fallen, me on the ground, Charles Dale on the whirling sprinkler head.

When I turned on the flashlight to look at the cut, he slapped me away, yelling at me through his sobs. "You could have turned it on *before* I fell." Though he was sitting practically on top of the sprinkler, both of us becoming more soaked by the moment, he wouldn't let me help him move away. Leaving the light with him, I made my way to the hydrant and shut off the water. In the darkness, Charles Dale sat with his hurt knee cocked up toward his face, his hands around the cut. He took a deep breath and blew into the sheltering circle of his fingers. I walked back to him, and he said between breaths, "We're going to be in big trouble. And it's your fault."

At my feet, he looked no bigger than David. He wore only a pair of short pajama bottoms. Wet through and through, they clung to his skinny thighs, making his legs look spindly and weak. His bare chest was whiter than his arms and legs, and as he bent forward, his rib cage caved into his abdomen, creating a hollow that looked too small to hold all the organs, blood, things necessary for life. Though I knew how tough he could be, had seen him handle wasps with no fear whatsoever, he now seemed only vulnerable and exposed. In the dim light, his torso was pearly, the color of a mussel shell forced open too soon, and it looked unattached to the tanned rest of him. A separate, defenseless being. And I wondered if I was doing the wrong thing by taking him into his house. Listening for cars, listening for any sounds from Lou Jean's, I squatted on the ground beside him and he let me take his hands away from his knee. "I know," I said. "I'll tell them."

I pulled him up and we started to his house. My plan was to go in, turn on all the lights, and make a lot of noise. And if confronted, swing the flashlight like a club.

No matter how hard I listened, how carefully I moved, it seemed that the only noise came from us, and that we made a lot of it. I circled the kitchen, turning on the overhead lights, the pierced copper fixture over the table, even the fluorescents fitted under the cabinets. I had to walk around Charles Dale, who was taking the time to look at his knee. "What do you want to show me?" he asked crankily as I passed.

"You'll see," I answered, struggling for a confident tone, realizing there was no way we could get upstairs without making noise. From the sheltering glow of the kitchen, the dining room darkness was hostile. Chair backs curved downward, a warning frown, and past it was the living room, then the stairs, the hall. We'd take it one room at a time, I thought, turning on each light as we went, chasing whoever was in there, driving ahead of us whoever was hiding, flushing them like quail, until we'd cornered them in Lou Jean's closet. Strengthened by my plan, I ran across the dining room to the far wall and flipped the switch. The chandelier over the table blazed, revealing only two people in the room, one of them staring at the other as if he doubted her sanity. "What is wrong with you?" Dried blood, dotted with grass, caked his knee and streaked his shin.

I shrugged, turning to the next dark room. "Come on."

"What did you do to your leg?" asked Charles Dale.

The living-room switch was just inside the door. When the room was lit and empty, I answered, "Cut it," and ran to the stairs.

Climbing them made plenty of noise, me clomping with my left leg to keep the weight off my right, Charles Dale asking questions and complaining. I pictured the intruder running back into the closet, frightened by our fervor. "I wish you'd just tell me," Charles Dale kept saying, followed by, "If your parents come home, they're going to see all the lights. Why are we turning on all the lights?"

At Lou Jean's door I told him, "Because somebody vandalized your mother's room. I found it when I came over to check the pickles."

"What do you mean?" He shot around me before I could answer, banging the door against the wall.

"Wait," I yelled, looking around the room as I caught up and grabbed his arm. "There's broken glass." Before I could chicken out, I ran to the closet door, put my bottom against it, and grabbed two corners of the cedar chest that sat close by. "There's no glass over here. Come help me." With me pulling and Charles Dale pushing, and with enough screeching of wood across tile to scare anyone, we managed to move the cedar chest in front of the door. Then we both sat down on it to catch our breath. "You think they're in there?" Charles Dale whispered. Blood dripped from the back of my leg onto the scraped tiles. In the closet, all was quiet, but in the kitchen, a door banged. Charles Dale's eyes were huge as we hopped up, him running to the window, me following. "Be careful. Can you see who it is?"

"I'll *tell* you who it is," said Mother. From the door, she took in the condition of the room and of the children in it. "What the hell are you two doing?" Beside her, Dad's face asked the same question. If he considered her cursing a surprise, if he even noticed it, he gave no indication. The charge to the window had made Charles Dale's knee bleed again, his face was streaked from crying, and he looked very close to losing it.

"It's my fault," I said.

Charles Dale lost it. "Somebody tore up my mother's room." His eyes roamed the damage as he sobbed open-mouthed, ragged gasps, and his chest collapsed again in the hollow. "They might still be in the closet. We blocked them."

It took two seconds for Dad to move the chest back to its place. He opened the door, stepped to the center of the closet, and with one sure motion, tugged the string attached to the overhead fixture. Light showered luggage, clothes, shoes, empty hangers, and Dad, revealing nothing more ominous than a tennis racket in a wooden vise.

Mother's words came through clenched teeth. "What happened?"

Charles Dale moved up close behind me. The least I could do was get him out of trouble. "I came over to clear the pickles," I said. "There was a light on and I came up to turn it off. When I saw what had happened, I went and got Charles Dale. He was in bed."

As if I weren't speaking or as if my words weren't worth hearing, Mother walked to the wall and touched the writing that scarred it. She ran a finger down a *D*, then smelled it. "Lipstick," she said. Then she bent and lifted something from the floor. Walking back to me, she held out an uncapped tube, still rolled to the fullest exposure, grit and a dust ball coating its waxiness. She looked at my lips. "What do you have to say for yourself?"

I didn't remember until Dad and Charles Dale stared at me too. Then I pressed my palm over my lips and tried to speak around it. "I didn't do it." My hand came away smeared red and smelling sweet. "I didn't," I said again.

"You get yourself home," Mother said. She grabbed my arm and started for the door. "And you stay home. This place is officially off-limits. I don't want either of you kids over here again."

Suddenly Charles Dale was between Mother and me, moving so quickly that he jolted me when he pushed us apart. He hung onto my arm with one hand, and shook the index finger of the other one at Mother. "I'll come over here anytime I want," he shouted. "It's my house, and you can't stop me." He pulled my arm into the space between his body and Mother's. "What are you going to do? Put bruises on my arm the way you did Kayla's?"

The only sound was his breathing. His fragile chest heaved, not with exhaustion but with energy, and it was as flushed as his face. His eyes were wide, and so were his lips, as if every part of him had to be open, uncovered, to pull in enough air to fuel his anger. He looked angry, but proud too, and he glanced at Dad and me, just for a moment took his eyes from Mother's face, as if to see if we were watching. Like a body builder who'd just lifted more weight than he'd ever thought possible, who wanted to be cool about it, who wanted to act as if it was no big deal but couldn't resist a peek around the gym to see who else might have witnessed. Against his ruddy exultation, Mother was pale.

Glass crunched under Dad's feet, and as he passed Mother, the look he gave her was questioning, suspicious, and perplexed, as if he didn't consider her incapable of such an act but was still surprised by it. He looked at my arm and so did I. In this light the crescents appeared nothing more than sunspots or the last remains of mosquito bites. Dad's confused gaze shifted to Charles Dale.

"What are you talking about?"

"She had bruises and cuts." The bravery in his voice gave way. "The day my mom went to the hospital." Before he could cry again, I began. With frustration. With the injustice of being blamed for something as horrid as destroying Lou Jean's room. And mostly with embarrassment. I hadn't wanted Dad to find out about my arm; I didn't want *anyone* to know. And I very much hated my mother. For the way she was. For her griping and manipulating and twisting us around. For the way she spun all of us into threads, stretching our nerves and our resolve and our desire for peace and harmony, pulling us thin and tight within her fingers and then weaving us back and forth across each other, some of us warp, some of us weft. Making us her own undeniable creation, the cloth of her latest plan, a fabric the color of bruised arms, burned cookies, angry faces, and departing taillights. I hated her for immediately blaming me for the wall, for automatically assuming my guilt. And I hated her for manipulating Lou Jean into driving across the Rio Grande that day, so that now and for his whole life, Charles Dale had to live with the knowledge that his own mother had almost done away with him. But more than anything else, I hated her for our unity, our similitude, because on the night she'd grabbed my arm, I had been like *her*. I had egged her on, goaded her, the same way she goaded Dad or Gran. Or me. I had wanted to push her, wanted to make her as angry as I was. I had wanted to hurt her, and ultimately to make her hurt me, so that she would be guilty of the larger crime. So that *she* would be undeserving of my love, and so that my love for and allegiance to Lou Jean would be justified. To divorce myself from her, to show how different we really were, I had copied her. When all I wanted was to be as little like her as possible, I had become her.

My arm supported by my brother's hand, I could now do what I'd set out to do that night. "I hate you," I told her, and my voice shook only a little. "Forever."

I expected her to slap me. I gritted my teeth and leaned into Charles Dale, waiting for it with dread and hope. The imprint of her hand would change my face, finally and forever making me both the right one and the wronged one, so that long after my skin returned to normal, after my blood returned to the surface, Dad and Charles Dale would look at me and remember what she'd done. And most of all, she would remember what she'd done. My face, if not guilt free then at least less guilty than hers, a reminder. Her fingerprints as condemning as if left on a jailhouse blotter.

When she didn't hit me, when neither arm lifted from her side, I realized that her own face was changing, was becoming sad and baffled and guarded, retreating, as if I were the one doing the hurting. It changed dramatically and drastically, instantaneously became someone else, making me wonder if Mother's face, the one I'd known through the years, had been not a real face but instead an illustration, painted on glass, on a window that now had opened, revealing the real face behind it. A face both right and wronged. Desperate, I said, "You made Dad leave. You put bruises on my arm. And most of all, you tried to make Lou Jean get an abortion."

Charles Dale released my arm so suddenly that it slapped against my thigh. The confusion on his face was terrifying, as if I'd revealed something hugely upsetting. We stared at each other. "But . . . you *knew*," I said. He *had* known. It was the reason he'd begun staying at our house, the reason he'd treated his mother so badly. My mother had *said* that Lou Jean had told him.

He shook his head. "No. You're wrong about that, Kayla."

Mother shifted, and her old face reappeared. Her sigh was heavy with accusation. The fact that I'd screwed up yet again was no surprise to her. The window had closed.

ᔮ 22 ᔮ

I was grounded, my parents' date had been a disaster, and I had hurt Charles Dale's feelings. He had stood up for me, and I had repaid him by announcing that his mother had tried to abort him. All I wanted to do was sleep, so that I could quit thinking about the coming Saturday, when the boys and Dad would be going to see Lou Jean without me. So that I could block out Dad's tires peeling rubber as he'd left the house, disgusted with all of us, no doubt. And most of all, so that I could forget how quickly Charles Dale had dropped my arm.

But my room was too hot for sleep, and I got out of bed and opened the door, hoping to pull breath through my lifeless window. Down the hall, another door opened, and I jumped back under the smothering sheet and closed my eyes. A moment later Charles Dale said, "Kayla."

He stood by my bed. "Come on."

In answer to my "Where?" he turned and started out of the room. I hopped out of bed and caught up with him.

Lou Jean's chimes hung dead as we walked down the dark sidewalk. The moon had gone wherever the wind had gone. The dog from the house next to the Howards' ran across the pavement and sniffed the backs of our legs, but Charles Dale just kept walking. "Where are we going?" I finally asked again, after even the dog had gone home.

"You'll see," was the only answer I got. The Howards' picture window was lit blue, and I hoped it wasn't Thad who was still up, knowing how thrilled he'd be to tattle. The sidewalk was warm and dusty under our bare feet. More than likely it was Mr. Howard, I thought, lying on their overtaxed sofa and watching a Civil War movie, the television coloring him his two favorite colors, blue and gray. I imagined him, sprawled like a foundered horse, having wiped out the refrigerator, nothing left in it but an open box of baking soda, the floor beside him now covered in empty olive jars, peanut cans, and chicken bones so clean a cat wouldn't have them. For the first time in a long time, I laughed out loud.

"Be quiet," Charles Dale said. He had put on a shirt after we'd gone back home, and I was glad. It covered the white of his torso, and its horizontal stripes made him seem stronger again, the Charles Dale who had leaped to my defense, challenging my mother, rather than the one who'd sat on the ground and sobbed. The one I'd wounded twice in one night.

We stopped in front of Mrs. Petersen's house, empty since she'd died the year before while giving a piano lesson to a fourth grader. Lou Jean had called her the kindest person on earth, so gentle that even as she'd died, she'd thought of the kid beside her on the bench, saying quickly, "I think I hear your mother out front," so that the kid was through the door before she fell. Only when she didn't come out for her paper the next day, when the neighbors went in and found her, did the kid remember that he had heard something fall as he'd walked across the

porch. He had thought it was Mrs. Petersen's fat Siamese jumping down from the top of the piano. He'd sat on the porch then,
waiting for his mother without going back inside, because he
knew the cat always jumped down from the piano when the lesson was over.

Charles Dale motioned for me to follow, and we walked
onto Mrs. Petersen's carpet grass, spongy and cool after the
chalkiness of the sidewalk. Even with Lou Jean's remembrance
of her, it seemed spooky to be in a dead woman's yard, not
twenty feet from where she had died, after midnight.

We moved in a diagonal direction to the dark line of oleanders that divided her property from the vacant lots at the end of
the street. Copying Charles Dale, I lay down on my stomach.
As he inched forward, using his elbows to pull himself, bit by
bit, back toward the sidewalk, I followed, hurrying a little to
come alongside him. "Be really quiet," he whispered again. His
voice sounded normal, maybe because I so wanted it to sound
normal. The last thing I wanted was for him to be mad at his
mother again, when she was improving, when he'd be going to
see her on Saturday. As we came to the last oleander, the front
edge of Mrs. Petersen's property, he touched me on the shoulder. Then he pointed to our left.

Under the streetlight, where the pavement ended and the
overgrown lots began, a mother skunk and two babies moved
peacefully, tails brushing the dusty white caliche behind them,
engrossed, with no idea we were only twenty feet away. In the
glow of the lamp, they were slick and rich, perfectly groomed,
as they bumped softly against each other, noses on the ground.
Their coats seemed to catch and hold light, as if made of gems
or jewels, moonstone white, onyx black. Something far grander
than fur on the back of a smelly animal.

Behind the skunks a lantana shivered, and from amidst its red and orange flowers poked a third tiny nose. Shaking its way out from under the plant, the baby paused at the edge of the lot, then waddled into the midst of the others and began catching its own crickets and moths. The crunching of dinner was loud, just as Charles Dale had promised two months before. There was no other noise, and there was no movement in the yellow blooms of the huisache tree that drooped over the skunks. Even the dryflies, which I knew must be attached to the tree's branches and which usually buzzed all night, like static from a radio left on too long, were quiet. Once in a while, a June bug smarter than the others would fly up into the huisache and away from the skunks' jaws, but even the sound of its wings, their usual whirring, was gone.

Beside me, Charles Dale lay as motionless as I, our chins resting on doubled fists. We watched the leisurely dining of the skunks long enough that I forgot the danger. My shoulders slackened, my chest and stomach eased into the lawn, and I let out a deep sigh, my relaxation marred only by a now-and-again worry about Charles Dale. Beside me, though, he seemed just as relaxed—until he spoke, his whisper harsh and scratchy: "I'm sorry your dad moved out."

All I could manage was "He's your dad too." Tears blurred my view of the mother skunk and one of the babies as they waddled back into the weeds, their sleek stomachs now brushing the ground. The other two skunks continued eating. The sharing of my father was the least I could offer Charles Dale.

"If it wasn't for me," he went on, as if I hadn't spoken, "he'd still be here. I should have stayed at home."

"You couldn't. Your mom was going away."

"I mean *before*," he said, too loud. The mother skunk

stepped back into the light, her nose in the air, her tail now halfway up as well. The babies stopped playing and moved to her side. Without taking my eyes from her, not daring to blink, I slowly moved the fist closest to Charles Dale, opened it, and laid it on his arm. I felt the wind then, as it came up from behind us, over our backs, and toward the skunks. The mother's tail raised even more.

"When I just sort of moved in," Charles Dale went on, oblivious to the skunk. "If I hadn't done that, my mom wouldn't be in the hospital. And your dad would be at home." I cautiously shook his arm, warning him.

"Just be still," he said, and his voice was impatient, irritated. "We're all right." A moment later the mother turned and followed her babies into the weeds, her erect tail the last thing we saw. Charles Dale pushed himself backward then, sitting on his heels. He jerked his head sideways to look at me. "I was mad at her for trying to get rid of me, even if she loved me too much to do it. Even if she went crazy when she saw that building, because it scared her so much what she almost did."

I sat up too, and I forgot the skunks. "You already knew? Before tonight?"

Charles Dale raised his hands from his knees and held them on either side of his face in a questioning gesture. "About your mom. About what almost happened. I didn't spill the beans?" The wind was blowing harder now, the oleanders bending ahead of it and away from us.

"Of course I knew." He looked down the street at Howards' house, dark now. "She told me. On the Fourth."

I fell back onto the lawn and looked at the sky. Like a star low enough to grab came the knowledge that I'd hurt Charles Dale only once that night, that I'd given him nothing worse than a cut knee, and I smiled. "So how come you acted so surprised when I mentioned it? How come you said it wasn't true?"

He lay back too. "I wasn't surprised by that, you idiot. I was surprised because you thought your mom was responsible." He plucked grass with one hand, dumping it on my face. "You ought to know your mother the saint better than that."

A flock of cattle egrets blew across us, low and white, voices raised to talk across the wind. "My mother's capable of anything."

"She isn't capable of *that*," Charles Dale answered. "Do you know cattle egrets sit on the backs of cows and eat ticks? The cows get rid of their ticks. The birds get something to eat. They have a symbiotic relationship."

"Quit using big words." The air grew quiet as the birds flew on. "So, if my mother didn't push Lou Jean into driving across that bridge, who did? She wouldn't have done it on her own."

His answer was slow. "Nobody made her do it. She was just too sad and confused. She thought it was the only thing that could make things right for everybody." He flipped onto his stomach and lay flat, his face half submerged in the grass. "And she was all by herself when she drove across that bridge."

I flipped too. "Except for you," I reminded him, and I hoped he'd take it the right way. "You were with her."

"Yeah. And the person in a car ten miles behind her, somebody who'd found out what she was going to do and decided to try to stop her."

The grass on my face was scratchy, and I sat up slowly, stiff from lying on the ground. "Who?"

"Someone who believes abortion is a sin."

"Carmen." It made sense now. How protective she was of Lou Jean. How she had immediately known that gray building, how her sense of danger had been so instantaneous, when she and Gran had turned that Mexico corner. How quickly she'd moved to us, holding David up to Lou Jean, her tiny arms strained with the effort of lifting a fifty-pound kid over her head.

How her poor body must have ached the next day. It was too much weight and too much worry for someone her age to carry. And in a way she'd carried it all summer—and still carried it. Having to get us up the day Lou Jean went to the hospital. Making sure my mother did nothing upsetting. Keeping the peace between Gran and Lou Jean's mother. Even now, she was the one calling Lou Jean's doctor, constantly checking on her, reporting back to the boys, carrying the weight for all of us. Sadly, I thought of Saturday, when the boys and Dad would go to San Antonio. When I would stay home. And when Carmen would get dressed up and go to church, inventing sins on the way.

Charles Dale flopped onto his back and put his hands behind his head. His voice was smug. "Nope." He crossed one leg over the other, kicking me with his bare toes.

His toenails dug into my knee. "Who, then?" I asked slowly.

"We-e-e-ll," he said, drawling the word. "Think of someone who believes she's entitled to some part of me. Think of chocolate-chip cookies. *I* don't want to think of them, but *you* can." He made a gagging sound.

I grabbed his foot and squeezed it. "My mother?"

"Ow," he said. "Congratulations. You're slow, but you get there."

I squeezed harder. "I don't believe you."

He kicked his foot free and stood up. Then he grabbed my arm, hauling me up with him. "Believe it or not," he said, dusting grass from his shorts, looking over his shoulder at his butt as if my buying his story was the last thing he cared about. "I'm tired." He started off toward the house.

"My mother?" I said behind him.

He kept walking. "She came driving up in this 1950 Mercury she had then, this big black mammoth car with silver teeth in its grill, and she parked right out in the street and ran in the door as if into battle, like the archangel Michael. She grabbed Mom and shoved her out the door. Yelling at the nurse, in English, of course, about God and unborn children and how the hottest fires of hell are reserved for abortionists."

"Was your mom already . . . ?"

"No. She was still in the lobby. She saw the whole thing. She said your mother looked like the Knight of Swords."

We neared Lou Jean's house. Dad had left her bedroom light on, and it shone in a little patch on the sidewalk. Past it, my own house was dark. I didn't want to believe it. I was ready to accept, even welcome, frailty in my mother, although it would be a long time before I baked cookies for her again. But, goodness in her, the idea that she had actually *helped* Lou Jean, made me uncomfortable, made me want to stay out all night, or at least until I'd had some time to adjust to the idea of Mother as savior.

It made sense, though, that Mother would see herself as some avenging angel, and that Lou Jean would see her as a figure from her tarot pack. And it made sense that in the silent house ahead, the one I wasn't yet ready to enter, Mother slept alone, as a saint would.

"You know what doesn't make sense, Charles Dale?" I asked. "All this time, and we never have gone to find what your mother left us."

In Lou Jean's room for the third time that night, I adjusted my back against the cedar chest. "Does Murray Ball have a girl-friend?"

Charles Dale leaned back against the French door. "Who wants to know?"

I launched a baby marshmallow at his head.

He dodged it, then plucked it from the clean floor and held it up for effect. "There's nothing better than when she makes us carrot-and-raisin salad with these." He ate it. "Unless it's eating them straight out of the bag."

I had no idea what most women, off to a mental facility, would leave behind as a surprise for the children they loved, but it made sense to us that it would be a giant bag of marshmallows.

It had taken us three hours to sweep up the glass, to scrub the wall, and to put clean sheets on the bed. Now, except for the missing lampshade and the faint pink stains on the plaster, Lou Jean's room looked normal.

"What are you going to call my dad? *Your* dad, I mean."

He reached into the bag between us. "I don't know. I might call him Phil." His full hand paused at his mouth. "But I might call him Dad."

"It's okay, you know. With me."

He leaned forward and looked back over his shoulder, out onto the balcony and up toward the bell tower. "How do you think she managed to get that bag up there? With her hands all wrapped up the way they were?"

I thought of Carmen again. "I'd guess she had some help." I picked up the note on the floor and thought of Gran. "This handwriting looks familiar."

He settled against the door again. "Do you think she's going to be okay?"

"I do. Look what the note says. She promises she'll be home. She says she'll make us salad." I looked at the bag, almost empty. "Are you counting?"

"Three hundred thirty-six. Including the one you threw at me. She also says for you not to be too hard on your mother."

I read the note again. "I'm going to try. It's hard when you're grounded."

He took one more handful, then tossed the bag to me. "I know who did it."

"I do too, but she'll never believe it." I ate the last six, then stood up. "One hundred sixty-two." I grabbed the dirty sheets from the floor.

"Three hundred ninety-two . . . wait a minute!" He reached into the bundle I held and dragged out a pillowcase. "Look at this." Centered on the pillowcase, like a new design, was a print. Clear and crisp, but small. The exact size of an outgrown Ked. My ticket to Austin on Saturday.

I handed him the sheets and took the pillowcase. "I'll take care of this," I said. "I'll wash it. I'll starch it. I'll even iron it. *After* I show it to Mother." I waved it in front of his face, careful not to smudge the print. "This pillowcase and I, Charles Dale, *we* have a symbiotic relationship."

The crickets still sang when I woke Saturday morning. I had set my alarm, determined to be showered, dressed, and waiting out front when Dad pulled up. I wanted one last chance to tell him that things could be different if he came home. Somehow, knowing that Mother, who was so capable of chicanery, of puppet-jerking us to get what she wanted and of incivility when she didn't, was also capable of gallantry, made me believe that they could work things out. Since Charles Dale had told me the truth about what happened in Mexico, I'd noticed some things about Mother. She wasn't very good at dealing with anything new. Once something was in her head, once she believed it was *this* way, the possibility that it might be *that* way threw her. She liked to think she *knew* things, and when the things she knew suddenly developed the appearance of being untrue, when it became possible that she *didn't* know things, that the things she *thought she knew* were in fact wrong, her confusion usually played out in anger.

But sometimes it didn't. Faced with a dirty pillowcase and an innocent and self-righteous daughter, she had turned sad. "Oh, that poor little boy. Bless his sweet deserted little heart."

I was flabbergasted. "Bless *his* heart? I'm the one that got blamed for it."

She shook her head, waving the silver spoon she was polishing. "He's just expressing his hurt and his anger," she protested, "in the only way he knows how." Her eyes went toward the noise of the living-room television. "Bless his heart."

"You said that already," I reminded her. "You just automatically assumed I did it."

"I'm sorry, Kayla." She motioned for me to come to her. She pushed me into the chair next to hers and stared at me. "I really am sorry," she reiterated. "But you shouldn't have been over there. Wearing her lipstick, for Pete's sake. After all she'd done."

I interrupted. "So, do I get to go to Austin on Saturday?"

She finished the spoon and stood. "Yes. You may go." She headed toward the living room. "I'd better see if David's hungry. He didn't eat much lunch."

"He colored on the walls," I reminded her, but in her confusion, she walked on. Since that day, she'd grown more and more confused. David was becoming a monster, and she didn't even see it, ignoring behavior that she'd have never tolerated in me. He wouldn't eat fruit or vegetables, pouting if he didn't get cheese or French fries. On Thursday he'd thrown a fit at the dinner table, tossing his hamburger across the table and screaming for a grilled cheese sandwich, and Mother had done nothing more than leave her own hamburger to cool while she melted butter and sliced cheese.

"You can't let him get away coloring on the walls, with writing cuss words," I'd told her. "Even if they are misspelled." She looked even weirder than normal. Again, she wore the pedal pushers that were part of the sailor outfit, but over them she'd donned a man's dress shirt. The cuffs kept slipping over her hands. I noted that this was the second day in a row that she'd chosen her wardrobe from *Dad's* closet.

"You can't blame David, Kayla, not with what his mother's done." Her voice was steady and sure, as if she knew this and *knew* she knew it. As if there was no confusion and no way she could be wrong. Lou Jean had intentionally hurt her boys, tearing the skin and flesh from her hands, checking into a mental hospital, for no other reason than to cause them pain. Mother talked continually about David's "rightful anger" at his "abandonment," even when I pointed out that he might be merely a spoiled brat who couldn't spell yet.

And she stared at him often, a look of wonderment on her face, as if she saw in him something she hadn't noticed before, some stellar quality just now surfacing, repeating in a sorrowful subdued half-voice, "Poor little tyke. Poor little fellow." When he ate a slice of apple at dinner, one *thin* slice, she'd bragged, "You're a good boy, David. A *very* good boy." The worst part came every afternoon at four o'clock, when she and David sat down on the sofa together and watched *Popeye*. She had started calling it their date, ignoring the fact that she spent much of the thirty minutes hopping up and bringing whatever her "date" demanded. Dry Cheerios in a bowl. Orange juice or Pepsi. More cheese.

So, on that Saturday morning, I was up early, forming reasons and arguments, all the things I'd say to Dad when he got there, all the things that would make him come home. The dim light of the hallway showed the boys still sleeping as I tiptoed past their room. Clothes in hand, I opened the bathroom door, looking forward to thirty minutes of thinking time. I'd have only a few moments alone with him, and I hoped it was enough to convince him that Mother needed him, to let him know how she'd seemed the last few days. Muddled rather than angry. Taken advantage of rather than in control.

A bright heat hit my face and blurred my vision. I could just make out Mother, standing in the middle of the bathroom, wearing one of our lace-trimmed towels and smearing cream on her face. In the steamy haze, her hair was curled tight to her head, making her face look big and bloated.

Every light in the room was on. "Hand me my robe, will you, sweetheart?"

Even her robe, hung on the back of the door, was damp. "What are you doing?"

"What does it look like I'm doing?" She slung herself forward and jerked the towel off her body, threw it over the back of her head, then stood and wrapped it, turban-style. Her naked shoulder blades stood out from her back, farther than her breasts did from her chest. In the bight heat, she seemed too white, as pale as the bathroom fixtures, the tub she'd just left.

"Why?" I asked.

She grabbed the robe, her gestures hurried and nervous, glancing at me as she pulled it up over her shoulders. "Why *what*? You're not making sense, Kayla." Surely she hadn't decided to go with us.

"Why are you up so early? Why are you getting dressed before daylight?" As far as I knew, she hadn't seen or spoken to Dad since Wednesday night. When he'd called to say what time he would pick us up, I had answered the phone and had been the only one to talk to him, relieved to hear his voice cheerful, relaxed again.

"I have things to do," she said. "Quit staring." She zipped up her robe with a quick decisive flourish, as if it were the final statement on the subject. Then she leaned into the sink, her face close to the mirror, and began tweezing her eyebrows, stopping when she realized I still stood there. "Go get dressed."

"But I wanted a shower."

"Oh." She resumed her plucking. "Okay. I'll be out in a minute."

An hour later, she was still in the bathroom. I'd knocked three times. The first two times she'd opened the door, once with a mascara wand in her hand, once with a comb. The third time, there'd been no response except the sound of the hair dryer and of Mother humming along with it.

Ten minutes before Dad was to be there, I gave up and hurriedly started dressing, pulling on the white shorts I'd ironed the night before. I wanted to be on the sidewalk waiting when he drove up, though I still didn't know what to say. The matching blouse was sleeveless, psychedelic orange with white polka dots and five white buttons shaped like surfboards. With one hand I tugged on sandals; with the other I buttoned the blouse, until I reached its hem and found only a broken nub of thread where the last button should be. I dropped to my knees and looked under the bed but found only a few dust balls and a single orange rubber band. I grabbed the rubber band, shoved it in my pocket, and jerked open the closet door. The floor was clean, no button. Searching the laundry room, the insides of the washer and dryer, I found no button. The bathroom was silent again, but in the guest room, the boys were up and talking.

I raced back to my room, unbuttoning the blouse, trying to think of something else to wear. The bathroom door came open and Mother's half-dry head appeared. "Why are you taking off that blouse?"

"Because there's a stupid button missing, and I can't find it," I said, hurling the shirt ahead of me through my bedroom door. "I must have knocked it loose when I ironed it."

"In the flashlight drawer. In the kitchen," said Mother.

"What's it doing there?"

"I put it there last night. You can sew it on. It won't take a minute."

"I'm going to be late now," I argued, covering my chest with my shirt and ducking into my room, as the boys' voices grew louder. "I spent too much time looking for the button that *somebody* put where I'd never find it. I'll wear something else."

"No. That's your nicest outfit. You can't go up there looking tacky."

"Why not? I'm going without a shower," I yelled, but I ran and got the button, watching the clock as I sewed it on. Mother ducked back in the bathroom.

I finished just as Dad's truck pulled into the drive. Tugging on the blouse, buttoning it as I went out my door, I ran down the hall. The boys were still in their room, and I hurried by it.

"Wait a minute," Mother called through the bathroom door.

"Now what?" Behind me, the boys' door opened. They were dressed and smiling, as if it didn't matter to them that none of us had brushed our teeth or washed our faces. I couldn't believe she was letting us go see Lou Jean in that condition. She *was* confused. I halted yet again in front of the bathroom door. The boys scooted around me, through the living room, and out the front door, yelling to Dad, "Doughnuts! We're starving!"

"I'm here," I muttered.

"Boy, you're in a bad mood." She still didn't open the door. "When you climb in the truck, ask your dad to come in for a second. I have something to discuss with him."

With all my heart, I wanted to clobber David. In the two or three minutes that Dad had been in the house, the brat had put his grimy shoe on my white shorts, frogged Charles Dale on the knee, and pronounced the two of us booger-brains. And the heat in the truck was miserable. Every time we opened the doors to let air move through, David shut them. If we tried to hold him, to keep him from climbing out, he screamed at the top of his lungs. Now he sat under the steering wheel, letting spit fall from his mouth, rubbing it into the dirt of the floorboard to form a sort of mud that he promised he was going to wipe on us, "when it's ready."

When he pronounced it done and held up a palm coated in the disgusting mess, then slithered out from under the steering wheel, waggling his hand toward us, I climbed over Charles Dale, opened the door and slammed it shut, then strode up the sidewalk and onto the porch. Somebody had to do something with this kid. The screen door was open, hung on one of David's million crayons, and I walked straight in the house, down the hall, and to the bathroom. Empty, the hair dryer silent, the light off, it was the room I had planned entering two hours earlier.

From my parents' room, then, I heard Dad's voice, one firm and unwavering word that vetoed whatever Mother had wanted to discuss with him: "No."

Great, I thought, *they're already fighting, and I haven't even gotten to tell him what I wanted to tell him.*

I swung through their door and stopped short, one foot away from Dad's back. When he didn't turn or acknowledge me, I reached out to touch his arm but stopped at the sound of his voice, whispery and sad: "It's too late for this." When he turned, so quickly that he startled me, his tennis shoe made a noise like the screen door's hinge, just before its final slam.

He grabbed my shoulders and spun me around and out of the room, but not before I saw Mother. Standing by their bed, eyes downcast as if searching the sheets, her hand slapped the ruffled eyelet of a pillow, as if angry at its presence. As if someone was in big trouble for placing the company sheets on her everyday bed. Her face furious but unflawed, her pageboy, for once, obedient, she had donned her third new look of the summer. As if she'd abandoned her recent *Vogue* look, her Women of the Great Depression, just as she'd abandoned her

Ladies' Home Journal on the day we'd moved here, she now embraced a radical new style. Red lips pouting, eyes sultry and veiled, her mascara black not brown, she looked just like the women on the pages of *Playboy*, where, everyone knew, makeup and hair were always perfect, but clothes were not allowed.

❧ 23 ❧

It wasn't as if I'd never seen Mother naked. I had seen her naked an hour earlier, when I'd stood at the bathroom door and wished I, not she, were inside it. She had never been especially modest, for all her puritanical ways. And I knew what sex was, knew what she had been trying to get my dad to do. Though I found it rather disgusting, and not very considerate, that she planned to do it while the boys and I sat in the hot pickup, hungry and unwashed, it didn't upset me. Instead it made me sad for her and, in some odd way, for me too. It all seemed off-kilter. I was used to Mother's getting what she wanted. What did it mean that she hadn't?

Dad too was annoying me. We weren't even to San Antonio yet, and he had asked three times if I was all right. He acted as if I'd received some great blow, been slammed into a windshield or thrown from a horse, as if Mother had done me some grave harm. Suddenly and seriously concerned about me, now that it was *Mother* who had done something wrong. When he'd told me he was leaving, when *he* was the one causing the problem, he'd been more concerned about my being mature and accepting, fair to Charles Dale.

Just out of Pearsall, we stopped at a Sinclair station so that Charles Dale could go to the bathroom. Dad sent David with him, then asked me a fourth time. "Quit asking me that," I said. I kicked at an empty doughnut bag, sending it to lie against the passenger door. "It's not like I haven't seen her naked before. Like I hadn't already seen her naked this morning, in the bathroom. Where I couldn't take a shower *or* brush my teeth *or* wash my hair or even my face because *she* was hogging the bathroom. It took her two whole hours just to get ready to stand around naked. For *you*." Charles Dale came out of the bathroom, and David, standing just outside the door, hopping from one foot to the other, dropped his hand from his crotch and ran in. "Wait for your brother," Dad called to Charles Dale.

"She really wants you to come back," I said. "She's trying."

Slouched in his seat, Dad's gaze just cleared the steering wheel, but his grip on it was tight and exemplary, at ten o'clock and two o'clock, as if we were in heavy traffic. "Being married to her hurts, honey." On the seat beside me lay a foil gum wrapper. I picked it up and wrapped it around my little finger, twisting its edge to form a wine cup, the way Dad had taught me when I was David's age. Dad watched, and tight little lines grew around his mouth, faint but sharp, as if sketched with a number 3 pencil. I stood the finished wine cup in my palm, and he picked it up. Then, he stared into it as if it were a teacup, with clear instructions for our lives.

David and Charles Dale ran toward us, David yelling to Dad about a blow-up dinosaur for sale inside the station. "It's Dino," he pleaded, "and it's only three dollars."

All that turmoil this morning, I thought, was for nothing. All my hurry and agitation, my getting up at the crack of dawn.

Nothing I said to Dad, none of my promises or apologies, would make one bit of difference. The boys grabbed the truck door, and the wine cup fell over. Dad gently righted it and held it out to me, as delicately as if it were a ladybug or an inchworm. I took it, wadded it up, and tossed it out the open door. "Being your daughter hurts too."

By the time we drove into San Antonio, David had realized he wasn't getting Dino, and he joined Dad and me in our gloom, leaving Charles Dale the only cheerful occupant of the truck. We passed the Butter Krust billboard, where bread spilled from its bag, every day of the year. A perpetually smiling blondhaired girl looked with wholesome greed at the pillowy white slices pouring onto the platter. David roused himself from his gloom. "Magic."

I turned and looked at the back of the sign, the spinning metal wheel that on the front was never-ending bread for a happy, smiling kid. On the back, it was only machinery, blackened and oily. A motor, a shaft, a disk, a light. On the front, it was an entire world, but on the back, it was nothing but parts, truth instead of magic. Like us. Anyone who drove alongside our vehicle and glanced inside would see a family, three kids and a father on a Saturday outing, on their way to the mall to buy Mom a birthday present, or maybe just giving her a morning to herself. Inside the truck, though, we were only parts. Parts of families. One kid with a sick mom and a dead dad. One kid with a sick mom and a dad he'd just learned of. One kid with a naked mom and a dad moving out.

"I wonder if that thing ever breaks down," Charles Dale said merrily. "I'd like the job of fixing it."

I thought about reminding him he was afraid of heights.

"Kayla," David said hopefully, "if you want that Dino, I'll get it for you." We were nearing Austin, and his desperation was growing.

"With what, David?" asked Charles Dale. "You just want it for yourself."

"Okay, David," I said. "I want it. You can buy it for me with your own money. The very next time we stop." He shut up.

Dad didn't say a word. Today, he wore creased slacks and a starched shirt, clothes that matched his older face. His eyes were on the city traffic, his hands back in military position. He suddenly flipped the truck's blinker and left the highway, stopping in the parking lot of another Sinclair. He pulled out his wallet and handed Charles Dale three dollars. "You and David go buy that Dino for Kayla." David's face held a mixture of excitement and apprehension as he climbed out. Dad turned in his seat, his back against the door. "Want to bet just how long that ugly green dinosaur is yours?"

"I don't want it." David looked back through the truck window, and I leaned my head back on the seat so I wouldn't have to see him. "But I'm keeping it, just the same."

The headliner above me had a new tear, a jagged rip that now pointed down like an arrow. Dad reached up and tapped it. "Guess who," he said.

I pushed his hand away and began working the ripped felt, pressing the arrow back up into place, trying to mesh the edges together. "I can handle Mother," I said finally. "But I can't handle her *and* David." The piece of fabric held for a moment, then fell again. "And I don't mind having Charles Dale for a brother. But I don't want David."

Dad started to speak, but I interrupted. "And if you tell me he's just a little boy who's lost his mother, I'll get out right now."

"I was just going to say that Lou Jean should be home in a week or two."

I let the fabric flop and looked at him. "How do *you* know when she'll be home?"

"Kayla, I have to get used to being without your mother before I can be with somebody else."

"You mean you're going to miss her?"

He reached over and began the process I'd just abandoned. "No. I'm not. But I'm going to miss you."

"Fourteen years and you're not even going to miss her?"

Charles Dale and David came out of the station, David trying to walk and blow up the dinosaur at the same time. "Boys," Dad called. "Use the bathroom before we leave. David, let me have Dino."

David gave us a murderous look as he pushed the dinosaur through the open window. "How come Kayla doesn't have to go?" When Dad didn't answer, he ran off, tongue pointed at me.

"Are you sure you didn't move into our house just to be near Lou Jean?"

"Did your mother tell you that?" When I didn't answer, Dad mashed the air out of the dinosaur and folded it up.

His voice was very clipped and short. "Yes, Kayla, I'm sure I didn't move here just to be close to Lou Jean. But it doesn't matter, you know, whether I'm sure. It matters whether *you* are." He opened the glove compartment and crammed the toy into it, struggling to close the door against all that green plastic. Then he sat back and looked straight through the windshield. "Your gran and I have talked this situation through. She and I would like you to alternate weekends. One at her house. One at mine."

"You mean I'd be with one of you every weekend?"

He nodded. His words were very short and quick, and he would not look at me. "If it's okay with you."

"What about if it's okay with Mother?" It was a stupid question. Mother, with all of her weekend plans, her youth fellowships, her Saturday altar-decorating and Sunday churchgoing, would fume about their making a decision without her, would gripe about Gran's bad influence, and would ultimately be glad for the freedom. But her reluctance, her dissension, would slow down the process a little bit, which, at that moment, seemed comforting.

Charles Dale came toward the truck, and David ran out from behind a gas pump and shoved him, trying to be first to get in. Taking it in, Dad said, "You know, Kayla, I really don't care whether its okay with your mother or not." Without a glance at us, Charles Dale whirled around and grabbed David's shirt between the shoulder blades, bunched the fabric in his fist, and used it to haul him to a standstill. In a voice he must have thought lower than it was, he said, "I've had it with you, you little shit." Every few syllables, he gave the shirt, and David, a good hard shake. "And you'd better be nice to Kayla, or I'll stick a hole in that dinosaur. I'll do it right at the seam, where nobody can tell." He gave him one last push, releasing the fabric so that David stumbled a couple of steps, astonishment on his face.

Dad nodded approvingly.

The drive through the hospital grounds was lined with crepe myrtles, at least a thousand of them, and not a single one knew it was August. Their bloom was lavish, dense fat flowers the color of a cooling sun, as if it were still June, the temperature only ninety-five or a hundred rather than one eleven. Their branches were pearl gray, smooth and shining like the inside of a shell. It must be good, I thought, for the people who stayed here, to walk under those blossoms and touch that bark, and I wondered if Lou Jean ever did. She might even now be standing under one of them, waiting for us, smiling at me the way she did when it was just the two of us in the kitchen, smiling because she was with Kayla the person; not Kayla the daughter of Phil.

Beside the truck, great-tailed grackles flew. Their wings and heads were the fiery blue-black of Mexican opals. Their calls to each other were loud, mocking, and squeaky. Like the laughter of a drunk with a bad cold. Suddenly, Charles Dale leaned hard against his door. "Stop, Phil," he said, his voice so quick and urgent that Dad stomped the brake. Charles Dale was out of the cab immediately, rushing to the nearest tree. Under its full branches he halted, hands on his hips, gazing up. "What is it?" called Dad. "What's wrong?" We craned our necks. Without answering, Charles Dale reached up and broke off a stem, so blossom-heavy that it drooped into his free hand. Cradling it like a queen's tiara, he walked back to the truck. "Thanks," he said, climbing in triumphant.

Dad's silence continued as we eased closer. The posted speed limit was twenty-five miles per hour, but our speedometer never climbed above twenty, and Dad's demeanor kept changing. One minute he fidgeted, turning the radio on then off, adjusting the rearview mirror, the side mirror. The next minute, he grew still, hands locked on the wheel, eyes ahead and jaw clenched, body sunk down into itself in a way that made him look dehydrated. The one thing he didn't do was look at me.

I had no idea what to say to Lou Jean. I wasn't even sure that I still wanted to be there. I kept thinking that Mother might be really sad right now, not just confused and sad about David and his motives, but genuinely despondent, that she might need me. And what if Lou Jean wasn't the same person? Or . . . what if she *was* the same but I'd been wrong about who she was, as wrong as my mother was about David? What if my mother was right about her? What if she'd been nice to me as a way of getting close to Dad? And what if therapy changed *all* of someone, not just the part that needed changing? There wasn't one of us who *hadn't* changed in some way, just because of our moving here. I was no longer a kid whose parents lived together. Mom was no longer someone who could flaunt having a husband. Charles Dale was no longer a kid without a father. And David was no longer cute.

"She's going to like my cookies better than that stupid flower," David told his brother.

"So what?" answered Charles Dale. "Kayla baked them."

Dad finally spoke. "Your mother might enjoy our visit more if everyone's polite." He pushed the accelerator a bit harder and settled back into his seat, as if dealing with bickering kids brought normalcy into the situation.

I tried to concentrate on the scenery. We rounded a sharp curve, and the trees stopped abruptly against a low rock wall that extended away from the road on either side. Along it grew peach and orange day lilies, with concrete benches interspersed. The benches were all occupied. People sat and talked to each other or sat solitary and gazed out at the grounds. Only one man sat alone *and* talked.

"David," said Charles Dale, "remember, it's not polite to stare."

In front of a long building of redwood and white rock, we turned right, circling the building until we came to a parking lot marked VISITORS. As if he'd parked there before, Dad headed for a spot that seemed to have no special significance, passing other, closer, available spots. He pulled in, shut off the engine, and spoke seriously to the boys, his face nervous. "Your mom's a lot better," he said, "but she may look a little different to you. Maybe a little thinner." He leaned onto the wheel so he could look around me, at David. "And she doesn't need to hear any arguments. Save them for later, okay?"

"Why do y'all tell *me* everything?" asked David. He scooted to the edge of the seat, leaning on the dash, looking past Dad's head, his face hard and impassive, still angry over the stupid dinosaur. Then his face changed, his left arm flew back and hit me, his elbow pushing into my midriff for propulsion, his right arm already reaching across Charles Dale for the door handle. "Mommy!" he screamed, and was out of the truck and running across the parking lot.

Lou Jean met him in the center of an empty parking place, dropping to hug him. "I've been watching for you," we heard her say. In the noonday sun, her gauzy dress was as white as some daytime eclipse, and I couldn't look at her. Instead, I stared at the place on the pavement where she knelt, where the fabric bunched and moved across the hot asphalt as if magnetized, its hem being soiled, melted tar already climbing it. Only when she saw Charles Dale walking toward her did she stand.

David clung to her waist. Charles Dale hugged her, then pulled back, sheepishly patting the top of her head in recognition of the fact that he was now the taller. One arm around his back, one around David's shoulders, she stood and held her boys. The hot, oily wind whipped her dress away from her knees, her hair about her face, and blew her smile across the parking lot to land on the hood of the truck. Dad put his arm around my shoulders and drew me against his side. Though he still didn't look at me, he said, "Let's go."

I followed him across the parking lot, asphalt squishy and squeaking under our shoes. His shirt was wet under the arms and down the spine, as if we'd not run the air conditioner since the last Sinclair stop. Even his head was damp. His arms, though, swung naturally at his sides, relaxed, with no more fidgeting. The grackles seemed to have followed us, were in every tree now, squawking and cackling.

Lou Jean hadn't yet looked at me. Like a woman greeting her returning war hero, she held her boys and looked straight at my father. Beside him, unseen and acknowledged, I might have been nothing more than the lame horse he'd thoughtfully climbed down from a mile back up the road.

Well, I thought, *at least I don't have to wonder what to say.*

If Dad didn't know what to say, he at least knew what to do. He leaned forward and kissed her cheek. When she reached and patted his shoulder, the sun flared on her scarred hands. Where the skin stretched tight across her palms, there were glints and flashes sharp as knife blades, and I stared at them, thinking how they must hurt, and wondering how she would use them, if she'd ever be able to cook or can. If she'd even want to.

She turned to Charles Dale. "Who said you could grow taller

than your mother?" She was laughing, and her laugh held the same rich warmth, like butterscotch kisses or melting chocolate. Just hearing it made me feel better. Then she bent to David. "And *you*. I hear you're on a new diet program." Even if her laugh wasn't for me, I wanted her to keep laughing. It sounded so normal, unaltered by all we'd been through. If she could laugh like *that*, then everything could be right again. She straightened and turned back to Dad. "You'll need to make a stop on the way home." His face, as she pushed him backward, was sober, as if he were being handed some crucial task and was required to meet the challenge with responsibility and care. When he was out of the way, she caught me in a hug every bit as fierce as the one she'd given the boys, and when she released me the skin on her hands looked brand new. Like baby skin, too tender for the sun or the wind or the heat or our eyes. She stuck one hand into a dress pocket, and I wanted her to leave it there, where it was sheltered and safe, but she pulled it out again, grabbed my own, and stuffed a folded five-dollar bill into it. "Buy jars," she said. "On your way through San Antonio, stop and buy jars. Because you *know* what we have to do the minute I get home."

Dad was a different man on the trip back. Cheerful. Grip on the steering wheel nonchalant, one hand at six o'clock, the other pulling my ponytail or thumping Charles Dale on the ear as he teased us about going into eighth grade. He was looking at me again. "Just practice for high school. That's what eighth grade is for." He asked Charles Dale if they still held the eighth grade Christmas Dance, the Valentine's Ball, and the graduation party, where he said he'd first kissed a girl. When Charles

Dale said yes, they did, and who was the girl, Dad laughed. "Nobody any of you know."

"Kayla might kiss Murray Ball," piped up David.

"Shut up, punk," said his brother.

I jerked open the glove box, grabbed the folded plastic, wedged it into the seat between Dad and me, and looked at David. "Thanks for reminding me. I'd forgotten about *my* dinosaur."

Dad's mood was so good that he only laughed. It improved even more when we turned onto our street and saw that Mother's car was gone. Dad let us out, said a quick good-bye, and backed out of the drive. At the curb, though, where he could not be blocked in by a returning vehicle, he stopped the truck, killed the engine, and called me over to the passenger window. "Are you going to be all right?" he asked. The lines around his mouth had disappeared while we were in Austin, had stayed gone all the way home, but now I could see them beginning, thin, quick strokes, fine and faint, as if someone were drawing them at this very moment, with a number 3 pencil.

"Hey, Dad?" I said. "I'm sure now."

"I'll call you every day," he said. Though his eyes were wet, the lines were growing shorter. "And you're staying with me next weekend. If your mother still hasn't taken you shopping for school, we'll go to San Antonio."

"I get to pick out all my own clothes?"

"Absolutely," he promised. "And, Kayla?" He leaned toward me, so that he had to look up into my eyes. "Remember, you have a brother."

"Yeah, I know." I raised the green plastic blob in my hand. "And Dino."

❧ 24 ❧

Climbing to the top of the mulberry tree while holding a coil of rope and a sweaty mass of plastic was harder than I'd expected it to be. My plan didn't seem as grand as it had on the ground. Halfway up, the crooks of my elbows scraped from their lock around the bark, I finally stopped and put the rope, which was really only a thin stretch of pigging string left over from my father's roping days, in my mouth. I went on, but I made no better time, because even though I now had a free hand, I kept having to stop and use it to wipe the spit, escaping past the rope and onto my chin. Thoroughly disgusted, swallowing continually, I moved slowly, wet splotches like bird droppings recording my progress up the trunk. I climbed as high as I dared, then stopped, wedged myself between two branches, and secured poor dumb Dino. With no desire to drop him, thus necessitating a trip down and, even worse, back up the tree, I very carefully draped his sad deflated body over the branch, then sat atop him. Below me, the television came on, immediately followed by the muted thunder of someone running through the house, David, no doubt, racing to flip the television channel away from whatever Charles Dale intended to watch. I listened, hoping to hear a thump, a scream, any indication that Charles Dale's earlier attitude with his brother, his apparent decision to no longer put up with the brat's behavior, was still in place. When no sound came, I leaned back against the tree trunk and took the drenched rope from my mouth.

Mother still wasn't home, and I kept wondering what she'd done after we'd left. If she'd thrown herself down on the bed and cried, brand-new black mascara smearing the company pillow-cases. Maybe she had even cried herself to sleep, slept all day, and just now gone to the church to arrange tomorrow's altar flowers. And then again, maybe she'd simply gotten dressed, made up the bed, and stormed out of the house, not sad, only angry, a scenario that seemed more likely—putting aside her husband's rejection, as quickly as she'd put the butter dish back in the refrigerator and the evening paper in the trash, and get-ting on to the more important task of making the gladioli stand proud among the carnations.

Laying one end of the rope across my hands and bringing the other up to join and wrap around it, I tried to think of times in my life, other than that day on the back porch, when I'd seen Mother cry. She hadn't cried when she'd miscarried babies, not even when she'd told me there'd be no more. And when she'd tried to "get" me a brother—or rather, Dad a son—and learned that the child would never be hers, that *he*, shock to the world, actually preferred his own mother, she still hadn't cried.

She hadn't cried the night Dad talked to Lou Jean on the phone, though she must have seen, as I did, the best part of Dad leave us, separate and change into something unrecogniz-able, something very different from what the three of us were, or had ever been, together. Something lighter and brighter, so that standing in the kitchen, under the garish and false fluorescent, he glowed like some just-born angel. No longer my familiar Dad. Not the playful Dad who tossed softballs and one-liners, not the cautious Dad who tested air and attitude before entering doorways, not the patient Dad who hated fighting and worshiped boxing. Instead, he seemed more the essence of the physical man he had been, hovering somewhere above and out of the reach of Mother's wrath. A light and lively vapor, easily and irrefutably able to enter a telephone receiver, slide through forty feet of phone line, and reappear next door, to glow in another woman's kitchen.

It was as if there was no place within Mother for sadness, all the room being taken up by anger. I looped the rope around my wrist, still trying to think of a time when I'd seen her cry. She might have cried when my grandfather died, so far in the past that I couldn't remember, but somehow I still could not picture her shedding tears, even at the death of her father. What I *could* see, what appeared in my mind, crisp and clear as one of Granddad's black-and-white photos, as solid and tangible as the branch I leaned against, was her fighting with Gran, each of them furious, insisting on having her way. In my mind, they stood on a huge map labeled THE FUNERAL, and around them the map was marked with *X*'s, signifying battles. The skirmish of how Granddad's body would be dressed. The struggle over what Gran herself should wear to the funeral. The battle over the service itself, what was appropriate, what wasn't.

The rope now ready, I laid it on my lap, freed Dino, and blew into the clear plastic mole that grew from his neck. The rope wasn't very long, and I wondered if maybe I should move to a lower branch. But his body filled sooner than I'd imagined, as if he couldn't wait to expand, and he lifted his head, raising it above my own so that I looked up at his painted red smile, which seemed so sincere and grateful. I slipped the noose over his neck.

The sun had disappeared, leaving a large scooped out bowl of red, peach, and turquoise, a reminder of itself, across the sky. I hooked Dino under my arm, stood and moved out onto a smaller branch, one that ran parallel to the ground, more visible from the house. A gust of wind came from the west, hot and dry, surprising me, bouncing the branch so hard that I sat and straddled it, hooking my feet around a crooked offshoot further down. When a car turned onto the street, I drew my feet back up, one hand clutching the limb before me, one hand clasping Dino.

I both wanted and didn't want the car to be Mother's, because I wasn't sure how I wanted her to *be* when she drove up. I wanted to see her, to know that she was all right, but if being all right meant she was angry, then I *didn't* want to see her. I didn't want her to be hurt, but I did want her to be sad, the way a normal person would be. Not as sad as Lou Jean, not so sad that she tried to hurt herself, but at least sad enough to cry, *normal* sad. The way it seemed you should be when your husband left you, when you'd messed up a whole summer for a lot of people.

I wrapped the free end of the rope around the branch, tied it in a double knot, and Dino dropped, smiling at me all the way down. When he ran out of rope, his body leveled and hung. No longer able to see his mouth, I pictured his look of shock and betrayal, the grim twist of his once-happy lips. His fat belly caught the wind and carried him out over the yard, and he twisted and turned, feet in front of and then behind him, a dance both crazed and cruel. His neck bent with each gust, the plastic crying against the rope so that I felt the first murmur of guilt.

The thought of David, though, stopped me from pulling the dinosaur up to safety. Only when the brat came out and saw him, could Dino go back to being himself, a happy plastic toy, a coercive harmless gimmick designed to make kids beg and adults buy fuel. All he had to do was walk out the back door, look up, and see the noose around Dino's neck, a knot to be proud of, fit for *Bonanza*. He had to realize that Dino, though we weren't really suited, though I was too old for him and he was too cheerful for me, was mine, that I could do anything I wanted to him. That high above David's unwelcome and demanding head, in a tree too tall for him to even *think* about climbing, Dino was all mine.

But he didn't come out. The floor vibrated no footsteps, the back door stayed closed, and the television chattered on, seemingly to itself. And Dino, as if tired of my childishness and ready for retribution, waited for the perfect wind and caught it just right. Riding it perfectly, flying so fast that I didn't see him, he slammed into me, rude and revengeful. The ridged seam of his back caught my neck, and his pointed green tail slapped my face. Its tip, quicker than reflex, dug into my open eye, and I bent my body backward, arching my spine to get away. My face banged against the trunk of the tree, its bark rougher than it looked, scraping my chin, driving a tooth into my lip, until I released my grip on the branch before me. My arms flew over my head, one trying to find the trunk, one try-

ing to push Dino away, and I lost my balance. My feet, the last
tether to the branch I straddled, came untucked, and I listed,
falling to the right, my elbow striking hard against a neighbor-
ing branch and my hand groping its way around it until finally,
I was able to secure myself, hanging on solidly. I trembled as I
held Dino the victor.

Surprise tears came, hot and painful against my scratched
eyeball. My head stuffed into the nest between the tree trunk
and the branch that had saved me, I let the tears slide off my
face and onto the dusty gray bark, filling the place where only a
moment before, there had been nothing but resolve, every bit
as dry and unyielding as my mother's.

Mother pulled into the drive, and I wiped my eyes to watch
her. She got out, reached into the backseat, and removed a
cardboard box and two small grocery bags. Only when she
kicked the door shut and caught the heel of her shoe in her
skirt did I notice what she wore. A navy blue shirtdress. Dotted
swiss, white bow at the neck, belt of matching fabric, and a
hemline halfway between her knees and ankles. I hadn't seen it
since we'd left Cameron.

She walked toward the house, shoulders hunkered around
her cargo, and her face wasn't sad, but it wasn't angry either.
Instead, curiously, it was expectant, cautious, and a little worried. As if she carried something important but disquieting,
something she wasn't quite sure about. She kicked the toe of
her shoe into the frame of the screen, making it bang so that
Charles Dale came and opened it for her.

I sat torn between waiting for David to come out and following Mother into the house. I wanted to know what could
be bought at a grocery store that could make my mother look

so nervous. When curiosity won out, I let Dino resume his dance, waiting to drop him until the wind was still. From the house came the clink of glass as Mother unpacked the bags. As I climbed down, I could see her through the back door, and her dress looked good on her. Old-ladyish. Familiar. The kind of dress she looked *herself* in. The kind she'd have tried to get my grandmother to wear to Granddad's funeral. I imagined Mother and Gran in Gran's kitchen, unpacking not groceries but casseroles, funeral food brought by neighbors. "I'm not old enough for that dress, Sarah Jo, but you are. You go ahead and wear it."

Moving back down the tree much faster than I'd climbed up, I could almost hear their words, loud and angry, until Mother surprised me. Stopping midsentence, midinsult, in the middle of our kitchen, which had somehow become Gran's kitchen, she looked down at her dress and began humming, the hum changing to words when she came to the chorus, "Then sings my soul, my Savior God to Thee." And as Gran turned away, hands empty, moving toward sandwich platters and relish trays, I heard her response, "And no goddamned maudlin hymn at the graveside."

Mother whirled toward her, ready to recite her usual words, take her usual role in the argument, but once more stopped and looked down at her dress. As if all alone, thoughtfully, reflectively, she dipped one hand to the fabric and skimmed the folds of dotted swiss. Her face was peaceful, her body at home in that dress, as if folds and dots and yards of fabric extending almost to her feet were enough to make her safe. A pleated and plain defense against the outrageousness that was her mother, the wit and wisdom that was my grandmother. She kept singing.

Behind her, I heard a familiar voice on the television, "You folks go on home now. Show's over." Calm, sensible words, the kind I imagined my grandfather might have used, living with those two. Then I heard the television, *our* television, switch off, heard thuds across our floor, David headed toward the kitchen. With the words of Ben Cartwright playing in my head, I climbed, once more, up the tree, and untied the damn dinosaur.

～ 25 ～

The pickle crock was the first thing I saw. Like a toddler in the middle of an intersection, out of place and ill at ease, it sat on our kitchen table. Mother, still in her dress, still unpacking bags, was so engrossed that she didn't hear me enter. She hummed as she worked, something so slow and hymnlike that I looked around the kitchen, even peeked through the door into the dining room, for the Gran I knew I'd only imagined. "What is this doing here?" I asked.

She answered without turning around, her voice pitched higher than usual. "I thought we'd do them together." From the sack, she removed a brand-new pair of canning tongs, a funnel, and a jar lifter. "I hope I got everything we need." Her voice was still squeaky.

I touched my pocket, scraping my finger against the outline of the bill behind it. "Lou Jean and I are going to do them. She gave me money to buy jars." Mother didn't answer, as if folding an empty paper bag and stuffing it into a drawer with countless others required her total concentration.

I sat down at the table and rubbed the crock, its cool white glaze comforting to my scraped palm. "I said we can't do them. How did you get this heavy thing over here, anyway?"

She walked across the kitchen, full skirt before her like some heralding trumpet, and sat down in the chair closest to mine. "Lou Jean won't be home for at least a few more days. These pickles will be ruined by then." Her voice was lower, and she kept her eyes on the dotted swiss between us.

I lifted the lid from the crock, and the smell of pickles filled the room. At the edges of the jar, away from the center, some of the pickles were a different color, a sign that they were getting soft. But the ones in the center looked fine. Mother leaned over the table and studied the inside of the crock, as if she'd been interested in canning her entire life. "What's the matter with you?" I asked. "You're acting weird. And why are you wearing *that* dress?"

Quickly she sat back, as if caught somewhere she shouldn't be, doing something she shouldn't do. Her hands fell into her lap, as if suddenly too heavy for her arms, then began moving in tandem over the fabric of her dress, brushing the tiny white nubs over and over. Though they moved at the same pace, their actions seemed different. One moved gently, lightly, as if it meant to soothe the material, but the other seemed to press against the cloth, almost to cling, as if it needed something, as if drawing strength. And only when I thought she hadn't heard my question, that she was too caught up in her own thoughts, in the pattern and feel of her dress, when I was about to ask again, in a voice loud enough to penetrate her homage, did she respond. Her voice was almost a whisper. "Because it suits me."

I thought about how right she was, and how hard it was to just *let* her be right. I knew I *could* let her, that all I had to do was say nothing. Out in the yard, watching her through the door, it had been so much easier to accept her difference, allow it. Now, with the almost-ruined pickles where they never should have been, on our chrome-and-Formica table instead of Lou Jean's ancient oak one, it wasn't so easy. "I guess," I finally allowed. "But you shouldn't have just gone into her house and gotten the crock. How'd you carry it, anyway?"

When again, it seemed she wouldn't answer, I got up and went to the refrigerator, poured a glass of milk, and started out of the room. "Kayla." Her voice was so low that merely turning toward her wasn't enough. I had to quit drinking, to stand very still, to hear. "I know Lou Jean wants to can the pickles with you. And I know you want to do with them her. But Gran doesn't think these pickles will last until then. And *she* thinks we should do them together. *And* she helped me carry the crock."

She watched me drink my milk, and I watched her watching me, saw her eyes take in my scraped neck and cheek, the eyes and lip I knew must be red. And she must have seen my own eyes register the redness of hers, the puffiness that matched mine. But she didn't say anything. She didn't protest or deny, made no effort at excuse. And she didn't make a fuss about how I looked, didn't ask what had happened. If she assumed, as she normally did, that I'd been doing something I shouldn't have been doing, she didn't mention it. She didn't ask why I'd been crying, and I didn't ask why *she* had. We simply stared at each other, almost as if accepting that scrapes and red eyes were personal matters, that we had no claim to the other's explanation.

I finished my milk, set the glass in the sink, and ran water in it. "Okay," I said, and Mother's hands quit their fidgeting.

❧ 26 ❧

It was well past dark when we finished. The crock, clean, scoured with baking soda to remove the smell, was back in Lou Jean's pantry, along with a dozen quarts of pickles. On our own table sat four more jars, one for Gran, one for Carmen, one for Dad, one for us. I stood at the table, drying the *Ball Guide to Canning*, which we'd retrieved from Lou Jean's when it became apparent we needed help and which had somehow taken a direct splash of boiling water. Mother, in her housecoat, stood at the sink soaking the dotted swiss in cold water, terrified that the brine she'd spilled down the skirt would bleach the color and leave a stain in the shape of Louisiana. "It's just saltwater and spices," I said for the fifth time. "No vinegar."

Her only answer was lifting the dress and giving it another slosh. From the corner of my eye, I saw David slip into the kitchen. He'd been in three times already, his gaze on the dinosaur that I'd left by the back door. With each trip, he'd eyed the beast, and me, more nervously. I knew he was gauging my mood, watching me as I worked, as if something in the way I lifted the steaming sterilized jars, the way I packed them full of pickles, or the way I lowered them, capped and shining, into the canner, might tell him just how much chance he had. And each time, he'd gone back to the living room, awaiting a better chance. Now, though, the hour close to bedtime, he eyed the clock as if he knew what it said. His desperation growing with each click of the second hand, he finally forgot all caution. "Kayla," he asked, stepping close to me, his upturned face artfully dismal, "are you really going to keep that Dino?"

He smelled sticky, like the Trix he'd eaten in front of the television, the Baby Ruths, his own, and half of his brother's, that I knew he'd had for dessert. "Yes, David, I am." He tuned up to cry, immediately looking to Mother for support. When she didn't look up from her wet dress, he left the room, slamming his crossed arms against his chest to clear up any doubt about his mood, casting significant parting looks over his shoulder: to me, outrage; to Mother, betrayal.

Only a few minutes later, he was back, a wad of construction paper in one hand, crayons in the other. He climbed into a chair at the end of the table and began drawing the devil. Triangular head, triangular eyes, triangular horns. A long forked tail. "How do you spell your name, Kayla?" he asked, and I laughed out loud. I spelled it for him as I dried dishes. Mother, finally satisfied that her dress was saved, lifted and wrung, then carried it, still dripping, to the laundry room. Passing David, she patted his head with one wet hand, a caress both absentminded and placating. A moment later, we heard the washing machine begin to fill.

"Are you tired, little boy?" Mother said on her way back through the kitchen. "Do you want me to rock you?"

He laid his head on one hand, a woebegone pose, pulling

out all the stops now that he had her attention. "I just wish I had that Dino," he said, voice pitiful, eyes on his listless sketching. I gave Mother a don't-even-think-about-it look, and she patted his head again, then went to her bedroom.

I heard Charles Dale switch off the television and go to bed and, still, I just sat there, watching David, who now scribbled alphabet letters, his sketch of me placed pointedly in the center of the table. "You should go to bed," I told him.

For answer, he began calling out the letters as he wrote them. "D . . . A . . . M . . ."

"You should have gotten your butt busted for that. And *I* almost got blamed for it."

Mother walked back in, her face free of makeup and shiny with cold cream. She sat down with us, planted her elbows on the table, and rested her chin on her quiet hands. I pointed at David's writing, the same three letters over and over, and she sat up straight and opened her mouth, but David shut her up. As he made the *D* and the *A,* he said softly but clearly, in a singsong, an upbeat, like a question, "David?" Then he made the *M* and, just as clearly, with a downbeat, sang the answer to his question, "Mommy."

I watched him repeat the process four times, feeling sadder, guiltier, each time. I was at the point of picking up a crayon and showing him how to write the complete words, almost the point of getting out of the chair and handing him the dinosaur, when I realized Mother was gone.

I found her in her chair, staring out the window. Through that entire summer, through new makeup and new wardrobe, through mental breakdowns and marriage breakups, through my growing as tall as she and Charles Dale growing taller than

Lou Jean, and no one buying any school clothes, she had returned to that chair over and over. And I still didn't know why. I still didn't know what Lou Jean had that Mother could want so badly. Bad enough to sit hour after hour and stare. I no longer believed it was Charles Dale. I never had believed it was David. And, somehow, I didn't think it was Dad.

The living room was silent. In late-night darkness, it seemed asleep, and its slumber was comforting. With the other rooms still confused, a child who belonged in another house sleeping in the guest room, another child who didn't belong sitting alone in the kitchen, scrawling poorly spelled love letters to his sick mother, with my parents' bedroom empty and Dad not even in the house, the living-room normalcy was solace.

Mother's knees were drawn up, tucked to the side against one arm of the chair, her feet pressed against the other arm. The way she looked made me nervous. Wedged in and grim, as if prepared for something unknown and frightening but inevitable. An astronaut, strapped into a rocket seat. An inmate, strapped into Old Sparky. She took a deep preparatory breath and let it out. "Just once," she said, so that I still struggled to hear her words. "Just once, I wish someone would choose me over her."

I plopped down on the sofa, wanting to comfort her, wanting to tell her that I preferred her, that given the choice, I'd have picked her any old day. The cushions gave off a comforting scent of air freshener, dust, and something sweet. I wanted to bury myself in them, to sink farther and farther until I was as recumbent as Thad Howard's father. Across the room, Mother was motionless. She'd drawn her legs up into the chair and was curled onto one side now, in a position that was fetal except for her head, tilted up to rest on the chair arm, her eyes level with the window.

"I . . . " I started. Mother didn't move. I tried to say the words in my mind—*I choose you*—but I couldn't even imagine them without seeing Mother's skeptical gaze returning to the room. Standing up, abandoning the hope of late-night solitude and television blue light, I returned to my room, dug under the clothes in my drawer, and pulled out the homecoming picture. Then I went back to Mother, switched on the pole lamp beside her chair, and balanced the photo on her canted knees.

❦ 27 ❦

"There sits my daughter," said Gran, "the saddest of sads." From my aluminum aerie, Mother looked anything but sad. Three rows from the bottom bleacher, she looked radiant, expectant, like a teenager before her first date, rather than a grown woman whose best prospect for fun was serving punch and cookies in a church basement. Sandwiched between two women twice her age and weight, she turned her head back and forth, like some curious bird, listening to one and then the other. Now and then, she laughed or offered her own comment. In her lap was her handbag. Resting against it was a notepad on which she occasionally scribbled, last-minute reminders, probably, for the big youth fellowship after tonight's game.

"She doesn't look sad to me," I said.

Gran continued her scrutiny. "I don't mean sad in an unhappy way. I mean pathetic. Unexplainable. She hangs out with women who've been dull their entire lives and tries to be just like them. Why does she *want* to be dull?"

"Maybe to be the opposite of you." Gran's hand came down to clamp my knee in a horse-eating-corn way. "And me—and *me*," I added. Twisting away from her and toward the safety of Carmen, I examined Mother's dress. New, selected especially for tonight, I was sure, something you'd find at Chatham's Department Store rather than Teens and Queens. A subdued and matronly green, it fit her. She looked like a woman who hadn't worn a sundress since kindergarten. "She doesn't look so bad," I said.

She gave me a look of mock disappointment. "And you were showing such promise." She jumped up simultaneously with Charles Dale, who sat on the other side of her. The crowd groaned, Gran's groan loudest, and I stood too. Carmen, so short that she knew standing was useless, remained in her seat and pulled on my arm. "What is it? What happened?"

Gran sat down, slapping her rolled-up program against her leg. Her voice was disgusted. "We fumbled. On our own thirty. God, I hate rebuilding years." I stood as long as I dared, nervous, scanning the admission gate for the twentieth time. Her eyes diligently on the field, as if it were her job to make sure the offensive team came off the field and the defensive team ran on, Gran asked Carmen, "When is that boy of yours going to get here? We need somebody who can hold on to the ball—I don't care if he *is* thirty-three years old. And Lou Jean could have brought her tail along. We could use the support."

Lou Jean had been home from the hospital for three weeks, a time we'd all spent getting used to things. She was getting used to washing her hands no more than ten times a day, the amount allotted her by the psychiatrist. I was getting used to a new school and new living arrangements.

This was my weekend with Gran. The boys were staying at

Carmen's house, part of a plan Gran and Carmen hatched while Lou Jean was in the hospital. Their concern was that Lou Jean needed free time, opportunities to get out of the house. As Gran put it, "Canning and cooking ain't a social life." Their plan was for the boys to stay with Carmen on the same weekend that I stayed with Gran, and they had sprung it on Lou Jean her first day home. The fact that their plan allowed for Dad and Lou Jean to be free on the same weekends had occurred to me, but I'd yet to see any evidence that they were spending time together.

Gran's yell was deafening, and she stomped on my foot as she leaped up again. "Time out, Coach!" Then in a softer voice, as she plopped back into her seat, "Jesus Christ, what's the man thinking?" She was aggravated, seemed to feel guilty, even, because she'd been late to the game, as if the Panthers couldn't play without her, as if their present poor performance was a result of her missing the kickoff. We'd made it to our seats ten minutes into the game, delayed by David, who had refused to go to the bathroom before we'd left Carmen's house, then had realized his mistake halfway to the stadium. Since coming home, Lou Jean had stringently enforced the cheese ban, so his bathroom habits were more consistent. There were still times, though, when he misinterpreted or refused to heed his body's signals, putting us all in jeopardy. Being late to the game was just one of the ways in which we all suffered.

Carmen, beside me, was nervous. She held out her hand, measuring the mist that had begun falling soon after we sat down. "I hope those roads aren't slick," she said for the fourth time. "I-35 will be packed between Dallas and Austin."

On the other side of her, David extended his tongue, catching the mist in his own way. On the other side of him sat an
empty Panthers stadium seat, its back folded down, to keep it
dry for Joey.

"Relax," Gran told her. "He's long past Austin by now."
Once more, I looked at the admission gate, knowing I'd recognize him and wanting him to hurry. Below me, Mother still
chatted, uselessly patting the frizz brought on by the rain. I
was afraid Joey wouldn't get here before halftime, when I had
to leave. The band members, evidently confident that the rain
would grow no heavier, were already putting on their hats, getting their instruments ready.

"It's a long way from Dallas," said Charles Dale, as if reading my thoughts. "He might not even make it before the
game's over." He suddenly jumped up, Gran following as if
tied to him, both of them screaming as the other team fumbled
and *we* recovered. When Gran sat back down, she wiped her
brow in an exaggerated way. "Thank God it's Hondo. They
lost all their seniors too."

It seemed to me that the whole first half had been this way,
one team losing the ball to the other, offense running onto the
field, defense running off, nobody scoring. And me trying to
watch both the game and the gate, determined to see Joey
when he came in, and most important, when he saw my
mother. Where she sat, two seats from the center aisle, he'd
walk right past her as he climbed the stairs to us. They couldn't
miss each other.

Mother had never mentioned the photo. About three days
after I'd laid it in her lap, I had casually asked, "Did Joey like
you in high school?" to which I'd received a curt "He was my

friend, Kayla. People can be friends without something else having to be involved." Of course, she was sitting in her chair at the time, and the quick flick of her eyes out the window made it clear what she meant by "something else." There was no further mention of him, but the following Saturday, when we'd gone to San Antonio to buy school clothes, Mother had wandered off to the Joske's perfume counter, and now a small bottle of Youth Dew sat in the bathroom cabinet. I had no idea if she'd bought it for him, whether she even knew he was coming tonight. But one thing was for sure. Although Gran's observations of her daughter were normally bull's-eye accurate, she was wrong in thinking her dull. Mother had to be the only woman in the stadium wearing a grandma dress and Youth Dew.

Probably, she had no interest in him. Being Mother, she probably believed that further relationships with men were off-limits. That because she was an almost-divorcée, her reputation and maybe even her soul were in jeopardy, and that their preservation was far more important than her social life. Still, I wanted to see the moment when she saw Joey and he saw her.

"What position did Phil play?" Charles Dale asked Gran. He pointed to the chain-link fence circling the field, which seemed to be the place where the young men in town stood to view the game. Dad stood with the others, wearing boots and a new silver-belly Resistol, talking and laughing, as if having once appeared on the field, he now was content to take his place beside it, to dress like the other men and compare, deride, and cheer the boys they watched. He reached up to brush the mist away from his brim. "He played wide receiver," said Gran. "And he'd better cover up that high-dollar hat."

"I wish *I* had a hat like that," said Charles Dale.

"If we win this game," promised Gran, "I'll *buy* you a hat like that."

David jumped down from his seat "Hey," he complained, his usual good manners in evidence. "What are you going to buy me?"

Gran gave him a look that put him back in his seat. "New underwear."

I was afraid that Joey wouldn't make it into the stadium before halftime. In sixth-period math today, I'd watched as a note was passed across three rows. When it landed on my desk, I'd read the name to see which direction to send it next and found it addressed to me. It was sent by Amanda Hughes, who shared a locker with me, and it said: "Murray wants you to meet him at the concession stand at halftime. Nod if it's okay." While the teacher was turned to the blackboard, I had nodded, not once but twice, to make sure anyone watching didn't miss it.

"It's almost halftime, Kayla," Charles Dale said, his voice so meaningful that Gran took her eyes off the game. For the role of matchmaker, he was running Amanda a close race.

"What's the deal about halftime?" asked Gran.

"Kayla's going to meet Murray Ball," said David. How did the kid know all this stuff?

"A boyfriend already, Kaylita?" asked Carmen. I glared at David, then turned to answer Carmen and saw, instead, her son. Even from across the field, he was easy to recognize, his black hair combed back and smooth, long enough to touch his shirt collar, and in the field lights it shone the way it did in the photo. He stood at the admission table, talking to the man handing out tickets. Only twenty-three seconds remained in the half.

"Kayla, we gotta go." Charles Dale stood and walked in front of us, slapping me on the knee as he passed. Joey was walking again, but in the wrong direction, away from us.

"Have fun," said Gran. She and Carmen still hadn't seen Joey, who stood outside the cinderblock restrooms until a little girl wearing a white shirt came out of the ladies' room and walked up to him.

"Kayla, come on," said Charles Dale, reaching for my arm. The girl stood on tiptoe, then reached up and straightened Joey's collar, and the movement raised her breasts until they brushed his chest. She was tiny, not much larger than Carmen, but she wasn't a little girl after all. I let Charles Dale pull me down the steps until I could no longer see Joey's head.

Behind us, David yelled, "Yeah, Kayla, hurry up. Murray wants to kiss you." And for the twentieth time, I regretted giving him that stupid Dino.

Mother waved as we passed. Her hair had at least frizzed in the right places, but she hadn't bothered to touch up her lipstick and I smelled no perfume. Leave it to her to wear only a saintly amount, so little that only an angel sitting on her shoulder could smell it. I bet the woman with Joey wore plenty of perfume.

On the walkway below Mother, I told Charles Dale to wait, and I squatted, retying my perfectly tied shoe. I could see Joey again. He was in the bleachers now, and he moved behind us, along the same walkway we traveled. He was less than three feet from the center aisle, four feet from Mother, the woman with him too tiny to be seen.

"Come on," said Charles Dale, pulling me upright again. Over his shoulder I saw Murray in front of the concession. He wore a pale pink oxford cloth button-down that made his eyes even bluer. Between him and us was Amanda, a serious smile on her face, delighted but sober with regard to her duties.

As we reached the last set of steps down to the concession, I turned once more and saw Joey reach that center aisle, take the first and then the second step. He turned his head to the left, looking down at someone in a seat close to the aisle. It had to be Mother he looked at, but just then Charles Dale dropped my hand and yelled, Granlike, "Oh, crap!" I craned my neck and saw the flash of one pearl earring as Mother's head tilted, maybe toward Joey and maybe only toward the woman on her left. Then I saw only a hundred gaping mouths as the crowd exploded, standing simultaneously as if joined at the hips, leaning out, almost over our heads.

Charles Dale's voice was disgusted. "Shoot. We lost it again. And they're within field-goal range." I strained on my tiptoes, the only person in the stadium looking *away* from the play, and saw Joey, now high in the bleachers. The woman was invisible. As he leaned down to hug his mother, I saw him glance over his shoulder, maybe looking at the field, where the poor old Panthers, their shoulders slumped but determined, had lined up in front of their own goal, or maybe looking no further than the third row of seats.

Just as the Hondo kicker sent the ball into the air, I saw Murray see me, and at the same time, I heard Gran's voice high above, her greeting to Joey, "About time you got here. Your mother was ready to send out a posse." And as the ball sailed dead even through the uprights, as if there was no place else it could have gone: "So you're the reason he's late. Well, I hope to hell you like football."

After all of the nights Lou Jean's house had sat dark, it felt great to see every light on. Gran and I had rushed there to pick up more shorts and underwear for David. "Insurance," Gran called it. Carmen and the boys had ridden home from the game with Joey and White Shirt. "Let's get *in* and *out* of here," said Gran, as we walked across the porch. "I want to get to Carmen's before they all eat the cake."

I shared her sense of hurry, though for a different reason. Murray was spending the night with Charles Dale. We had spent the second half of the game talking, creating an island in the stream of people going to and from the concession stand, and after only thirty minutes, I was ready to see him again. But once inside the house, we couldn't find Lou Jean. "Where *is* she?" asked Gran, roaming the rooms and flipping lights off. "Good thing she's rich." I was about to remind her that she herself kept the air-conditioning running in rooms she never used, when through the kitchen door I saw Lou Jean. In a lawn chair at the edge of the garden, where Bermuda grass changed to bare soil, she sat with her back to the house. Her hand absentmindedly brushed the browning leaves of the tomato plant beside her. I walked out the back door and across the lawn.

She wore a matching skirt and peasant blouse. Black and silky, the outfit was ringed with wide satin ribbons of every color. The full skirt overflowed the chair and spilled to her ankles, and below it, her toes, nails freshly painted, peeked from a pair of Mexican sandals. The stadium lights still burned, giving the yard a dim glow. When she reached up and pushed me into another chair, ribbons dangled from the sleeve of Lou Jean's blouse, draped my hand, and wafted perfume.

From indoors, we could hear Gran still tromping through the house. I made a move to get out of my chair, to go and tell her where we were, but Lou Jean stopped me. Her voice was very quiet. "She'll wander out here eventually."

Something about this wasn't good. It was too much like the nights earlier in the summer, when she sat solitary in the darkness, accompanied only by the endless drone of dryflies and the occasional lonely owl. "Why are you sitting out here in the dark?" I tried to make my voice teasing and playful. Despite the fact that she had seemed fine, that not once since she'd returned had she failed to pass my daily scrutiny, it would be a long time before I didn't worry.

Her failure to answer now concerned me, as did the fact that she wouldn't look at me. Her head lifted and her gaze traveled above mine, across the alley, over the tree tops and *away*, past even the stadium lights, as if she could see something way out in the country. We could hear the car horns of people still leaving the game, the celebratory honks of the Hondo fans.

I tried again. "Want to go with us to Carmen's? She made an orange-slice cake. Gran says it won't be as good as yours, so she'll probably eat only three pieces."

Lou Jean shook her head, sighed deeply, and finally looked at me. "What I'm doing out here in the dark," she said slowly, "is thinking."

"What about?"

"About what's right." Her gaze never left mine, so that when she said the next part, I wondered if I'd done something. "And about what's wrong. About being very careful not to hurt people you care about." She kept staring at me, harder than she had that first time we'd sat at her big oak table, when she'd gazed at me as if what I had to say at that moment was more important than *anything*, when she'd said, *So. Tell me about Kayla.*

The sound of the cars was spreading, from the stadium and out through the streets, as people made their way home or to parties, my mother to the church, my dad to the river camp. Of course, I was bothered by the fact that I might have hurt Lou Jean in some way, but more than that, I was confused. I would *never* hurt her, I never willingly did anything but good things for her. And Lou Jean, whose home was a haven of few rules and relaxed behavior, was not easily offended. *What* could I have done?

Behind her, the kitchen light flipped off and Gran sailed down the steps and toward us. "You might let somebody know," she called. She flounced up and jerked me out of the chair, plopped down into it, and pulled me onto her lap. "What are you two in such deep meaningful conversation about?" Through all the hubbub, as I rose and fell, was jostled and rearranged to facilitate Gran's comfort, Lou Jean kept her eyes fixed on mine, her smile tiny and nervous, but *there*, so that by the time I was seated again, Gran's strong arms squeezing the air from my middle, I knew that I wasn't the one Lou Jean thought capable of causing hurt.

"So." Gran eyed Lou Jean's outfit. "You've joined the Ballet Folkórico?"

No one said anything. "You coming with us to Carmen's?" Still, Lou Jean didn't answer, and as the stadium lights popped off, one by one, I realized she was waiting for me.

Before the last one went out, in what I hoped was enough light for Lou Jean to know my smile was for her, I said, "She's putting up the last of the tomatoes."

Gran, of course, was indignant. "At ten o'clock on a Friday night?"

Lou Jean and I both nodded, and Gran responded as only *she* would to a woman who'd just come home from a psychiatric hospital: "You are one sick human."

Gran and I were in the car, down the street, and into the melee before I realized that Gran's smart comment had covered real concern. A carload of teenagers pulled out in front of us and she berated her closed window. "Watch out, you little dumbasses!" When the car sped away from us, she still muttered. "Friday night, and she gets all dressed up to sit in the dark." As we entered a particularly raucous intersection, Gran added our horn to the chaos. "Why don't all you idiots go home? Canning tomatoes, my rear."

We passed the First Baptist Church, where Mother's car sat in the parking lot, surrounded by old-lady Oldsmobiles and matronly Mercuries. Despite all my attempts to change things, Mother was a single woman with no foreseeable chance for a date. Realizing that, I felt a slight pang of something. Not loss or loneliness, and not exactly nostalgia. More a sense of the sadness we *should* feel, she and Dad and I, as we let go of *us,* of our family the way it had been, in order to cling to the way we were going to be.

"I can't believe she's all dressed up and sitting in the dark." We passed the Dairy Queen and then Beto's Bar, the neon colors discoloring Gran's face and worsening the worried set of her mouth. "Did she say anything to you?"

Though I felt guilty, I shook my head no, staring fixedly at the red dash lights. A tiny insect, a beetle or ladybug, crawled across the speedometer, moving from the 20 to the 30, trying to find its way to the glow. I wondered if Lou Jean had left her house yet.

Odd, how so much could center on one woman. Mother, though she'd never see it that way, had let go of our family for nothing more than the chance to one-up her old rival. To settle some ancient competition that mattered to no one but her. And though I knew I *should* be sad, had spent much of the summer sad, at this particular moment I couldn't *feel* the sadness, because after all was said and done, Dad's leaving, our combined but separate attempts to bring him home, our ferocious battles, tonight Mother was at the church, and there she'd be tomorrow and Sunday. Arranging flowers. Decorating altars. Offering soda and scripture and impromptu sermons on celibacy. All the things that I knew and recognized in her. All the things that made her my mother.

She probably believed that Dad had let go of our family for a chance with Lou Jean, but I wasn't sure. Even though at that moment he was at the river, pouring wine or dusting the coffee table or brushing his teeth or his hair, doing whatever men do to prepare for their first date in fifteen years, there had to be more to his leaving. On three occasions: the night he'd talked to her on the phone, the morning she'd left for the hospital, and the day he'd taken us to Austin, I had seen his reaction to Lou Jean. And, yes, each time, he changed, became a man secure, strong, at peace. How could he not want to be with her?

But in the weeks since he'd left, I had seen him probably twenty times without her. And he seemed just as fully at peace without her as with her. Every line was gone from his mouth. His youthful garments, his jeans and tennis shoes and ball gloves and Dairy Queen bags, fit his face better than they ever had.

And I? I was both like my parents and different from them. With my patent lie to Gran, "She's canning the last of the tomatoes," I too had laid down our family and the last tiny hope to go back to the way we had been. Not for peace of mind, as my father had, and not to rival Lou Jean, as my mother had, but for Lou Jean's happiness. She was no longer sitting alone in that festive black dress. She was on her way to show it off.

"I wonder if I should call her doctor." With each step of the beetle, Gran's concern grew. I'd have to tell her as soon as we reached Carmen's house. If she continued this worrying, their evening would be ruined. The two of them would huddle in the kitchen, whispering, fretting, and pasting on brave smiles when one of us wandered in. They would consume no cake, and after waiting so long for Joey's visit, Carmen would not be able to enjoy it.

In a normal family, at this moment, a kid would be sad that her dad had a date. She would resist it no matter how much she cared for the woman. She certainly wouldn't have lied to make it possible. And in a normal family the dad, not the date, would be the one to tell the kid, to seek her understanding. But our family was no longer normal, if in fact it ever had been. So it made perfect sense, and was only a *little* sad, that Lou Jean was the one to tell me, just as it made sense that the house she now traveled to, the house where my father lived, belonged to his mother-in-law.

But I kept thinking I *should* be sad, that it should upset me to think of them there together, to think of my dad kissing a woman other than my mother, to think that someday he might even marry her. The boys, then, and not *I*, would live with him. Maybe I was just putting it off. Maybe the sadness was going to hit me later, at the most embarrassing moment, when I was in the school cafeteria eating Wednesday's enchiladas or Friday's fish. Or in Spanish class or the locker room. Or when I was with Murray.

I glanced guiltily at Gran's sad face, thinking that in a normal family a kid wouldn't wait even a few miles to tell her beloved grandmother something that would ease her worry.

I'd probably break down and cry when the sadness hit me, embarrass myself, change Murray's mind about liking me. It would be fitting punishment for how I was punishing Gran. The minute we got to Carmen's, before we even got out of the car, I would tell her. I wouldn't wait a moment longer.

I would tell her as soon as she parked the car, and then I would go in and eat cake and talk to Murray and Charles Dale and Joey. I'd be very nice to White Shirt to make up for how I was treating Gran. But until then, until we made it through this traffic and across town, I would keep my mouth shut. Because for the first time all summer and for the next fifteen minutes, I knew something that someone else didn't. And there was *no* sadness in that.

South of
Reason

Cindy Eppes

A Readers Club Guide

ABOUT THIS GUIDE

The suggested questions are intended to help your reading
group find new and interesting angles and topics for
discussion for Cindy Eppes' *South of Reason*. We
hope that these ideas will enrich your
conversation and increase your
enjoyment of the book.

For a complete listing of our Readers Club
Guides, or to read the guides online, visit
http://www.SimonSays.com/reading/guides

A Conversation with Cindy Eppes:

Q: Where did the inspiration for *South of Reason* come from? Are there any other writers you looked to for guidance? What prompted you to tell this story in particular?

A: My husband and I were driving west on I-10 from San Antonio toward El Paso. Somewhere between Junction and Sonora was a wooden sign hanging on a fence. The sign read *Goat's Milk Soap Very Mild*. I began thinking about who would need such a mild soap. Many people enjoy it, but who would actually *need* it? What came to mind was a middle-aged woman who bought the soap for her elderly mother who washed her hand too much. But when we returned from our trip and I sat down to write the story, the narrator had changed. Who then told the story was a thirteen-year-old girl who was concerned about her beautiful, kind, and enchanting neighbor who also suffered from a hand-washing compulsion. I looked at what Alice McDermott had done with child narrators, at *To Kill a Mockingbird,* of course, and also at the child narrator that Richard Russo created in *The Risk Pool.* I was prompted to tell this story simply by the voice of Kayla. It was believable, and fun to follow.

Q: How long have you been working on *South of Reason*? Have you explored the issues in the book in any other stories or unpublished novels?

A: I worked on *South of Reason* for four years. The issue of "family" that is not joined by blood but by desire to spend time together is one I continue to explore. The novel I am now working on holds the same issues.

Q: You must have been fairly nervous about publishing your first novel. Have you been pleased with the reader's reactions to your book? What did your family think of the novel? Have any of your friends recognized themselves in your work?

A: Reader's reactions have been both gratifying and mystifying, because, as a first-time author, it is still amazing to me that people *read* my book. My family all liked it, even my brother, whose taste normally runs to fiction with more blown-up cars and bodies in the street. None of my friends have recognized themselves in the book, but they've recognized the places where we grew up. I consider myself very fortunate to still be close to friends I grew up with, people who were at my earliest birthday parties. And we still gather at the river, all of us floating along on somebody's barge until we stop and everyone jumps in. We fish, barbecue, and tell stories, just as we did as kids, and I think they couldn't help but recognize if not the exact places, places very much like the places we all love.

Q: **The novel takes place in your home state of Texas. Do you feel you got to know your home better by writing this novel? What aspects of Texas were most important to the characters in the novel, and which aspects did you feel were most important to convey to people who haven't lived there before?**

A: I didn't get to know my home better, but I got to *be* in my home, at least in my head, while I wrote it. I grew up in the brush country of south Texas. I now live in east Texas, a very beautiful place, but I do miss the mesquite and prickly pear world. Writing the novel let me "be" there every day. I think the characters in the novel show an appreciation for the outside world, the natural environment in which they live. A lot of the book takes place out of doors, and I wanted to convey that sense of a world that can be so hot and dry it seems hostile but is so beautiful that people stay out in it as much as possible. I also wanted to convey the culture of that part of the world, which is in America, is part of Texas, but is so close to Mexico that sometimes it feels that a new culture is formed, a blend of the two. Call me sentimental, but I think the place is special, and I hope the reader gets a glimpse of it.

Q: **Gran has a lively and spirited personality. How did you develop the material you used to characterize her? Have** you known anyone who inspired you to create Gran? Do her personality traits serve a purpose within the novel? Is she a role model?

A: The material to characterize Gran came just as the material to characterize Kayla, Lou Jean, and all the others, by daily work and then rework, but the inspiration came from my grandmother and great aunt. The two of them lived with my great uncle, sometimes harmoniously, most of the time not, but they always had fun. The two were very different, my grandmother was very small but so direct. She could take charge of an out-of-control moment in a heartbeat. My aunt was taller, very irreverent. In many ways, they were like Gran and Carmen. Writing the scenes where the two of them argue and laugh together was like being home again. I think Gran has good sense, despite all her playfulness and maybe *because* of all her playfulness. She diffuses intense situations with her humor, and what she does in the scenes, she does in the novel. A book that deals with obsessive-compulsive disorder, abortion, family disintegration could easily be depressing and boring, but Gran perks things up. I think Gran is a role model. She is a leader. On the other hand, she isn't perfect.

Q: In chapter 15, Gran tells Kayla, "You know, there's always a reason why people do the things they do." Do you believe this is true? How did you determine your characters' motivations? Do you feel that understanding their motivations is key to a deeper understanding of the novel?

A: I do think there has to be a motivation for what we all do, although learning this in writing was difficult. I tend to begin stories with a place. If I can see a place and I want to *be* in that place, I begin a story. Then I see the people who are in it. Then I see the people do something, a plot begins. And then *finally* I begin to think of motivation, *why* these people are doing what they're doing. If we as readers don't understand the motivations of a character, how can that character be believable? I think we have to understand motivation in order to "attach" to the character, to care about what happens.

Q: What made you choose the title *South of Reason?* Do you feel that the title sums up an important aspect of the novel, or describes a mental place the characters inhabit?

A: The title "South of Reason" came from a line in the book. After the move to Rosalita, when Kayla's parents are acting so odd, she feels that she and they, leading the moving van, have moved to a place not intended, *south of reason*. I think the title sums up not the mental place of the characters so much as the question of what is reasonable behavior and what isn't. Is Lou Jean, who lies down on the floor with the kids but listens to every word of the children, south of reason, or is Sarah Jo, in outward appearance the model wife, mother, and Christian but inwardly so jealous that she moves across the state and next door to her husband's old lover? What is reason and where is it?

Q: To what extent does the tension between Sarah Jo and Lou Jean drive this novel? While writing the novel, did you derive energy from their dynamic relationship? To what extent did their interactions set up the pace and the plot for the other characters?

A: I think this novel was driven by a number of tensions, not only between Sarah Jo and Lou Jean, but by Sarah Jo's tension with Kayla, with Rose, with Phil, and finally with herself when she begins to realize that she can't create someone different from who she is. There is a great deal of energy that comes from two people with such a long history of competition and animosity living door-to-door.

Q: What did you think of the publishing process? Was it what you expected? Do you feel that your book changed significantly as it was edited? Did you write this book with publication in mind?

A: The publishing process was very intriguing, more complicated than I expected, all these different "parts" of the process taking care of their specific duties. The editing was delightful, in large part to my editor, who had the same vision for the book that I did. Though she'd never been to south Texas, she seemed to understand it, and the suggestions she made, I think, only enhanced the sense of place. Of course, I wrote it with the hope that some day it would be published. I can't imagine anyone who doesn't. But I also believe that you can't dwell on publication while writing. The focus *has* to be on the work, on making it better and better and struggling with it until it's the best in can be, or you're simply so exhausted that you want someone to come take it off your hands. *Then* you think about publication.

Q: When did you first begin writing? Have you always wanted to write a novel? What writing techniques did you develop over the course of writing *South of Reason*? Any advice for aspiring writers?

A: I wrote my first poem at six. With the number of written words available to the average six-year-old, you can imagine that it wasn't very good. I've read novels since I learned to read, but I can't remember when I first thought that I might write one. Maybe at graduate school when my advisors looked at the short story that became *South of Reason* and suggested I try stretching it. I was very fortunate in being accepted to the Warren Wilson MFA Program for Writers. I don't claim to be objective, I believe it must be the best in the country, and I'm really proud of being a graduate. While there, and while writing this novel, I learned the importance of revision. I can't believe that any work is what it can be until it is revised. There may be some first drafts that became great works of fiction, but I don't know of any. Revision unlocks what's going on in characters' minds, it allows the writer to come to know them, it changes what they do. It's where the *AHA!* shows up in the writing process. My advice is to commit to a certain amount of writing time each day, even if you only produce a page a day, a half a page, and then revise, revise, revise.

Reading Group Questions and Topics for Discussions

1. Kayla's voice is smart, witty, and often youthfully naïve. Although she is amazingly observant for her years, how does having such a young narrator affect this story? Why does Cindy Eppes opt for a voice that, to some extent, distances us from the adult world of Rosalita, while also giving us hints of it? How would the story have been different told through the voice of Sarah Jo, or Lou Jean?

2. After her family moves back to Rosalita, Kayla observes, "I seemed to be the only one in the house getting any older." What does it mean to be "getting older" in this novel, aside from simply aging chronologically? Are there some characters who are incapable of becoming older? Why? Gran comments "Just because someone is eighteen, or twenty-one, or thirty-three, does not make her a grown up." So, what does make one a grown up? Is Kayla a grown up by the end of the story (or at least on her way)?

3. What role does religion play in the world of this story? Specifically, how is Christianity viewed? What role does the church play in Sarah Jo's life, and why do you think she attends? Do other characters address religion in other ways, perhaps less formal or conventional ways? Discuss the idea of "faith" and how it manifests in the different characters. Is there a difference between being religious, and being spiritual?

4. The outside world of appearances and the inner world of thoughts, feelings, and emotions do not mesh well in the south of the late 60's. In what ways does this conflict seem to disturb the people in this book? Does it disturb some more than others? Why? Does Sarah Jo's ability to keep her emotions behind a calm layer of reserve seem deceptive to you?

5. In many ways, this is really a story about the struggle between past, present, and future. While these characters inhabit the world of the present, they cannot seem to break free—and in some cases do not want to emerge— from their past. Which characters do you see as the most haunted by their pasts? By the end of the novel, do you think anyone has truly broken free from the things that happened to them long ago? Is the budding relationship between Kayla's father and Lou Jean representative of an inability to shake the past, or is it something else? Is it

possible to re-visit the people from your past in a fresh way?

6. *South of Reason* is a story that deals with secrets. The characters struggle with their own sense of truth in a world that seems to encourage them to lie in the interests of propriety. Discuss the illusive nature of "truth" and the concept of "right and wrong" as presented in this story. Do any characters seem to have a firm grasp on what it means to be honest?

7. The concept of family permeates this novel and there is a sense that family is not so much comprised of the people who are blood relations, but of people who understand each other and make one another feel comfortable (keep in mind the relationship between Gran, Carmen, and Lou Jean). Discuss the ways that the idea of "family" shapes, alters, and helps determine the fate of the different characters in this novel.

8. On pages 172 and 173 Kayla and Charles Dale talk about the trees in Texas and compare them to trees in more temperate climates. How does their discussion reveal their perception of their lives in Texas and the lives of other characters? How does the author use the Texas landscape to emphasize the issues that matter most to Kayla and Charles Dale?

9. Focus on the different mother/daughter bonds in this novel (Gran and Sarah Jo, Kayla and Sarah Jo), paying close atten-

tion to the way that attitudes, behaviors, and modes of thinking are passed down between the generations. Do you think a reconciliation is possible between Kayla and her mother? How about Sarah Jo and Gran? Do mothers and daughters have a "symbiotic relationship" like the one that Charles Dale describes cattle and cattle egrets having on page 223?

10. Although Kayla is doing her best to accept her new family situation at the end of the story, it is apparent that she has some mixed emotions. How did you feel about her father's leaving, and his decision to start seeing Lou Jean again? Do you think this novel ends on a positive note? Where do you envision the characters in ten years?